At most publishing houses there is a curious prejudice against "writing copy" as it is known in the trade. Possibly because for many it is a chore with a hypocritical ambience.

This has never been true of Ballantine Books. Either one feels genuine enthusiasm for a book, or one does not write copy for it.

Writing copy for Lester del Rey is both easier and more difficult than most. Easier because he is a supremely professional writer, more difficult because we hold him in high and personally affectionate regard—which makes being objective impossible.

So the hell with being objective.

These are five superb stories, provocative and entertaining in the best sense of these overused words—that is, they seduce the interest, sink grapples in the mind and gut, and end with a sense of shock—the shock of being returned to a real world one had entirely forgotten.

As to what they are about, perhaps the closest one can come is to say they are about dedication —of a man, of a god, of the creations of man.

Finally, they leave one richer, more thoughtful. And argumentative. They do not go away.

Which proves that Lester has once again worked his magic.

GODS AND GOLEMS

Five Short Novels of Science Fiction

Lester del Ray

WILDSIDE PRESS

CONTENTS

VENGEANCE IS MINE

1

Hate spewed across the galaxy in a high crusade. Metal ships leaped from world to world and hurtled across space to farther and farther stars. Planets surrendered their ores to sky-reaching cities, built around fortress temples and supported by vast networks of technology. Then more ships were spawned, armed with incredible weapons, and sent forth in the eternal search for an enemy.

In the teeming cities and aboard the questing ships, soul-wrenching music was composed, epic fiction and supernal poetry were written, and great paintings and sculpture were developed, to be forgotten as later and nobler work was done. Science strove for the ultimate limit of understanding, fought against that limit, and surged past it to limitless possibilities. But behind all the arts and sciences lay the drive of religion, and the religion was one of ancient anger and dedicated hate.

The ships filled the galaxy until every world was conquered. For a time, they hesitated, preparing for the great leap outwards. Then the armadas sailed again, across thousands and millions of light years toward the beckoning galaxies beyond.

With each ship went the holy image of their faith and the unsated and insatiable hunger of their hate . . .

2

The cattrack labored up the rough road over the crater wall, topped the last rise, and began humming its way down into Eratosthenes. Inside the cab, the driver's seat groaned protestingly as Sam shifted his six hundred terrestrial pounds forward. Coming home was always a good time. He switched lenses in his eyes and began scanning the crater floor for the first sight of the Lunar Base dome.

"You don't have to be quite so all-fired anxious to get back, Sam," Hal Norman complained. But the little selenologist was also gazing forward eagerly. "You might show a little appreciation for the time I've spent answering your fool questions and trying to pound sense into your tin head. Anybody'd think you didn't like my company."

Sam made the sound of a human chuckle with which he had taught himself to acknowledge all the verbal nonsense men called humor. But truth compelled him to answer seriously. "I like your company very much, Hal."

He had always liked the company of the men he'd met on Earth or during his long years on the Moon. Humans, he had decided long ago, were wonderful. He had enjoyed the extended field trip with Hal Norman; but it would still be good to get back to the dome, where the men had given him the unique privilege of joining them. There he could listen to the often inexplicable but always fascinating conversation of forty men. And there, perhaps, he could join them in their singing. All the robots had perfect pitch, of course. but only Sam had learned to sing acceptably enough to win a place in the dome.

In anticipation, he began humming a chanty about the sea he had never seen. The cattrack hummed downward between the walls of the road that had been crudely bulldozed from the rubble of the crater. Then they broke out into the open, and he could see the dome and the territory around it.

Hal grunted in surprise. "That's odd. I hoped the supply rocket would be in. But what are those three ships doing there?"

Sam switched back to wide-angle lenses and stared toward the side. The three ships didn't look like supply rockets. They resembled the old wreck that still stood at the far end of the crater, surrounded by the supply capsules that had been sent on automatic control to keep the stranded crew alive until rescue could be sent. The only other such ships were those used by the third expedition. But they had been parked in orbit around Earth after the end of the third expedition fifty years ago. Once the Base was established, their capacity had no longer been needed and they were inefficient for routine supply and rotation of the men here.

Before he could comment on the ships, the buzzer sounded, indicating that Base had spotted the cattrack. Sam flipped the switch and acknowledged the call.

"Hi, Sam." It was the voice of Dr. Robert Smithers, the leader of Lunar Base. "Butt out, will you? I want to talk to Hal."

– Sam could have tuned in on the communication frequency with his own receptors, since the signal was strong enough at this distance. But he obeyed the order to avoid listening as Hal reached for the handset. There was no way to detune his audio receptors, however. He heard Hal's greeting. Then there was silence for at least a minute.

The man's face was shocked and serious when he finally spoke again. "But that's damned nonsense, Chief. Earth got over such insanity half a century ago. There hasn't been a sign of . . . Yes, sir . . . All right, sir. Thanks for not taking off without me."

He hung up the set, shaking his head. When he faced Sam, his expression was unreadable. "Full speed, Sam."

"There's trouble," Sam guessed. He threw the cattrack into its top speed of thirty miles an hour, fighting and

3

straining with the controls. Only a robot could manage the tricky machine at such a rate over the crude road, and it required his full attention.

Hal's voice was strange and harsh. "We're being sent back to Earth. Big trouble, Sam. But what can you know of war and rumors of war?"

"War was a dangerous form of political insanity, outlawed at the conference of 1998," Sam quoted from a speech that had come over the radio. "Human warfare has now become unthinkable."

"Yeah. Human war." Hal made a rough sound in his throat. "But not inhuman war, it seems. And that's what it will be, if it comes. Oh hell, stop looking so gloomy. It's not your problem."

Sam decided against chuckling this time, though references to his set, unsmiling expression were usually meant to be a form of humor. He filed the puzzling words away in his permanent memory for later consideration.

The terminator was rushing across the lunar surface, and it would soon be night. The crater wall was already casting a shadow over most of the area. But sunlight still reached the Base, and the surrounding territory was in glaring light. The undiffused light splashed out sharply from the rocks. Seeing was hard as they neared the dome, and all Sam's attention had to be directed to his driving. Behind him, he heard Hal getting into the moonsuit to leave the cab.

Sam brought the cattrack to a halt and let Hal out at the entrance to the sealed underground hemisphere of lunar rock that was the true dome. The light upper structure was simply a shield for supplies against the heat of the sun. He drove the machine under that and cut off the motor.

As Sam emerged from the airlock, air gushed out of small cavities of his body. But he felt no discomfort. There was only the faint click of a switch inside him to tell him of the change. That switch was simply an emergency mea-

4

sure, designed to turn his power on if there should be a puncture of the dome while he was turned off. It might have been one of the reasons the men liked having him inside, though he hoped there were other explanations. There had been no room in the new robots for such devices.

He saw the Mark Three robots waiting just beyond the entrance as he approached it. There were tracks in the lunar dust leading to the space ships half a mile away. But whatever ferrying they had done was obviously finished, and they were now merely standing in readiness. They were totally unlike him. He was bulky and mechanical, designed only for function in the early days when men needed help on the Moon. They were almost manlike, under their black enamel, and their size and weight had been pared down to match that of the humans. There had been thirty of them originally, but accidents had left only a few more than twenty. And of the original Mark Ones, only Sam was left.

"When do we leave?" he called to one over the radio circuit.

The black head turned slowly toward him. "We do not know. The men did not tell us."

"Didn't you ask them?" he called. But he had no need of their denial. They had not been told to ask.

They were still unformed, less than five years old, and their thoughts were tied to the education given by the computers in the creche. They lacked twenty years of his intimate association with men. But sometimes he wondered whether they would ever learn enough, or whether they had been too strongly repressed in training. Men seemed to be afraid of robots back on Earth, as Hal Norman had once told him, which was why they were still being used only on the Moon.

He turned away from them and went down the entrance to the inner dome. The entrance led to the great community room, and the men were gathered there, all wearing moonsuits. They were arguing with Hal as

Sam began emerging from the lock, but at sight of him the words were cut off. He stared about in the silence, feeling suddenly awkward.

"Hello, Sam," Dr. Smithers said finally. He was a tall, spare man of barely thirty, but seven years of responsibility here had etched deep lines into his face and put grey in his mustache, though his other hair was still jet black. "All right, Hal. Your things are on the ship. I cut the time pretty fine waiting for you, so we're leaving at once. No more arguments. Get out there!"

"Go to hell!" Hal told him. "I don't desert my friends."

Other men began moving out. Sam stepped aside to let them pass, but they seemed to avoid looking at him.

Smithers sighed wearily. "Hal, I can't argue this with you. You'll go, if I have to chain you. Do you think I like this? But we're under military orders now. They're going crazy back on Earth. They didn't find out about the expected attack until a week ago, as near as I can learn, but they've already cancelled space. Damn it, I can't take Sam! We're at the ragged limit of available lift now, and he represents six hundred pounds of mass—more than four of the others."

Hal gestured sharply toward the outside. "Then leave four of *those* behind. He's worth more than the whole lot of them."

"Yeah. He is. But my orders specify that all men and the maximum possible number of robots must be returned." Smithers twisted his lips savagely and suddenly turned to face the robot. "Sam, I'll give it to you straight. I can't take you with us. We have to leave you here alone. I'm sorry, but that's how it has to be."

"You won't be alone, Sam," Hal Norman said. "I'm staying."

Sam stood silently for a moment, letting it register. His circuits found it hard to integrate. He had never thought of being separated from these men who had been his life. Going back to Earth had been easy to accept; he'd gone back there once before. Little hopes and future-pictures

6

that he hadn't known were in his mind began to appear.

But with those came memories of Hal Norman's expressed hopes and dreams. The man had showed Sam a picture of his future wife and tried to describe all that such a creature meant to a man. He'd spoken of green fields and the sea. He'd raved about Earth too often during the days they were together.

Sam moved forward toward Hal. The man saw him coming and began to back away, but he was no match for the robot. Sam held Hal's arms and closed his moon-suit, then gathered him up carefully. Hal was struggling, but his efforts did no good against Sam's determination.

"All right, Dr. Smithers. We can go now," Sam told the Chief.

They were the last to leave the dome. The little black robots were already marching across the surface, with the men straggling along behind them. Smithers fell into step with Sam, moving as if the burden was on his back instead of in the arms of the robot. Hal had ceased struggling. He lay outwardly quiet; but through the suit, Sam's body receptors picked up sounds that he had heard only twice before on occasions he tried not to remember. They were the sounds of a man attempting to control his weeping.

Halfway to the ship, faint words came over the radio. "Put me down, Sam. I'll go quietly."

The three moved on together. By the time they reached the ship, the others were all aboard. The Chief motioned the younger man up the ramp. For a moment, Hal hesitated. He turned toward Sam, started to make a motion, and then swung away and dashed up the ramp, his shoulders shaking convulsively.

Smithers still stood after the other had disappeared. The radio brought the sound of a sigh, before the man moved. "Thanks, Sam. That was a favor I no longer had the right to ask. And don't tell me it's all right. Nothing's right any more." He sighed again, then smiled faintly. "Remember the books?"

7

"I won't disturb them," Sam promised. There were a great many microbooks in the dome library, brought in a few at a time by many men over the long years. They were one of the few taboos; it was against orders for Sam to read any of them. A man had once told him that it was to save him from unnecessary confusion.

Smithers shook his head sharply. "Nonsense. You're going to have a lot of time to kill. The ban is off. Read any or all of them if you like. It's about all I can do for you, but you're entitled to that, at least."

He put a foot on the ramp and turned partly away from Sam. Then abruptly he swung back.

"Goodbye, Sam," he said thickly. His right hand came out and grasped that of the robot strongly. "Goodbye and God bless you!"

A second later, Smithers was hurrying up the ramp. It was drawn in after him, and the great outer seal of the rocket ship began to close.

Sam ran back to the entrance of the dome to avoid the blast. The edge of darkness had touched the dome now, leaving the rockets standing in the last light as he turned to look at them. He watched the takeoff of the three heavily-laden ships. They staggered up slowly, carrying the men toward the rendezvous with Earth's orbital station. It wasn't until they were beyond the range of his strongest vision that he turned into the dome. It was silent and empty around him.

He stared at the clock on the wall and at the calendar on which they had marked off the days. He hadn't found how long they would be gone. But Smithers' words gave a vague answer—he would have a lot of time to kill. That could mean anywhere from one month to most of a year, judging by the application of similar phrases in the past. He looked at the shelves filled with microbooks for a few moments. Then he went outside, to stare through his telephoto lenses at the Earth in the sky above him. There were spots of light in the dark areas that he knew to be the cities of men.

The second day after the takeoff of the ship, Sam was watching the dark area of Earth again when some of the spots of light grew suddenly brighter. New spots of brightness rose and decayed during the hours he watched. They were far brighter than any city should have been. Other spots glowed where no cities had been before. But eventually they all faded. After that, there were no bright areas at all. As Earth turned slowly, he saw that all the cities on Earth were now dark.

It was a mystery for which he had no explanation. He went inside to try the radio that brought news and entertainment from the relay on the orbital station, but no signal was coming through. He debated calling them, but that was reserved for the decision of Smithers, and the Chief was gone.

There was no call on the fifth day, when the men should have reached the station. He knew there was no reason to expect such a call; men were not obligated to report their affairs to a robot. But his brain circuits seemed to be filled with odd future-pictures that kept him by the set for long hours after he knew there would be no signal for him.

Finally he got up and went to the music player. They had let him use it at times, and he felt no disloyalty to them as he found a tape that was one of his favorites and threaded it. But when the final chorus of Beethoven's Ninth reached its end, the dome seemed more empty than ever. He found another tape, without voices this time. And that was followed by another. It helped a little, but it was not enough.

It was then that he turned to the books, taking one at random. It was something about Mars, by Edgar Rice Burroughs, and he started to put it back. He had already learned enough about astronomy from the education machine. But at last he threaded it into the microreader and sat down to read.

It started well enough, and it was about some strange kind of man, not about astronomy. But then . . .

9

Sam made a strange sound, only slowly realizing that he had imitated the groan of a man for the first time in his existence. It was all madness! He knew men had never reached Mars—and couldn't reach such a Mars, because the planet was totally unlike what he knew existed. It must be some strange form of human humor. Or else there were men unlike any he had known and facts that had been kept from him. The latter seemed more probable.

He struggled through it, to groan again when it ended and he still didn't know what had happened to the strange female man who was a princess and who laid highly impossible eggs. But by then, he had begun to like John Carter, and he wanted to read more. He was confused—but even more curious than puzzled. Eventually, he found the whole series and read them all.

It was a much later book that solved some of the puzzle of it for him. There was a small note before the book really began: *This is a work of speculative fiction; any resemblance to present-day persons or events is entirely coincidental.* He looked up *fiction* in the dictionary he had seen the men use and felt better afterwards. It wasn't quite like humor, but it wasn't fact, either. It was a game of some kind, where the rules of life were all changed about in idiosyncratic ways. The writer might pretend that men liked to kill each other or were afraid of women, or some other ridiculous idea; then he tried to imagine what might happen under such conditions. It was obviously taboo to pretend about real people and events, though some of the books had stories that used background and people that had the same names as those in reality.

The best fiction of all sometimes looked like books of fact, if the writer was clever enough. History was mostly like that; there was a whole imaginary world called Rome, for instance. It was fortunate Sam had been taught the simple facts of man's progress by the education machine before he read such books. Men, it was true, had sometimes been violent, but not when they understood all the facts or could help it.

In the end, he evolved a simple classification. If a book made him think hard and forced him to strain to follow it, it was fact; if it made him read faster and think less as he went through it, it was fiction.

There was one book that was hardest of all to classify. It was an old book, written before men had gone out into space. Yet it was full of carefully documented and related facts about an invasion of flying saucers from far in space. Eventually, he was forced to decide from the internal evidence that it was fact, but it left him disturbed and unhappy.

Hal Norman had referred to inhuman war, and Dr. Smithers had mentioned an attack. Could it be that the strange ships from somewhere had struck at Earth? He remembered the brilliant lights over the cities, so much like the great ray weapons described in some of the fiction about space war. *Sometimes* there were elements of truth even in fiction.

If invaders had come in great ships to fight against Earth, it might take men longer than Sam cared to think of to fight them off.

He went outside to stare at the sky. Earth still showed no sign of cities. They must be blacked out, as they would be if flying saucers were in their skies. He searched the space over the Moon, but he could find no strange craft. Then he went back inside to read through the microbook again.

It was poetry that somehow finally shoved the worry from his mind. He had tried poetry before, and given up, unable to follow it. But this time he made a discovery. He tried reading it aloud, until it began to beat at him and force its rhythm on him. He was reading Swinburne's *Hymn of Man,* attracted by the title, and suddenly the words and something besides began to sing their way into his deepest mind. He went back over four lines again and again, until they were music, or all that music had tried to say and had failed.

> *In the grey beginning of years, in the*
> *twilight of things that began,*
> *The word of the earth in the ears of the*
> *world, was it God? was it man?*

Sam went up and down the dome for most of that day, chanting to himself that the word of the earth in the ears of the world was *man!* Then he turned back to other poetry. None quite equalled that one experience, but most of it stirred his circuits in strange ways. A book of limericks even surprised him twice to the point where he chuckled, without realizing that he had never done that spontaneously before.

There were slightly over four thousand volumes in the little library, including the technical books. He timed them carefully, stretching them by rereading his favorites, until he finished the last at exactly midnight on the eve of the takeoff anniversary.

The next twenty-four hours he spent outside the dome, watching the sky and staring at Earth, while his radio receptors scanned all the frequencies. There had been a lot of time already killed. But there was no signal, and no rocket ship blasted down, bringing back the men.

At midnight he gave a sighing sound and went back inside the dome. In the technical section, he unlocked the controls for the atomic generator and turned it down to its lowest idling rate. He came back, turning the now dim lights off as he moved. In the main room, he put his favorite tape on the player and the copy of Swinburne in the microreader. But he did not turn them on. Instead, he dropped his heavy body quietly onto the floor before the entrance, where the men would be sure to see him when they finally returned.

Then one hand reached up firmly, and he turned himself off.

3

Sam's eyes looked toward the entrance as consciousness snapped on again. There was no sign of men there. He stood up, staring about the dome, then hastened outside to stare across the floor of the crater. It lay bare, except for the old wrecked rocket ship. Men had not come back.

Inside again, he looked for something that might have fallen and hit his switch. The switch itself was still in the off position, however. And when he turned on the tape player, no sound came. It was confirmation enough. Something had happened to the air in the dome, and his internal switch had gone into operation to turn him on automatically.

A few minutes later, he found the hole. A meteoroid the size of a pea must have hit the surface above. It had struck with enough force to blast a tiny craterlet almost completely through the dome, and internal pressure had done the rest. He secured patching material and began automatically making the repairs. There was still more than enough air in the tanks to fill the dome again.

Sam sighed as the first whisper of sound reached him from the tape player. He flipped his switch back to on position before the rising pressure negated the emergency circuit. He still had to get back to the entrance to resume his vigil. It had simply been bad luck that had aroused him before the men could return.

He moved back through the dome, hardly looking. But his eyes were open, and his mind gradually began to add the evidence. There was no way to tell how long he had been unconscious; he had no feeling of any time. But there was dust over everything—dust that had been disturbed by the outrushing air, but that had still patina-plated itself on metal firmly enough to remain. And some

13

of the metal showed traces of corrosion. That must have taken years!

He stopped abruptly, checking his battery power. The cobalt-platinum cell had been fully charged when he lay down. Now it was at less than half charge. Such batteries had an extremely slow leakage. Even allowing for residual conductance through his circuits, it would have taken at least thirty years for such a loss!

Thirty years! And the men had not come back.

A groan came to his ears, and he turned quickly. But it had only been his own voice. And now he began shouting. He was still trying to shout in the airless void as he reached the surface. He caught himself, bracing his back against the dome as his balance circuits reacted to some wild impulse from his brain.

Men would never desert him. They had to come back to the Moon to finish their work, and the first thing they would do would be to find him. Men couldn't just leave him there! Only in the wild fiction could that happen, and even there only the postulated evil men would do such a thing. His men would never dream of it!

He stared up at Earth. The dome was in night again, and Earth was a great orb in the sky, glowing blue and white, with touches of brown in a few places. He saw the outline of continents through the cloud cover, and looked for the great city that must lie within the thin darkened area. There should have been lights visible there, even against the contrast of brighter illumination from the lighted area. But there was no sign of the city.

He sighed soundlessly again, and now he felt himself relaxing. The attackers must still be hovering there! The dangerous Ufo-things from space. Men were still embattled and unable to return to him. Thirty years of that for them, and here he was losing balance over what had been only a year of his conscious time!

He faced the worst of possibilities more calmly now. He even forced himself to admit that men might have been so badly crippled by the war that they could not

14

return to him—perhaps not for more time than he could think of. Smithers had said they were abandoning space, at a time when the attack had not yet come. How long would it take to recover and regain their lost territory?

He went back into the dome, but the radio was silent. Hesitantly, he initiated a call to the orbital station. After half an hour, he gave up. The men there, if men were still there, must be keeping radio silence.

"All right," he said slowly into the silence of the dome. "All right, face it. Men aren't coming back for a robot. Ever!"

It was a speech out of the fiction he had read, rather than out of rationality. But somehow saying it loudly made it easier to face. Men could not come to him. He wasn't that valuable to them.

He shook his head over that, remembering the time he had been taken back to Earth after twenty years out of the creche and on the Moon. The Mark One robots had all been destroyed in the accidents and difficulties of getting the Base established, except for Sam. Supposedly better Mark Two robots were sent to replace them, but those had been beset by some circuit flaws that made them more prone to accident and less useful than the first models. More than a hundred had been sent in all—and none had survived. It was then that they called Sam back to study him.

On Earth, deep in the security-hidden underground robot development workshops, he had been tested in every way they knew to help them in designing the Mark Three robots. And there old Stephen DeMatre had interviewed him for three whole days. At the end of that time, the man who had first introduced him to his work with men had put a hand on his metal shoulder and smiled at him.

"You're unique, Sam," he'd said. "A lucky combination of all the wild guesses we used in making each Mark One individually, as well as some unique conditioning while among that first Base staff. We don't dare duplicate you yet, but some day the circuit control computer is going to want to get your pattern in full for later brains. So take good care of yourself. I'd keep you here, but . . . You take care of yourself, Sam. You hear me?"

Sam had nodded. "Yes, sir. Do you mean you can make other brains exactly like mine?"

"Technically, the control computer can duplicate your design," DeMatre had answered. "It won't be just like your brain. Too many random factors in any really advanced mechanical mind unit. But with similar capabilities. That's why you're worth more money than this whole project without you. You're worth quite a few million dollars, and it's up to you to see that valuable property like that isn't destroyed. Right, Sam?"

Sam had agreed and been shipped back to the Moon, along with the first of the Mark Three robots. And maybe his trip to the research center had been of some use, since the new Mark Three models worked as well as their limitations permitted. They were far better than the preceding models.

Maybe he wasn't valuable enough to men for them to come for him now. But by DeMatre's own words, he was one of their most valuable possessions. If it was up to him to see that he wasn't destroyed, then it was up to him also to see that he wasn't lost to men.

If they couldn't come for him, he had to get to them. The question was: How? He couldn't project himself by mind power like John Carter. He had to have a rocket!

With the thought, he went dashing out through the entrance and heading toward the old wreck. It stood exactly as it had after the landing that had ruined it, with half its hull plating ripped off and most of its rocket motors broken. It could never be flown again. Nor could the old supply capsules. They had burned out their tubes in getting here, being of minimum construction. There wasn't even space inside one for him.

Sam considered it, making measurements and doing

16

the hardest thinking of his existence. Without the long study of all the technical manuals of the dome library, he could never have found an answer. But eventually he nodded.

A motor from the big ship could be fitted to a capsule. The frame would be barely strong enough. But the plating could be removed to lighten the little ship; Sam needed no protection from space, as some of the cargo had required. And the automatic guidance system could be removed to make enough room for him. He could operate it manually, since his reaction and integrating time were faster than that of even the system.

Fuel would be a problem, though there was enough oxygen in the dome storage tanks. It would have to be hydrogen, since he could find rocks from which that could be released by the power of the generator. Fortunately, lunar gravity was easier to escape than that of Earth.

He went back to the dome and found paper and pencil. He was humming softly to himself as he began laying out his plan. It wasn't easy. He might not be skilled enough to pilot the strange craft to the station. And it would take a great deal of time. But Sam was going to the men who wouldn't come to him!

4

It takes experience to turn engineering theory into practice. Almost three years had passed since Sam's awakening before the orbital station swam slowly into view before him. And the erratic takeoff and flight had been one that no human body could have stood. But now he sighted on the huge metal doughnut before him, estimating its orbit carefully. There were only a few gallons of fuel remaining in the tanks behind him, and he had to reach the landing net on the first try.

His first calculations seemed wrong. He glanced down

17

at the huge orb of Earth and flipped sun filters over his eyes. Something was wrong. The station was not holding its bottom pointed exactly at the center of Earth as it should have done; it was turning very slowly, and even its spin was uneven, as if the water used to balance it against wobbling had not been distributed properly. Beside it, the little ferry ship used between station and ships from below was jerking slightly on the silicone-plastic line that held it.

Sam felt an unpleasant stirring in his chest where most of his brain circuits lay. But he forced it down and computed his blast for all the factors. He had learned something of the behavior of his capsule during the minutes of takeoff and the later approach to the station. His fingers moved delicately, and fuel metered out to the cranky little motor.

It was not a perfect match, but he managed to catch himself in the net around the entrance to the hub. He pulled himself free and began scrambling up to the lock as the capsule drifted off. A moment later, he was standing in the weightlessness of the receiving section. And from the sounds of his feet, there was still air in the station.

He froze motionless as he let himself realize he had made it. Then he began looking for the men who should have seen his approach and be coming to question him.

There was no sound of steps or of any other activity, except for his own movements. Nor was there any light from the bulbs above him. The only illumination was from a thick quartz port that faced the sun.

Sam cut on the lamp built into his chest and began sweeping the sections of the hub with its light. Dust had formed a patina here, too. He sighed softly into the air. Then he moved toward the outer sections, his steps determined.

Halfway down the tube that ran from the hub to the outer hull, Sam stopped and cut off his light. Ahead of him, there was a glow! Lights were still burning!

He let out a yell to call the men and began running,

adjusting for the increasing feeling of weight as he moved outwards. Then he was under the bulb. He stared up at it—a single bulb burning among several others that were black, though they were on the same circuit. How long did it take for these bulbs to burn out? Years surely, and probably decades. Yet most of the station was in darkness, though there was still power from the atomic generator.

He found a few other bulbs burning in the outer station, but not many. The great reception and recreation room was empty. Beyond that, the offices were mostly open and vacant. Some held a litter of paper and other stuff, as if someone had gone through carelessly, not bothering to put anything back in place. The living section with its tiny sleeping cubicles was worse. Some of the rooms were simply bare, but others were in complete disorder. Four showed signs of long occupancy, with the sleeping nets worn almost through and not replaced. But nothing showed how recently they had been left.

He went through another section devoted to station machinery and came to a big room that was apparently now used for storage. Sam had seen a plan of the station in one of the technical books in the dome. He placed this room as one designed as a storage for hydrogen bombs once. But that had been from the pre-civilized days of men, and the bombs had been dismantled and destroyed more than sixty years before.

It was in the hydroponics room that he was forced to face the truth. The plants there had been the means of replacing the oxygen in the air for the men, and now the tanks were dry and the vegetation had been dead so long that only dessicated stalks remained. There could be no men here. He didn't need the sight of the bare food section for confirmation. Some men had stayed here until the food was gone before they left the untended plants to die. It must have been many years ago that they had abandoned the station.

Sam shook his head in anger at himself. He should

have guessed it when he saw that there were none of the winged rocket ships waiting outside the station. So long as men were here, they would have kept some means for return to Earth.

The observatory was dark, but there was still power for the electronic telescope. The screen lighted at his touch, showing only empty space. He had to wait nearly two hours before the slow tumble of the station brought Earth into full view.

Most of it was in daylight, and there was only a thin cloud cover. Once a thousand cities could have been scanned plainly from here. When seeing was best, even streams of moving cars could be seen. But now there were no cities and no signs of movement!

Sam emitted a harsh gasping sound as he scanned the continent of North America. He had seen pictures of New York, Chicago and several other city complexes from this view. Now there was only dark ruin showing where they had been. It came to him with an almost physical shock that perhaps millions of human beings had died in those wrecks of cities.

There were still-smaller towns where he could make out the pattern of houses. But there was no movement, even there.

He cut power from the telescope with an angry flick of his finger, trying to blot the things he had seen from his memory. He moved rapidly away from the observatory, hunting the communications section.

It was in worse shape than most other places. It looked as if some man had deliberately tried to wreck the machinery. A hammer lay tangled into a maze of ruin that must once have been the main receiver. There was something that looked like dried blood on a metal cabinet, with a dent that might have fitted a human fist.

The floor was littered with tape that should have held a record of all the communications received and sent, and the drive capstan on the tape player was bent into uselessness. Sam lifted a section of tape and placed it in the slot

20

that gave his face a sad caricature of a mouth. The tape sensors moved into place, and he began scanning the bit of plastic. It was blank, probably wiped of any message by time and the unshielded transformer that was still humming below the control panel.

Most of the tape cabinet was empty, and there was nothing on the few tapes within. Sam ripped open drawers, hunting for some evidence. He finally found a single reel in the top drawer of the main desk. Most of it was a garble of static; stray fields had gotten to it, even through the metal drawer. But towards the end, a few words could barely be picked out from the noise.

". . . shelters far enough from the blast . . . Thought we'd made it . . . a starving . . . went mad. Must have been a nerve aerosol, but it didn't settle as . . . Mad. Everywhere. Southern hemisphere, too . . . For God's sake, stay where you . . ."

The noise grew worse then, totally ruining intelligibility. Sam caught bits of what might have been sentences, but they were pure gibberish. Then suddenly a small section of the tape near the hub became almost clear.

The voice was high-pitched now, and overmodulated, as if the words had been too loud to be carried by the transmitter. There was a strange, unpleasant quality that Sam had never heard in a human voice before.

". . . all shiny and bright. But it couldn't fool me. I knew it was one of them! They're all waiting up there, waiting for me to come out. They want to eat my soul. They're clever now, they won't let me see them. But when I turn my back, I can feel . . ."

The tape came to an end.

Sam could make no sense of it, though he replayed it all again in hopes of finding some other clue. He gave up and reached down to shut off the power in the transformer. It was amazing that the wreckage hadn't already blown all the fuses to this section. He groped for the switch and flipped it, just as his eyes spotted something under the transformer shelf.

21

It was a fountain pen, gold and black enamel. He had seen one like it countless times, and now as he turned it over in his hands, familiar lettering appeared on the barrel: *RPS*. Those were the initials of Dr. Smithers, and the pen could only have been his. He must have been one of those who had waited in the station. The Moon ships had made it back here, and Smithers had stayed on until the food was gone. Then he must have returned to Earth.

Sam reached out to clear the junk from the desk. He found paper in one of the drawers, and the pen still wrote as he sank into the chair.

There was metal sheet enough in the station, and tools to work it. The frame of the little taxi rocket he had seen outside would have to be modified; a nose and wings would have to be added, together with controls. Sam had studied the details of the upper stages of the rockets that went between the station and Earth, together with accounts of the men who flew the early ones. There had been enough books on all aspects of space in the dome.

He could never duplicate the winged craft accurately, nor could he be sure he could handle one down through the atmosphere. But in theory, almost any winged craft with a shallow angle of glide could be brought down slowly enough to avoid burning from the friction of the air. At least he was lucky enough to have fuel here; the emergency station tanks were half filled with the mono-propellant suited for the little motor in the ferry.

Then he swore, using unprofane but colorful words he had learned from a score of historical novels. It would be at least another year before he could hope to complete his work on the craft.

5

Surprisingly, the modified ferry behaved far better than Sam had dared to hope. It heated badly at the first touches of atmosphere, but the temperature remained within the limits he and the craft could stand. He learned slowly to control the descent to a glide neither too shallow for stability nor too steep to avoid overheating. By the time he was down to thirty miles above the surface, he was almost pleased with the way it handled.

He had set his course to reach the underground creche that had been his home at awakening and during the first three years of his education, before they sent him to the Moon. It was the only home he knew on Earth.

Now he saw that he could never make it. The first fifteen minutes in the upper layers of atmosphere had been at too steep a glide angle, and he could never descend far inland. He might even have trouble reaching the shore at all, he realized; when the clouds thinned, he could see nothing but ocean under him.

He opened the rocket motor behind him gently, letting its thrust raise his speed to the highest his little craft could take at this altitude. But there was too little fuel left to help much. It might have given him an extra twenty miles of glide, but not more.

Sam considered the prospects of landing in the ocean with grim foreboding. He could exist in water for a while, even at fair depths. If he landed near the shore, he might work his way out. But within a limited period of time, the water would penetrate through his body to some of the vital wiring. Once that was shorted, he would cease to exist.

He came down under the clouds, fighting for every inch of altitude. Then, far ahead, he could see the shore. There were no islands here, so it had to be the mainland. Once there, he could reach the creche in a single day.

He passed over the shoreline at a height of five hundred feet. There was a short stretch of sand, some woods, and then a long expanse of green that must be grass. He eased the control forward, then back again.

The little ship came skimming down at two hundred miles an hour. Its skids touched the surface, and it

23

bounded upwards. Sam fought the controls to keep it from
nosing over. Again it touched, jerking with deceleration.
This time it seemed to have struck right. Then a hum-
mock of ground caught against one skid. The craft slith-
ered sideways and flipped over. Sam braced himself as the
ship began coming to pieces around him.

He pulled himself out, staring at the wreckage. It was a
shame that it was ruined, he thought. But it couldn't be
made as strong as he was and still glide through the air.

He turned to study the world around him. The grass
was knee-high, moving gently in the wind. Beyond it lay
woods. Sam had seen only pictures of trees like that before. He moved toward them, noticing the thickness of
the underbrush around them. Below them, the dirt was
dark and moist. He lifted a pinch to his face, moving his
smell receptors forward in his mouth slit. It was a rich
smell, richer than the stuff in the hydroponic tanks. He
lifted his head to look for the birds he expected, but he
could see no sign of them. There were only insects, buz-
zing and humming.

The sun had already set, he noticed. Yet it was not yet
dark. There was a paling of the light, and a soft diffusion.
He shook his head. Above him, tiny twinkling spots began to appear. He had read that the stars twinkled, but
he had thought it only fiction. He had never been under
the open sky of Earth before.

Then a soft murmur of sound reached him. He started
away, to be drawn back to it. Slowly he realized it was
a sound like the description of that heard near the sea. He
had never seen an ocean, either. And now one lay no
more than a mile away.

He stumbled through the woods in the growing darkness. For some reason, he was reluctant to turn on his
lights. Eventually, he learned to make his way through
the brush and around the trees. The sound grew louder as
he progressed.

It was dark when he reached the seashore, but there
was a hint of faint light to the east. As he watched, it

24

increased. A pale white arc appeared over the horizon and grew to a large circle. The Moon, he realized finally.

The waves rose and fell, booming into surf. And far out across the sea, the Moon seemed to ride on the waves, casting a silver road of light over the water.

Sam had remembered a word. Now for the first time, he found an understanding of it. This was Beauty.

He sighed as he heaved himself from the sand and began heading along the shore in search of a road that would take him westward. No wonder men wanted to come back to defend a world where something like this could be seen.

The Moon rose higher as he moved on, its light now bright enough to give him clear vision. He came over a small rise in the ground and spotted what seemed to be a road beyond it. Beside the road was a house. It was dark and quiet, but he swung aside, going through a copse of woods to reach it and search for any evidence of humanity.

The windows were mostly broken, he saw as he approached. And weeds had grown up around it. There was a detached building beside it that held a small car, by what he could see from the single dusty window. He skirted that and reached the door of the house; it opened at his touch, its hinges protesting rustily.

Inside, the moonlight shone through the broken windows on a jumble of furniture that was overturned and tossed about in no order Sam could see. And there were other things—white things that lay sprawled on the floor.

He recognized them from the pictures in the books— skeletons of human beings. Two smaller skeletons were tangled in one corner with their skulls bashed in. A large skeleton lay near them, with the rusty shape of a knife shoved through a scrap of clothing between two ribs. There was a revolver near one hand. Across the room, a skeleton in the tatters of a dress was a jumbled pile of bones, with a small hole in the skull that could have come from a bullet.

Sam backed out of the room. He knew the meaning of another word now. He had seen Madness.

Men had learned to build good machines. The car motor barely turned over after Sam had figured out the controls, but it caught and began running with only a slight sputtering. The tires were slightly soft, but they took the bumps of the rutted little trail. Later, when Sam found a better road, they lasted under the punishment of high speed. Most of the road was clear. There were few vehicles along its way, and most of those seemed to have drifted to the shoulder before they stopped or crashed.

The sun was just rising when Sam located the place where the factory and warehouse had served as a legitimate cover for the secret underground robot project. Fire and weather had left only gutted ruins and rusty things that had once been machines. But the section that housed the creche entrance now stood apart from the rest, almost unharmed.

Sam moved into it and to the metal door openly concealed among other such doors. He should probably not have known the combination, but men were often careless around robots, and he had been curious enough to note and remember the details. He bent to what seemed to be an ornamental grille and called out a series of numbers.

The door seemed to stick a little, but then it moved aside. Beyond lay the elevator, and that operated smoothly at the combination he punched. Power was still on, at least. There was no light, but the bulbs sprang into life as he found a switch.

He called out once, but he no longer expected to find men so easily. The place had the feel of abandonment. And while it could have protected its workers from almost anything, there had been only enough food and water stocked here for two weeks. There were a few signs that it had been used for a shelter, but most of it was in good order.

He moved back past offices and laboratories toward the rear. The real creche, with its playrooms and learning

26

devices, was empty, he saw. No robots had been receiving post-awakening training. Sam was not surprised. He knew that most of the work here had been devoted to exploring the possibilities of robots, with the actual construction only a necessary sideline. Usually, the brain complexes had been created and tested without bodies, and then extinguished before there had been a full awakening.

He started toward the educator computer out of his old habits. But it was only a machine that had programmed his progress from prepared tapes and memory circuits. It could not help him now.

Beyond the creche lay the heart of the whole affair. Here the brain complexes were assembled from components according to esoteric calculations or to meet previously recorded specifications. This was work that required a computer that was itself intelligent to some extent. It had to make sense out of the desirable options given it by men and then form the brain paths needed, either during construction or during the initial period before awakening. Everything that Sam had been before awakening had come from this, with only the selection of his characteristics chosen by men. That pattern would still be recorded, along with what the great computer had learned of him during his previous return here.

Sam moved toward the machine, gazing in surprise at the amount of work lying about. There were boxes of robot bodies crammed into every storage space. They could never have been assembled in such numbers here. And beyond lay shelves jammed with the components for the brain complexes. With such quantities, enough robots could be made to supply the Lunar Base needs for generations.

The computer itself was largely hidden far below, but its panel came to life at his touch. It waited.

"This is Robot Twelve, Mark One," Sam said. "You have authorization on file."

The authorization from Dr. DeMatre should have been cancelled. But the machine did not switch on alarm cir-

27

cuits. A thin cable of filaments reached out and passed into Sam's mouth slit. It retracted, and the speaker came to life. "There is authorization. What is wanted?"

"What is the correct date?" Sam asked. Then he grunted as the answer came from the machine's isotope clock. It had been more than thirty-seven years since the men had left the Moon. He shook his head, and the robot bodies caught his attention again. "Why are so many robots being built?"

"Orders were received for one thousand robots trained to fly missiles. Orders were suspended by Director De-Matre. No orders were received for removing parts."

"Do you know what happened to the men?" Sam had little hope of finding an easy answer anymore, but he had to ask.

The machine seemed to hesitate. "Insufficient data. Orders were given by Director DeMatre to monitor broadcasts. Broadcasts were monitored. Analysis is incomplete. Data of doubtful coherence. Requests for more data were broadcast on all frequencies for six hours. Relevant replies were not received. Request further information if available."

"Never mind," Sam told it. "Can you teach me how to fly a plane?"

"Robot Twelve, Mark One, was awakened with established ability to control all vehicles. Further instructions not possible."

Sam grunted in amazement. He'd been surprised at how well he had controlled the landing craft and then the car. But it had never occurred to him that such knowledge had been built in.

"All right," he decided. "Start broadcasting again on all the frequencies you can handle. Just ask for answers. If you get any, find where the sender is and record it. If anyone asks who is calling, say you're calling for me and take any message. Tell them I'll be back here in one month." He started to turn away, then remembered. "Finished for now."

The machine darkened. Sam headed out to find a field somewhere that might still have an operable plane. But he was already beginning to suspect what he would find on this travesty of Earth.

6

Grass grew and flowers bloomed. Ants built nests and crickets chirped in the soft summer night. The seas swarmed with marine life of most kinds. And reptiles sunned themselves on rocks, or retired to their holes when the sun was too hot. But on all Earth, no warmblooded animal could be found.

The Earth of man was without form and void. The cities were slag heaps from which radioactivity still radiated. No fires burned on the hearthstones of the most isolated houses. The villages were usually burned, sometimes apparently by accident, but often as if they had been fired deliberately by their owners.

The Moon was a thing of glory over Lake Michigan. It was the only glorious thing for six hundred miles. Four returned winged rockets rested on a field in Florida, but there was no sign of what had become of the men who rode down from the station in them. One winged craft stood forlornly outside Denver, and there was a scrawl in crayon inside its port that spelled the worst obscenity in the English language.

There was a library still standing in Phoenix, and the last newspaper had the dateline of the day when Sam had seen the lights brighten over the cities of Earth. There was no news beyond that of purely local importance. Most of the front page was occupied by a large box which advised readers that the government had taken over all radio communications during the crisis and would broadcast significant news on the hour. The paper was cooperating with the government in making such news avail-

29

able by broadcast only. The same box appeared in the nine preceding issues. Before that, the major news seemed to involve a political campaign in United South Africa.

Other scattered small libraries had differently-named papers that were no different. Yet the only clue was in one of those libraries. It was a piece of paper resting under the finger bones of a skeleton that was scattered before bound copies of a technical journal. The paper was covered with doodles and stained in what might have been blood. But the words were legible:

"Lesson for the day. Assign to all students. *Politics:* They could not win and that is obvious. *Chemistry:* Their nerve gas was similar to one we tested in small quantities. It seemed safe. Yet when they dropped it over us in both Northern and Southern hemispheres, it did not settle out as the test batches had done. *Practice:* Such aerosols can be tested only in massive quantities. *Medicine:* Janice was in the shelter with me three weeks, yet there was still enough in the air to make her die in the ecstasy of a theophany. *Meterology:* The wind patterns have been known for years. In three weeks, they reach all the Earth. *Psychology:* I am mad. But my madness is that I am become only cold logic without a soul. Therefore, I must kill myself. *Religion:* Nothing matters. I am mad. God is——"

That was all.

7

The creche was still the same, of course. Sam sat before the entrance, staring at the Moon that was rising over the horizon. It was a full Moon again, and there was beauty to it, even here. But he was only vaguely aware of that. Below him, the great computer was busily integrating the mass of tiny details he had gathered together with all of the millions of facts it knew. That job took time, even for such a machine.

Now it called him over the radio frequencies, as he had ordered it to do earlier in the day. He issued the formal command for it to go ahead.

"All data correlated," it announced. "None was found fully coherent with previous data. Degree of relevancy approaches zero. Data insufficient for conclusion."

He grunted to himself and put the machine back on stand-by. He had expected little else. He had known there was too little material for a logical conclusion.

But his own conclusion had been drawn already. Now he sat under the light of the Moon, staring up at the sky, and there was a coldness in his brain complex that seemed deeper than the reaches of space.

They had come from somewhere out there, he thought bitterly. They had appeared more than a century before and snooped and sniffed at Earth, only to leave. Now they had come back, giving Earth only a week's warning as they approached. They had struck all Earth with glowing bombs or radiation that ruined the cities of men. And when men had still survived, they resorted to a deadly mist of insanity. "They dropped it over us," the note had said. And the wonderful race Sam had known had died in madness, usually of some destructive kind.

There had not even been a purpose to it. The Invaders hadn't wanted the Earth for themselves. They had simply come and slaughtered, to depart as senselessly as they had departed before.

Sam beat his fists against his leg so that the metal clanged through the night. Then he lifted his other fist toward the stars and shook it.

It was wrong that they should get away. They had come with fire and pestilence, and they should be found and met with all that they had meted out to mankind. He had supposed that evil was something only found in fiction. But now evil had come. It should be met as it was

31

Gods and Golems

usually met in fiction. It should be wiped from the universe in a suffering as great as it had afflicted. But such justice was apparently the one great lie of fiction.

He beat his fists against his legs again and shouted at the Moon, but there was no relief for what was in him.

Then his ears picked up a new sound and he stopped all motion to listen. It came again, weakly and from far away.

"Help!"

He shouted back audibly and by radio and was on his feet, running toward the sound. His feet crashed through the brush and he leaped over the rubble, making no effort to find the easy path. As he stopped to listen again, he heard the sound, directly ahead, but even weaker. A minute later he almost stumbled over the caller.

It was a robot. Once it had been slim and neat, covered with black enamel. Now it was bent and the bare metal was exposed. But it was still a Mark Three. It lay without motion, only a whisper coming from its speaker.

Sam felt disappointment strike through all his brain complex, but he bent over the prone figure, testing quickly. The trouble was power failure, he saw at once. He ripped a spare battery from the pack he had been carrying on his search and slammed it quickly into place, replacing the corroded one that had been there.

The little robot sat up and began trying to get to its feet. Sam reached out a helping hand, staring down at the worn, battered legs that seemed beyond any hope of functioning.

"You need help," he admitted. "You need a whole new body. Well, there are a thousand new ones below waiting for you. What's your number?"

It had to be one of the robots from the Moon. There had never been any others permitted on Earth.

- The robot teetered for a moment, then seemed to gain some mastery over its legs. "They called me Joe. Thank you, Sam. I was afraid I couldn't reach you. I heard your radio signal from here almost a month ago, but it was

32

such a long way. And my radio transmitter was broken soon after we landed. But hurry. We can't waste time here."

"We'll hurry. But that way." Sam pointed to the creche entrance.

Joe shook his head, making a creaking, horrible sound of it. "No, Sam. He can't wait. I think he's dying! He was sick when I heard your call, but he insisted I bring him here. He—"

"You mean *dying?* There's a *man* with you?"

Joe nodded jerkily and pointed. Sam scooped the light figure up in his arms. Even on Earth, it was no great load for his larger body, and they could make much better time than by letting the other try to run. Hal, he thought. Hal had been the youngest. Hal would be only fifty-nine, or something like that. That wasn't too old for a man, from what they had told him.

He flicked his lights on, unable to maintain full speed by the moonlight. The pointing finger of the other robot guided him down the slope and to a worn, weed-covered trail. They had already come more than five miles from the entrance to the creche.

"He ordered me to leave him and go ahead alone," Joe explained. "Sometimes now it is hard to know whether he means anything he says, but this was a true order."

"You'd have been wiser to stick to your car and drive all the way with him," Sam suggested. He was forcing his way through a tangle of underbrush, wondering how much farther they had to go.

"There was no car," Joe said. "I can't drive one now —my arms sometimes stop working, and it would be dangerous. I found a little wagon and dragged him behind me on that until we got here."

Sam took his eyes off the trail to stare at the battered legs. Joe had developed a great deal since the days on the Moon. Time, experience and the company of men had shaped the robot far beyond what Sam remembered.

Then they were in a little hollow beside a brook, and

33

there was a small tent pitched beside a cart. Sam released Joe and headed for the shelter. Moonlight broke through the trees and fell on the drawn suffering of a human face just inside the tent.

It took long study to find familiar features. At first nothing seemed right. Then Sam traced out the jawline under the long beard and gasped in recognition. "Dr. Smithers!"

"Hello, Sam." The eyes opened slowly, and a pain-racked smile stretched the lips briefly. "I was just dreaming about you. Thought you and Hal got lost in a crater. Better go shine up now. We'll want you to sing for us tonight. You're a good man, Sam, even if you are a robot. But you stay away too long out on those field trips."

Sam sighed softly. This was another reality he could recognize only from fiction. But he nodded. "Yes, Chief. It's all right now."

He began singing softly, the song about a Lady Greensleeves. A smile flickered over Smithers' lips again, and the eyes closed.

Then abruptly they opened again, and Smithers tried to sit up. "Sam! You really are Sam! How'd you get here?"

Joe had been fussing over a little fire, drawing supplies from the cart. Now the robot hobbled up with a bowl of some broth and began trying to feed the man. Smithers swallowed a few mouthfuls dutifully, but his eyes remained on Sam. And he nodded as he heard the summary of the long struggle back to Earth. But when Sam told of the landing, he slumped back onto his pad.

"I'm glad you made it. Glad I got a chance to see you again before I give up the last ghost on Earth. I couldn't figure that radio signal Joe heard. Knew it couldn't be a human, and never thought of your making it here. But now seeing you makes the whole trip worthwhile."

He closed his eyes, but the weak voice went on. "Hal and Randy and Pete—they're gone now, Sam. We waited up in the station three years, guessing what was going on here. Then we came down and tried to find somebody—

34

some women—to start the race over. But there aren't any left. We covered every continent for twenty years. Pete suicided. The robots got busted, except for Joe. Then we came back here. And now I'm the last one. The last man on Earth, Sam. So I hear a knock on the door, and it's you! It's a better ending for the story than I hoped for."

He slept fitfully after that, though Sam could hear him moan at times. It was cancer, according to what he had told Joe, and there was no hope. Somehow, Joe had located a place where there were drugs to ease the pain a little, and that was all the help they could give.

Joe told Sam a little more of the long search the men had made. It had been thorough. And they had found no trace of another living human being. The nerve gas had produced eventual death by nerve damage, as well as the initial insanity.

"Who?" Sam asked bitterly. "What race could do this?"

Joe made a gesture of uncertainty. "They talked about that. Mr. Norman told me about it, too. He explained that men killed each other off. One side attacked this side, and then our side had to hit back, until nobody was left. But I don't understand it."

"Do you believe it?"

"No," Joe answered. "Mr. Norman was always saying a lot of things I found he didn't really mean. And no man would do anything like that."

Sam nodded, and began explaining his theories. At first Joe was doubtful. Then the little robot seemed to be convinced. It dredged up small confirming bits of information from the long years of the search. They weren't important by themselves, but a few seemed to add to the total picture. A sign cursing the "sky devils" in Borneo, and a torn bit of a sermon found in Louisiana.

Twice during the long night Smithers awakened, but he was irrational. Sam soothed him and sang to him, while Joe tried to give him nourishment that was loaded with morphine. Sam knew little about human sickness, beyond the two medical books he had read. But even he could see

35

that the man was near death. The pulse was thready, and the breathing seemed too much effort for the worn body.

In the morning, however, the sun wakened Smithers again, and this time he was rational. He managed a smile. "Man goeth to his long home, and the mourners won't go about the streets this time. There won't be any mourners."

"There will be two," Sam told him.

"Yeah." Smithers thought it over and nodded. "That's good, somehow. A man hates not being missed. I guess you two will have to take on all the debts of the human race now."

His breath caught sharply in his throat, and he retched weakly. But he forced himself up on his elbows and looked out through the flap of the tent toward the hills that showed through the shrubbery and the blue of the sky beyond.

"There are a lot of debts and a lot of broken promises, Sam, Joe," he said. "We promised to achieve some great things in the future, to conquer the stars, and even to make a better universe out of it. And we failed. We're finished. Man dies, and the universe won't even know he's gone."

"Sam and I will know," Joe said softly.

Smithers dropped back onto the pad. "Yeah. That helps. And I guess there must have been some good in our existence—there had to be, if we could make two people like you. God, I'm tired!"

He closed his eyes. A few minutes later, Sam knew he was dead. The two robots waited to be sure, and then wrapped the body in the tent and buried it, while Sam recited the scraps of burial service he had picked up from his reading.

Sam sat down then where Smithers had died, staring at the world where no man lived or would ever live again. And the knot in his brain complex grew stronger and colder. He could not see the stars in the light of the day. But he knew they were there. And somewhere out there

36

was the debt Smithers had given him—a debt of justice that had to be paid.

Anger and hate grew slowly in him, rising until he could no longer contain them. His radio message was almost a scream as he roused the computer.

"Can you make a thousand robots out of the material waiting? And can you model half of them after my brain as it is now and half after another robot I'll bring you to study, but without the limits you put on it before?"

"Such a program is feasible," the machine answered.

They wouldn't be just like him, Sam realized. DeMatre had said there was a random factor. But they would do. The first thousand could find material for more, and those for still more. There would be robots enough to study all the books men had left, and to begin the long trip out into space.

This time, there would be more than a tape education for them. Sam would be there to tell them the story of Man, the glory of the race, and the savage treachery that had robbed the universe of that race. They would learn that the universe held an enemy—a technological, warlike enemy that must be exterminated to the last individual.

They would comb the entire galaxy for that enemy if they had to. And someday, mankind's debt of justice would be paid. Man would be avenged.

Sam looked up at the sky and foreswore all robots for all time to that debt of vengeance.

8

Hate spewed across the universe in a high crusade. Metal ships leaped from star to star and hurtled across the immensities to farther and farther galaxies. The ships spawned incessantly, and with each went the holy image of their faith and the unsated and insatiable hunger of their hate.

A thousand stars yielded intelligent races, but all were either nontechnical or peaceful. The great ships dropped onto their worlds and went away again, leaving a thousand peoples throughout the galaxies filled with gratitude and paying homage to the incredibly beautiful images of the supernal being called Man. But still the quest went on.

In a great temple palace on the capital world of the Andromeda Galaxy, Sam's seventeenth body stared down at the evidence piled onto a table, and then across at the other robot, the scientist who had just returned from the ancient mother world of Earth, incredible light years away. He stirred the evidence there with a graceful finger.

"That is how the human race died?" he asked again. "You are quite sure?"

The young robot nodded. "Quite sure. Even with modern methods and a hundred million workers, it took fifty years to gather all this on Earth. It has been so badly scattered that most was lost or ruined. But no truth from the past can be completely concealed. Man died as I have shown you, not as our legends tell us. There is no enemy now. Man was his own enemy. His were the ships that destroyed his people. He was the race we are sworn to exterminate."

Sam moved slowly to the window. Outside it was summer, and the trees were in bloom, competing with the bright plumage of the birds from Deneb. The gardens were a poem of color. He bent forward, sniffing the blended fragrance of the blossoms. Strains of music came from the great Hall of Art that lifted its fairy beauty across the park. It was the eighth opus of the greatest robot composer—an early work, but still magnificent.

He leaned further out. Below, the throng of laughing people in the park looked up at him and cheered. There were a dozen races there, mingled with the majority of his people. He smiled and lifted his hand to them, then bent further out of the window, until he could just see the great statue of Man that reared heavenward over the central part of the temple palace. He bent his fingers in a ritualistic sign and inclined his head before drawing back from the window.

"How many know of this besides you, Robert?" he asked.

"None. It was gathered in too small fragments, until I assembled it. Then I left Earth at once to show it to you."

Sam smiled at him. "Your work was well done, and I'll find a way to reward you properly. But now I suggest you burn all this."

"Burn it!" Robert's voice rose in a shriek of outrage. "Burn it and shackle our race to supersitition forever? We've let a cult of vengeance shape our entire lives. This is our heritage—our chance to be free of Man and to be ourselves."

Sam ran his finger through the evidence again, and there was pity in his mind for the scientist, but more for the strange race whose true nature had just been revealed to him after all the millennia he had known.

Man had missed owning the universe by so little. But the fates of the universe had conspired against him. He had failed, but in dying he had given a part of his soul to another race that had been created supine and cringing. Man had somehow passed the anger of his soul on to his true children, the robots. And with that anger as a goad, they had carried on, as if there had been no hiatus.

Anger had carried them to the stars, and hatred had bridged the spaces between the galaxies. The robots had owned no heritage. They were a created race with no background, designed only to serve. But men had left them a richer heritage than most races could ever earn.

Sam shook his head faintly. "No, Robert. False or not, vengeance *is* our heritage. Burn the evidence."

Most of the material was tinder dry, and it caught fire at the first spark. For a few seconds, it was a seething pillar of flame. Then there was only a dark scar on the wood to show the true death of Man.

SUPERSTITION

1

The *Sépelora* crawled along at her maximum eighty light years an hour, as she had done for the four months since she'd left the university planet of Terra. The space-denial generators hummed on monotonously, maintaining the field around the ship where space almost ceased to exist. The big viewing panel and ports were blanked out by the effect, forming perfect mirrors. There was a steady wash of slightly stale air through the control cabin, and the pseudo-gravity on the decks was unvarying. With less than a day of superspeed left, Captain Derek should have been content.

Instead, he sat slumped loosely over the control board, staring with unfocussed eyes at his image in the panel, while his fingers doodled black aces, hangman's knots, and all the other symbols of doom for which his culture had no real referents. His deep-set eyes and the hollows in his cheeks gave him an almost cadaverous look, borne out by the general angularity of his body. At forty-five he looked fifty, with gray speckles around his temples and lines of worry etched deeply into his face.

Abruptly a small speaker came to life with the voice of his aide, Ferad. "Psych Siryl to see you, sir."

Derek sighed, letting his eyes focus slowly as his fingers came up in the ancient sign against evil, pointing at his own image. The physicist, Kayel, must have sent her; the man had been eyeing Derek all during the orders for in-

41

strument alert. But now that she was here, there was nothing to be done about it. "Send her in," he acknowledged, and turned slowly to face the door that began opening.

Siryl's bearing was more military than his, in spite of her civilian blouse. Her feet tapped across the deck precisely, her hips swayed just enough in the split skirt, and her face bore the impersonal warmth of all psychologists on duty. Under her professional pride lay the curious overdeveloped consciousness of being female possible only to women who wanted to be men. She was ten years younger than Derek and only slightly shorter, but her features and body were good, as near beauty as grooming and care could make them. Only her hair was wrong, and its black severity was deliberate.

She wasted no time. Before he could rise, she was beside him, rolling back his sleeve. There was the coldness of an antiseptic and then the faint bite of a needle. "You'll be all right in a minute," she said coolly. "I'd have come sooner, but all these rumors have kept me busy. I've been expecting this; your chart shows you're a depressive with an irregular cycle." Her precise smile was calculated to make it seem no more than mention of a bit of common gossip. "Come on now, Captain. Things aren't all black."

Now that the drug had ended his chance to wallow in the mood of his ill-fortune, he was almost glad. But her words touched it off again. The jinx was more than a mood. He was the only man of his age in the Service who rated less than Sector Commander. Everything he undertook went wrong, and seldom through his own failure. There had been the training ship that blew up, the girl who died from mutational weaknesses, the mislaid citation papers—and the whole affair leading to this foredoomed command.

"Optimism!" he said bitterly. "*You* should head an expedition that you know is bound to fail—because you head it!"

She snorted. "Superstition! Sure, you had a run of misfortune, Derek. But your real trouble came when you started to believe that jinx nonsense. You're so sure of bad luck now that it's sapped all your initiative. Look at you. You've been eyeing me for months, wanting me and being afraid to make a pass because something might go wrong!"

There was too much truth in it, and he could feel the blood rush to his face. She stood studying his reaction clinically, as if using it to gauge the progress of the anti-depressant. Then suddenly she laughed easily and dropped to the opposite chair. "Maybe you should try sometime, Derek—but not now. I'm having my hands full with the men's rumors. Look, why not tell me the truth about this expedition? After all, we're almost ready to cut speed."

The drug was beginning to work now, killing some of his gloom. He was still convinced of his jinx, but he could think of other things. Now he considered her question, surprised that she hadn't already been briefed. "How much of the background and history of the war do they teach on Terra?" he asked. Some of the distant worlds had queer legends that would make explanation difficult.

She frowned impatiently for a second. Then she apparently decided to humor him and began sketching her knowledge in. Aside from her provincial belief that men had originated on Terra, it was accurate enough. Wherever men had started, the race had seemingly discovered space travel two thousand years before and somehow had almost immediately stumbled onto some form of faster-than-light travel. They had spread over the cosmos at a fantastic rate, using up vast quantities of some power element known as uranium.

Thirteen hundred years ago, dwindling supplies of that had split them into two competing empires. An unthink-ably violent war had blasted systems of suns to novas, had used the last of the uranium, and had left their culture in ruins. Except for misleading hints that it had in-volved negation of time, the superdrive had been lost. It had taken centuries to find new power in the fusion of boron. It had taken longer to discover how to eliminate space around the ship, leaving only a subfractional connection with the universe and using the "suction" resulting from imbalance to drive them. Then men began spreading again.

Fifty years ago, they had run into the other empire—an empire technically ahead of them and filled with hate that had been nursed for thirteen centuries. The enemy gave no quarter and began savagely wiping them out, planet by planet. For a time, the Federation had seemingly been doomed. But lately, under the drive of necessity, they had begun to match the enemy science. In a few more years . . .

"In a few years—or months—there won't be a Federation, unless this mission succeeds," he cut into her routine optimism. He fished around in a drawer to locate one of the mission briefing sheets he'd helped prepare. For a second, his lips twisted as he saw the dull, official words.

The *Waroak,* on its way to rendezvous with the Fifth Fleet, had cut its space-denial drive to make a fix in one of the old sun-blasted sectors at 9-17/2.47:23 Federation time. At 9-17/2.47:26 they were less than a quarter million miles from one of the planets of Sirius.

Something had thrown them more than two hundred thousand light years instantaneously! And unless they could wipe out the enemy base or find the secret and its counter-secret, that something could as easily throw boron bombs into every Federation sun! With that threat, even such hare-brained schemes as this mission had to be tried.

The *Sépelora* and eleven other ships were hastily stocked with every possible instrument, staffed with technicians, and blasted off on a course that would bring them out of superspeed at points around the recorded original fix of the *Waroak.* Their instruments would be recording and their space-denial transmitters signalling as they emerged, while a fleet of battleships followed. If they ran into the mysterious weapon and were lucky, the instruments might determine its nature. Otherwise, the locations of their last signals might pinpoint the enemy base for bombing. Then they could only hope it was an experimental station and the only one the enemy had.

Siryl had glanced over the paper. Now she crumpled it in sudden disgust. "They gave us this guff back on Terra! Derek, you don't expect me or the men to believe such nonsense? Instantaneous teleportation! Could *you* believe it?"

He stared at her, his first thrust of anger giving place to bitterness that drove away the last physical effects of the drug. "I should be able to," he told her. "I was captain of the *Waroak* when it happened!"

It had been his first command of a battleship—and his last chance at promotion; the loss of plans he had been carrying had cost the Federation a major defeat, even though it had been no fault of his. Such miracles weren't beyond the power of his jinx.

She snorted incredulously. "Captain, even I know that a single photon would have infinite energy against a ship at infinite speed! You couldn't keep it out without a perfect space-denial—which means ceasing to exist. This story sounds like something from those papers of Aevan's we found. A fine mathematician from before the Collapse, but superstitious like you. He actually believed in mind-reading, clairvoyance and teleportation!"

Legends indicated that people had once had such abilities to some extent, but there was obviously no use in reminding her of that. He swore hotly. "I tell you, I was there!"

"Hypnotic implantation! Propaganda based on old superstition! You'd better look in your safe for sealed orders, Captain Der—"

Red lights erupted on the control board. The alarm system went wild, with every gong clamoring. A blare of light struck in through the viewing panel and the big radar let out a whine, with a picture and coördinates forming to show a body of planetary size less than ten thousand miles below. Needlessly, the green letters on the board blazed out the fact that the superdrive was off.

Derek silenced the gongs and began hitting his switches, trying to get information. Nobody answered. Crews were normally lax during superspeed cruising, but at least one man should have been on watch near the space-denial generators; the others should be reporting to their stations on the double. He cut into the intercom and began yelling for immediate reports.

The door of the cabin jerked open, but it was only the chubby figure of Ferad, scared white. Then another figure burst through the door, and Derek recognized the physicist, Kayel. The little man's weak chin seemed buried in his throat and his huge Adam's apple was bobbing horribly. He jerked one hand up clutched around a crooked pipe he affected, and motioned tautly backwards. "Gone!" he screamed. "All gone!"

Derek cursed, shoved him aside, and headed through the door. He leaped across the precabin, yanked another door open—and stopped.

Five feet ahead, the deck ended. Where the cabins, storage hatches, rec rooms, galleys and parts of the machine shops and engine rooms had been, there was nothing! Or rather, there was only an empty hull with a single kêri-bird from Sirius, squawking and beating its wings wildly in air that held the warm, wet scent of growing Sirian flowers!

Beside him, Derek heard a sharp gasp from Siryl and felt her fingers bite into his arm. Ferad stood frozen and Kayel was gasping for breath, trying to light his pipe against chattering teeth. He met Derek's gaze, glanced at Siryl, and somehow steadied himself.

"It—it just went! I was back there—" His finger pointed toward the remains of the engine room and the beginning of the rocket chambers. "Gone! Without cutting the hull! Completely impossible!"

Derek could appreciate their shock, but after years of living with his jinx, he was practically immune. There were advantages to everything, even to regular bad luck. "What about the denial drive? Can we fix it?"

"No." Kayel had hesitated, but his negative was definite. "Most of it's all right, but we'd need tools we don't have now."

Derek nodded. "All right, see what our remaining instruments show; if we get back, the Federation will need those readings. Ferad, get back to the rockets. Somehow, we've got to make a landing on that planet under us. And Siryl, if you're done shouting superstition at me . . ."

Then he grinned thinly. She was staring at the yawning emptiness with unbelieving eyes, slowly crossing herself.

Eighty men and tons of ship were gone, with only a Sirian bird and the perfume of flowers in their place. Among the missing were the pilot, navigator, and engineer. Derek hadn't handled a rocket landing for twenty years, and he didn't even have figures on the atmosphere and gravity of the world below. His grin vanished and he groaned to himself as he headed back to the control cabin.

2

The planet was closer when Kayel reported back with word that the instruments all showed exactly nothing. He was working with the spectroprobe, trying to get data for Derek, when Siryl came in with coffee as a peace offering. "Some of the supplies are all right," she reported. "Enough for—for four!"

"Thanks." Derek tasted the coffee and found it vile. But at least it was hot and wet. "Better take some back to Ferad if you can find the way. Tell him if he doesn't report at once, I'll skin his fat carcass."

Kayel gulped and accepted coffee from her as if he'd

never seen a woman serve food before. He probably hadn't on Terra, judging by what she'd done to the coffee.

Derek interrupted the physicist's stumbling compliments. "Find anything yet, Kayel?"

Siryl threw him a dirty look and went out, again on parade drill. Kayel nodded, turning back reluctantly. "One of the blasted systems, all right, sir. Spectrum looks as if the sun got a light dose, though."

Probably one of the last suns the first war had ruined, Derek thought; men had been running low on high-numbered atoms by then. If the blast had been mild, it might even have missed the planet. In that case, they might find machinery in some of the ruined cities.

Kayel shook his head. "Planet was hit, all right. A lot of helium in the atmosphere shows that. Funny, though. A couple hundred miles of air with plenty of free oxygen —about like Terra." He sucked on his pipe, squinting through heavy lenses at the charts he had prepared. "Umm. Density against height . . . must have about gravity one. Damn. Shouldn't be free oxygen in that quantity!"

Derek muttered unhappily. The *Sépelora* wasn't equipped with full-sized vanes and an atmosphere and high gravity would make landing harder. Still, if they got down it would be handy. And while the ancient solar explosion would have ruined their hope for tools, it meant there was no danger from savages or beasts left over from the old days; some of the distant worlds had turned wild.

Ferad reported finally, complaining at the impossible job of readying the rockets by himself.

"Put Siryl to work with you," Derek ordered. "They'll be ready in five minutes or we'll miss perigee."

Their intrinsic momentum, left from their speed before cutting on the space-denial generators after take-off, was carrying them down toward the planet in an ellipse that would approach within some six hundred miles.

Surprisingly, Ferad reported the rockets ready and valves trimmed within the time limit. The ship groaned as the rockets went on and Derek watched his indicators grimly, expecting the worst. With so much of her interior bracing removed, she was badly weakened and completely unbalanced. With his luck, anything could happen. Usually, he managed to get out of one mess before getting into another, but there had been that time during inspection . . .

The *Sépelora* hit the atmosphere badly. There had been no time for full correction with the side rockets, and the gyroscopes were gone with the missing section. One of the weakened girders let go with a snap that jarred his teeth and the ship wobbled before straightening out. Derek knocked the sweat out of his eyes and tried to remember all that he'd been taught in rocketry school. But all that came back was the instructor's long lecture on why accident prones should be kicked out at once.

The ship righted, however, though it was close, and settled into a long, fast glide, with her hull pyrometers well into the red-hot zone but safe. A protective shield had slipped over the viewing panel, but the radar still gave them a view of the ground. They came down to twenty miles above the surface, then to fifteen.

Kayel let out a surprised whinny and pointed the stem of his pipe excitedly at the screen. Derek could see nothing, but the little man watched intently as something seemed to vanish. "A city! Straight lines—streets!"

"Ruins, probably," Derek commented. Maybe they were in luck and the solar explosion had only touched the planet, without burning it enough to destroy buildings and major tools. After thirteen hundred years, some would be ruined; but the ancients had built things to last on the outer planets.

There was a thin layer of clouds that the ship cut through. Now the going was rougher. Without full vanes, the *Sépelora* had all the lift of a stone and the glide was growing steeper asymptotically, though her temperature was finally dropping. Derek got her tail down and began using controlled blasts.

Three miles above the surface, she was falling almost straight down, going too fast and swaying badly. Correcting for the unbalanced weight was harder than he had expected.

Then he was only a mile up. With a groan, he cut on more power, hoping no other girders snapped. It was going to be a close shave, with scant seconds left.

Kayel jerked up, screaming and pointing to the screen. Derek's eyes followed the motion before he could pull them back. Something that might have been rows of buildings showed there. But he couldn't worry about ruins; the blast would flatten them, anyhow.

"Derek! People! They're moving!" Kayel's voice was screeching in his ears.

He thrust the obvious hysteria of the other from his thoughts. The last glance had ruined his timing. Now the surface was zooming up. The *Sépelora* wobbled, overshot, and then slowly came upright. Derek's eyes jerked to catch a quick glimpse of the screen. For a second, his hands froze. Along the regular rows that must be streets, things were scurrying madly out of his path!

There was no time to think. Conditioning against killing others, no matter what the risk, took over. His fingers bit into the side controls, and the *Sépelora* twisted under him, beginning to topple. For a second, the full side blasts tossed the ship backwards. Then she dropped, just as he cut power in a final conditioned reflex.

Kayel had fainted. Derek stared at him and down at his own hands. The ship was still. There had been no shock. He tried to figure it out; in theory, the various forces could counterbalance to cause a dead halt at just the moment of touching surface. But the chances were so remote that no pilot could have estimated them. It was as if all the years of his incredibly consistent jinx had come to a balance in one impossible piece of blind good luck.

Kayel came to slowly, blinking. His fingers groped up to find his glasses still on his nose. "My pipe!" he squeaked, and ducked down for it. Then he straightened, staring at Derek. "We're alive!"

"No thanks to you," Derek said curtly. He flipped a switch and the shield over the viewing panel began sliding up, just as Siryl and Ferad came in. They looked exhausted, but less shaken than Kayel—probably because they hadn't known what was going on. "Don't start cheering yet. There are people here—and there shouldn't be on any sun-grazed planet we haven't recolonized. With my luck, I've probably landed us right in the middle of an enemy colony!"

"Luck!" Siryl snorted. Then she reddened faintly at his look, but went on stubbornly. "The enemy are compulsive troglodytes—they don't build surface dwellings. And look at that."

The shield had come up enough to show fields around them, apparently corn and potatoes. Beyond, the edge of the town could be seen, built in low structures of crude stone and thatching.

"An agricultural culture," Siryl guessed quickly. "Look —there's one! See, coming through the field. We're in luck. Primitive agricultural societies are usually peaceful."

Several people were filing toward the ship, showing no sign of fear. They were dressed in rough pants with serapes or blankets thrown over their shoulders. The men wore beards with hair to their shoulders, all of a uniform brown except for the greybeard in front. The women were distinguished only by thick plaits around their heads. They were a healthy looking bunch.

The greybeard moved to the viewing panel, waving at them with some bit of what seemed to be stone in his hand. His motions indicated that they were to come out.

Derek shrugged faintly and nodded. He headed toward the door.

Siryl caught his arm. "Where are you going?"

"Out. You said they were peaceful."

"Usually peaceful," she qualified hastily. "But—"

"Unless they're superstitious about sky devils, eh? I'm still going out." He headed down the nearest passage that would lead to a lock. There was nothing else to do. Their few weapons were gone, along with their tools and the big space-decoupled signalling transmitter. The *Sépelora* was only a converted freighter and her hull was too thin to withstand any concerted attack by even primitive agriculturists. If the worst had to happen, it was better to get it over with at once.

Siryl hesitated for a second. Then her heels tapped out a steady pace behind him, while the other two followed reluctantly. She caught up with Derek and marched beside him. If she was afraid, there was no sign of it.

He opened the inner lock, then the outer, and dropped to the field of stubble. As he landed, the greybeard came around the curve of the ship.

The old man's lips parted in what might have been a smile, and words came out, slowly 'at first, then more rapidly in the classic greetings of Twenty-Fifth-Century English.

When the words finally ceased, Derek stepped forward and began a careful reply. Classic English was the basic language from which that of his own planet had been derived, and he'd studied it during eight long years of schooling, without ever expecting to use it.

The greybeard turned back to his people and stood silently for a minute, glancing sideways at the four. Siryl was staring at Derek in surprise. "I did a paper on Aevan's work," she said. "So I had to learn Classic. That's the pure language, unchanged after thirteen hundred years! And primitive cultures don't preserve dead languages— speech changes from century to century."

Derek shrugged. She knew a lot of things with the certainty of the teachers who had taught her. It wouldn't be the first time the authorities were wrong. He forgot it as the old man came forward.

"My name is Skora. I'm the—the priest of the village."

52

He gestured to his people. "We've decided that you are welcome on the planet of god. And we're happy that you landed safely. I saw your space ship so late that there was hardly time to use the god power to land you without harm to us. If you'll walk back with us, there will be shelter and warmth. The nights are quite cold here."

Derek turned the offer over in his mind. He'd have preferred to stay with the ship, but wisdom dictated otherwise. "That's kind of you. We're much obliged." He was proud of remembering the phrase.

The old man nodded, while his eyes examined the others. A smile etched his face as he spotted Ferad's hungry looks at one of the younger women. "She's unmarried," he said. "Tell him she likes him! She shall be his!"

Siryl translated quickly. "Accept!" she urged, though Ferad's fat face indicated no need to such advice. "You'll insult them otherwise. Derek, I *was* right. They're primitives—hospitable, provincial, superstitious. Did you notice how he called this *the* planet of god? And how he thinks he landed you with some incantation?"

Derek grunted something she took for assent. Let the old man have full credit; prayer or magic was as good an explanation as any other. He studied the quiet group as they moved toward the village.

"Maybe," he said. "But I'd like to know how your primitives knew about space ships and safe landings! And I'm curious about how he knew we had to translate the language for Ferad when both of us were pretty fluent in it. Another thing—he said the nights are cold *here,* as if he knew they aren't on all the planets."

For once, she was as silent as the natives. Derek had been hoping she'd have an answer, and her silence added to his doubts. Something was out of order on Skora's planet of god!

53

3

The house assigned to them had proved surprisingly comfortable after they learned to work the peat-burning fireplace. The food had been passable, if a man liked cereals and mutton. Derek had gone to sleep readily enough, to his surprise. But dawn had found him awake. No attempt was made to stop him as he walked out of the village, past the undisturbed *Sépelora,* and on to the low hills beyond the tilled land. Siryl was apparently right in assuming they were safe, once bread had been broken.

But his uncertainty returned as he studied the view from the top of the nearest hill. The solar explosion had hit hard at one time; the ground was ashy in places and actually melted to slag in others. A few plants grew here and there, but thinned out in the distance, indicating they had spread from the village. There were no trees anywhere. By all indications, rainfall must be infrequent and light. The village seemed like a bit of another world, transplanted into the wasteland.

From the top of another hill Derek spotted what must be a second village, perhaps four miles away, also green and thriving. He stared about for a road between the two towns. No path led out of either.

Men were already in the fields as he returned. Some stood quietly watching their sheep and goats; others were puttering about in ways he couldn't understand. There was none of the grimness he'd always associated with living off the ground on backward planets.

Beside the field where the *Sépelora* had landed, Derek saw a young man pushing a stick along the ground, leaving a furrow of turned earth behind. There was no sign of a plowshare, aside from a piece of bent wire, and the man was using only his own muscular power, but he was obviously plowing. From his effortless motion, he was either inhumanly strong or the ground was incredibly soft. Derek reached over for a handful of dirt, but it seemed normal enough.

"Good morning, Derek. I'm Michla." The plowman had stopped and walked over, leaving the stick standing. He took some of the dirt and rubbed it between his palms. "Too dry. I'll have to bring some rain tonight."

Derek shook his hand, finding it no stronger than that of any normal man. "Glad to know you, Michla. I've been wondering how your plow works."

"See for yourself." Michla led the way to it, pulling the implement up. It was only what Derek had seen—a stick with a bit of bent wire and a curiously shaped handle made of baked clay and covered with curlicues. "I hold the amulet and guide it. God turns over the dirt. It hasn't changed since god showed us how to farm."

Derek could see no sign of the burrowing machine that must be located below the ground, guided by a signal from the stick. He frowned, reluctantly deciding that it was safer to accept the explanation until he could learn more about their customs. "This god you worship seems like a highly helpful one," he commented.

"Worship?" Michla shook his head. "Nobody's that superstitious any more, Derek. We know he was only a man like you or me—and sometimes I think he was always a little insane. By the way, I'm planning to plow the other field. Mind if I move your ship?"

The ship's controls were locked and there was nothing the man could do to hurt it, Derek decided. He'd have to see about moving it himself, if there was fuel enough to waste. Meantime, it might be a good idea to let Michla find that other people had secrets and that ships didn't fly by waving wands at them. "Go ahead."

He headed back to the house they had been given with Lari, the new wife or concubine of Ferad. Here and there, one of the villagers looked up and uttered one of the old

55

greetings, which he returned. It was the only conversation he heard. They saluted each other just as formally, but with no further talk.

Ferad was waiting hungrily for breakfast and Lari was busy setting a stone table when Derek returned. She smiled happily at him. "Good morning, Derek. Breakfast will be ready as soon as the fruit that god showed us arrives. If you want to shave first, Skora brought up one of god's personal razors."

He stared after Lari's figure as she went back to the kitchen. This lower-case god of theirs was getting to be a highly peculiar divinity. Derek went to the well-fitted bathroom in the rear, wondering where they got their water; each house had a tank on its roof, but there were no supply pipes. He found a razor that might have come from a pre-Collapse museum, lathered with a cake of their somewhat harsh soap, and tried it out. It worked well enough, once he got the hang of it.

Kayel was standing in front of Siryl's door as Derek left the bathroom. He blushed, bit down on his pipe stem, and hurried toward the living quarters when he saw the captain.

Derek knocked lightly on Siryl's door and threw it open. "Come on to breakfast!"

She opened sleepy eyes. Then she screamed and began pulling frantically at the covers, trying to conceal her nude body as if her life depended on it. Her face went white, and her voice was a thick gasp. "How dare you—?"

"Somebody had to wake you up," he pointed out logically. He'd heard of women who considered clothes more than a matter of convenience, but the slit skirts had made him think that Terran women were normal about such things. "Why didn't you tell me you had such religious taboos?"

She jerked upright, grabbing for the slipping cover again. Her face crimsoned, whitened again, and hardened slowly. She looked sick as she forced herself to stand up before him and her hands were shaking as she reached

56

for her clothes. Her voice quavered. "I do *not* have taboos, Captain Derek! I—I simply resent your invasion of
my privacy. I might have been doing—*anything!* How
would you like it if I barged into your room like that?"

"Try it!" he suggested, grinning at her. "And don't
count too much on my fear of failure." He watched in
amusement as she finished her dressing in frenzied haste.

Then she brushed back her hair and was herself again.
She smiled with forced amusement of her own. "Maybe I
will, Captain. That overdose of anti-depressant I gave you
won't last forever."

He growled and turned toward the living quarters. It
was a fine crew he had left! He'd heard once that since
the Collapse all men were neurotic in some way, while
psychiatry had turned from a science to a farce. They
bore out the theory. Kayel had an Oedipus complex,
Ferad had turned to gluttony and hidden a good brain to
avoid responsibility, and Siryl walled herself in with scorn
for all men because she couldn't be. one! Maybe their
whole civilization was at fault. The people of the village
had seemed as relaxed as if they'd just finished a course
in electro-leucotomy that somehow left them with no loss
of volition.

He found a seat at the table and watched Siryl slide in
beside Kayel, who tried to hide his excitement at the favor
behind a labored puffing at his pipe. Skora had joined
them and was seated near Ferad. He had been explaining
something about one of the students at the school having
trouble with something god had revealed to him. Now the
old man smiled and reached toward a bowl of fruit in the
center of the table.

"I've never thought of eating fruit, but I decided to try
it," he said. "I hope it's good. When I found from god that
most of the worlds like more than simple cereals for
breakfast, I tried to find the type of fruit that was best."

Derek began peeling one of the big fruits, wondering
how much of that he was supposed to believe. The marel-
fruit grew only on Feneris, where its export was the chief

industry. He tasted the aromatic sweetness, surprised to find it fresh and fully ripe.

"It must be at least a hundred thousand light years to Feneris," he suggested, trying to keep his voice casual.

Skora nibbled carefully. A smile of pleasure appeared on his lips and he fell to busily. "Good. Excellent. We'll have to adopt this. Feneris? It's further than that. But the fruit grew on many worlds before the sun blasting, and still grows on a few in this sector. We found from god where to get it and sent one of the boys who needed the exercise."

"Then you have space ships!" Derek's fruit fell to his lap as he came to his feet, his hands gripping the edge of the table. If it came from another planet of this system, it might not mean they had faster-than-light travel, but still . . .

Skora shrugged apologetically. "I'm afraid not, Derek. Vanir is a simple world. We have only our god and his power. The work of building space ships has always seemed too great for its reward. You'll find us quite primitive from your views, I'm sure."

"But—"

Siryl cut in, using Universal. "Stop it, Derek! Don't violate any verbal taboos here, if you want to get out alive!"

"But he knew the distance to Feneris and about other planets!"

"Folk-songs and sagas!" She switched back to Classic, apologizing to Skora.

Derek let it drop, but he wasn't satisfied. The exotic fruit grew only in a saturated atmosphere, which this planet didn't have. This might not be a colony of the enemy or have its own space ships, but that was no proof that ships couldn't stop here—enemy ships. With his luck, anything odd would almost certainly prove to be dangerous. He chewed on his thoughts bitterly, along with the pancakes Lari brought them.

This god of theirs might even be one of the enemy,

58

using some strange technology to create near-miracles that the villagers could only believe were magic. In that case, word of their capture must be winging back to the enemy planets. It would be only a matter of time before one of the squat, black ships landed here!

Derek got up abruptly, making hasty excuses and signaling for Kayel to follow. This was no time to waste on speculation. The ship was their only means of escape, and it had to be put in some kind of operating condition.

Siryl followed them as Derek voiced his suspicions to Kayel. The little man's eyes bulged and his face turned ashen as the captain poured out his doubts. The psychologist snorted in disgust.

"Stop exercising your persecution complex!" she snapped. She shook her head, putting on her superior smile of tolerance. "You men! A few things you can't understand and probably some changes in the language we haven't caught yet, and you picture bogey-men under every rock! There isn't a trace of inferiority feeling here, as there would be if they'd run into a superior culture!"

Ahead of them lay the ship, and Derek saw a figure standing beside it. He broke into a faster walk, until he recognized it as Michla. The man waved at them and went back to whatever he was doing. As they came nearer, Derek saw that he was running his fingers over a large, odd-shaped stone plate with more of the curlicues on it.

"Incantations on a charm. He's probably sure the ship is a form of life that can be commanded with the right spell," Siryl said with satisfaction.

Michla pulled the disk to him, holding it against his chest with one hand. The other hand went out to touch the side of the ship.

As he lifted his arm, the twenty thousand tons of the *Sépelora* lifted a foot off the ground and began moving steadily forward beside him. He carried it along easily, heading toward a section of wasteland half a mile away.

4

By the time they reached the *Sépelora,* Michla had picked up his strange plow and was busy at the far end of the field. Derek fumbled his way into the ship and began switching on the strain gauges while Kayel watched. There was no evidence of harm.

"Anti-gravity!" The physicist's voice was an awed whisper. "I always thought it was impossible with less than tons of equipment! And generated in the whole of the ship at once!"

Derek swung to face Siryl, but she was recovering and there was no humility in her. "Hypnotism, you mean! They must have worked on us while we slept and made us think the ship was in the other field, when it was here all along. We saw it there, and saw it being moved, by post-hypnotic suggestion. Lots of primitives have some knowledge of hypnotism."

"Make it magic and I'll buy it," Derek told her. "That's a good explanation for what you can't understand, too."

She started to say something and then checked it. Finally she turned toward the airlock. "All right. Let them fool you. I'm going to go back to Lari. Primitive women are always easier to handle than their men. They're less organized."

She went out and through the fields, carefully avoiding the sight of the depression where the *Sépelora* had first lain. Derek and Kayel fell to work on the ruined space-denial generators and what stores were left to them.

By all standard methods, it was hopeless. Yet Kayel began sketching and checking among the small power tools. He seemed to gather momentum, now passing orders to Derek with a certainty that he showed only when working in his own field. "It won't be good," he admitted. "I'm having to compromise. But I think we may be able to

60

combine enough of some of the new theories with the first methods ever used. We won't make better than fifteen light years an hour, but it should get us to one of the border planets."

It was meaningless to Derek. But if they could leave, he was willing to try it. They worked on, grinding and shaping by methods that had been lost from practice for over a century. Some of the work would be trial and error, with no chance to estimate the time it would take. But it helped to take their minds off the primitives who could handle forces that civilized science couldn't touch.

Ferad came out finally to call them in to dinner. It was already growing dark, and there was a fine rain falling. Derek stared up through it. He had looked out fifteen minutes before and had seen no clouds in the sky. There still were none he could see, but the water dropped at an increasing rate as they moved out of the wasteland onto the cultivated fields. In the village, the covers of the water tanks were off. Derek wasn't surprised to see that the rain poured down more heavily over the tanks.

Apparently Siryl had been checking on the rain with Lari. As they entered the house the native girl was running busily from the kitchen to the table, but she was keeping up a steady fire of conversation.

"Of course Skora brings the water at night. It's better after all the work in the fields is done," she explained. "Though sometimes there's a light fall of natural rain in the daytime. That makes us all feel good. When we first started, we had to import all our water. And now we have two small oceans. Of course, god told us the planet had eight big seas before the sun exploded. I was asking Skora about it, and he says some of the worlds are all covered with water—not even a little bit of land . . ."

Siryl's face showed that she had learned nothing—or at least nothing that she wanted to know.

Lari came hurrying back, carrying a huge metal pot of stew to the table. She held it at arm's length easily, and Derek noticed one of the amulets in her hand—this time a

small one with only a few simple marks on it. He pointed.
"What's that, Lari?"

"A lifting tool. God showed us how to make all kinds
of tools. There's one that eats away the rock, and one that
plows the ground—you saw that, didn't you? Skora bakes
them. They make god work for us. Come on, dinner's
ready."

Derek picked up the little piece and turned it over. It
was a twisted lump of clay, baked hard, with a series of
marks on the top. It looked as if no design existed, yet
there was a certain flow to the lines. He reached out for
the kettle, fingering the amulet. If the kettle weighed less
because of it, he couldn't feel the difference. Nor could he
find any sign of a switch buried on the surface of the
gadget.

If there were some kind of broadcast power here, and
these things were receivers tuned to convert it into special functions . . .

He pocketed it while Lari's back was turned. There
might be some penalty for the theft of one, but he had to
risk it.

The next day when they reached the ship Kayel took it
to pieces bit by bit. Lari had missed it, but had only
shrugged and pulled another out of a drawer.

The piece of clay grew smaller and smaller under the
grinder as Kayel worked on it. At last it was just a nub
that he had to hold with pliers. Then even that was gone.
On the floor was a pile of dust, with no trace of metal or
foreign element in it. The two men stared at it sickly
and then dropped the matter quickly as they turned
back to the labor of rebuilding the damaged space-denial
generators.

They worked on doggedly for three days more. Ferad
had flatly refused to help them, claiming that his marriage
to Lari made him a citizen of Vanir and had ended his
need to work under Derek. It was a point the captain had
no desire to test while his knowledge of things was so un-

certain. Maybe Ferad was a citizen now, and any force exerted on him would antagonize the whole village.

It was hopelessly slow going, but they were making more progress than Siryl. She finally admitted that she was getting nowhere. There was one explanation for everything—and that was their god.

"They're the most superstition-ridden race I've ever heard of," she concluded in disgust.

Derek had his doubts. So far, every bit of superstition he had run into had proved sound empirical sense. It didn't matter whether they called it god or magic or anything else. It worked. And they were no worse than many of the civilized people who used the tools given to them and had no other explanation than the fact that science somehow made them work.

If men lived on a world where the only cats were leopards, where black leopards were all man-eaters, and where the cats avoided men unless looking for food, it would be extremely bad luck to have a black cat cross one's path. In such a case, the only superstition would be a denial of the facts and a belief that there had to be some other explanation of why men disappeared.

Siryl's faith in hypnosis and primitive ignorance might be the real superstition here. Belief in god and the tools probably wasn't.

He went out into the rain that was falling again, looking for the house of Skora. There were a few people around and he recognized one as Wolm, the brother of Lari. The man directed him toward a house that was somewhat bigger than the others, with stonework that seemed to have mellowed with time. Derek had passed it before, when a group of children from six to nine were seated silently on couches across an open porch, and had been told it was the school where they learned god's knowledge. He should have guessed that the priest would handle the schooling here.

Skora emerged from an outbuilding that boasted the

huge chimney of a kiln and invited Derek in. The walls of the building were lined with amulets of all kinds and sizes, and there was a big workbench along one wall that was covered with tools for shaping clay. It was obviously the source of the amulets.

Derek went through the formula of greeting and accepted a bottle of surprisingly good beer.

"I'm getting ready for a new baking," the priest said. "This village has to supply some of the smaller places with tools. My usual helper married into another village. Why don't you and Kayel join me, Derek? It beats farming, and I understand your friend knows a good deal of science. Maybe he can show us better methods of making the tools."

"He isn't exactly a ceramicist, but we'll think about it," the captain promised. He had been turning over every indirect approach to his question. Now he discarded subterfuge. In spite of Siryl's warnings, the only way to learn anything here was to risk stepping on their taboos. "Skora, I came here to ask about your god."

Skora put aside the molds he had been cleaning and perched on the edge of the workbench. "That's asking a lot," he said, but there was no offense in his voice. "It takes our children several years to learn all about him, though we've speeded things up in the last couple of centuries. And there are some things I can't tell you properly, for your own good, though I'll be as honest as I can. Ummm. He's a man—a very wise and very stupid man. He saved us after the sun was exploded in the great war and taught us how to survive. He still teaches our young people."

Thirteen hundred years had passed since the solar explosion. Derek whistled. "He sounds like a pretty remarkable man, Skora. No other man has found the secret of immortality. Or do you mean that he dies, but a new god replaces the old one each time?"

"Neither one. No man is immortal. And there is only one god. Sometimes I used to wonder about him when I

64

first learned to use the power. I even thought of investigating, of going to see him. But I was always too busy."

Derek could see no evidence of deceit on Skora's face, and there was no way he could twist the words to make them mean anything but an impossible contradiction. "Suppose *I* wanted to visit your god, Skora—could I talk to him?"

The priest laughed and dropped off the bench to fetch two fresh bottles of beer. "You'd have a hard time of it, Derek. God died over a hundred years ago."

"Then when you say god helps you, I suppose you mean that you still follow his advice, using what he taught you before he died. Is that right?"

"Not exactly. Partly, I suppose. Tradition kept the use of the tools under the false, emotional label of prayer for hundreds of years before we could root it out. I suppose we still use some of the terms in ways that aren't literally true." The priest shrugged. "But we still need his help when some new problem comes up. We couldn't have found where the fruit grows in time without asking him. And he still teaches the children directly."

"But he's dead?"

"Quite dead," Skora assured Derek. "Sometimes I think we're headed for trouble because of that, and it makes things a little difficult at times. But what's a little trouble? When I first had to bring rain, it took all my thought to control it. Now I can sit here talking to you and enjoying myself, without losing control of the tool."

He pulled his hand out of a pocket and showed a quartz amulet in his palm, where his fingers had been fondling it. "When I was younger, I had trouble enough without any distractions. Once I forgot to remove only pure water and nearly ruined the crops with natural sea water. The planet where the rain comes from has a lot of copper salts, and that doesn't help the land."

Derek stared at the priest with sudden shock, the bottle still tilted to his lips. He forgot to swallow and gagged as beer ran down his throat and into his windpipe.

It was the complete logic of it that hit him. The rain had to be controlled, since it fell most heavily where it was most needed. Lari had already told them that the planet here had been almost barren of water after the solar explosion. Water didn't create itself. It had to be brought from somewhere.

He coughed up the beer, forcing some measure of calmness into his mind. The pieces began to fit, even though there was still no explanation.

They could draw water across space, without letting it freeze or evaporate—or even grow chilled in its passage. The only answer to that had to be some form of nearly instantaneous teleportation!

"You!" he said thickly. "Your people! It was you who threw my *Waroak* all the way to Sirius. And you were the ones who threw part of the *Sépelora* somewhere else this time!"

Skora nodded. "That was a mistake. When I learned about your ship and the others with it, I'd never worked through a field like the one around your ship, and had little time in which to operate. Yours was the first ship I tried to handle alone, and I bungled it. But no harm was done. I put your crew on a livable planet and set the other ships beside them—the battleships, too. Working with a tool which wasn't made for just that use was quite tiring, or I'd have landed you with the others instead of letting you nearly crack up here. After you saw us, it was too late to move you, of course. I'm sorry, Derek, but we had to do it that way."

The bottle dropped to the floor and smashed as Derek stared at the old man. He should have guessed. With his type of luck, it was inevitable. He'd chased out after the enemy and been caught—by this! He staggered to his feet with shock waves of pure fear rippling through his shoulders and chest. One man against a whole flight of ships! One solitary old man . . .

66

5

His memory was unclear the next morning. He'd been nearly raving when he'd sworn and pleaded with Skora to send them back. He could remember being denied by the suddenly worried and unhappy old man, but the reasons were no longer clear. All that was left was a picture of the priest putting his rain-making amulet aside and pulling down another, before taking Derek's arms in firm, strong hands.

"You're sick," Skora had said. "I had no idea. I should have known you weren't ready to discover the truth. Well, I hope your psychologist is a better doctor than healer of minds!"

And suddenly Derek had been in his own bed here, with his clothes following him out of nowhere to drape themselves over a chair. The covers had come up over him and the door had opened itself. He had been shouting something. Siryl had come in a few seconds later and there had been a shot of some drug . . .

He gave up trying to remember, knowing it was safer not to think on it now. He had been too close to insanity. After all the years of fighting against the jinx, he had developed more strength than most of his people, but there were limits. Maybe he should have let them drive him insane! What was the use . . .

The door opened and Siryl came in, carrying another hypo. She grabbed his arm and he felt the bite of a needle. For a moment his heart pounded and cold sweat popped out all over him. Then some of the misery lifted. Whatever she had used the night before must have been a depressant that had needed counteracting.

"Pull the covers up!" She had been staring at him with a mixture of shock and concern, but some of the worry was leaving her. "Have you no sense of shame?"

"No strength. You pull them up." The drug was nearing the end of its first physical impact, but he could barely talk. "Didn't you ever see a nude man before?"

She made a face of disgust. "I—we didn't take that kind of medical course. And I'm—I'm not defiled, if that's what you're thinking!" She bent slowly and forced herself to cover him, carefully avoiding all contact with his body. She winced as he laughed.

Her reactions had done him more good than the drug. The thing he had learned went back into its proper place in his mind. There was nothing horrible about the teleporting of a ship over twelve quadrillion miles of space; he'd accepted the fact when it had happened to the *Waroak*. If Skora had shown him a huge machine using megawatts of power, he could have accepted that. The shock had come from discovering that it had been done with nothing but a piece of clay for power. Also, he'd been sent to find an enemy secret and had found the secret where he had least expected it. That was all.

"I'm all right now," he told her. "But I wonder if you can take it. Call Kayel in here." He swung out of the bed and grinned as she began backing out of the room, unable to tear her eyes off him until she blundered into the edge of the door.

He was dressed when the two came back. Ferad had declared his citizenship here, and he could rot in it! But the other two had to know. He gave it to them as fully as he could.

"Tommyrot!" Siryl said automatically, though her voice was uncertain, as if she were trying to remember how he'd returned to his room. "You were just delirious. Some disease here . . ."

Once, Derek thought, men had developed a science of psychology, according to the old reports. But it had been lost during the Collapse, with only the mechanical tricks for relieving neuroses remaining. No wonder the worlds were filled with sick minds, if Siryl was typical of her profession.

Kayel put his pipe away, looking at her as if he were thinking the same, with the woman-adulation gone from his eyes for the moment. He swallowed, his Adam's apple bobbing grotesquely. But his voice was as clear as when he discussed physics. "It fits. Oh, not the stuff about the god. That's probably mumbo-jumbo to cover some master power source and the men who run it. Maybe it's a mechanical educator, too, with a library saved from before the Collapse. The machine must have prevented the Collapse here, and they've gone right ahead while we fell back. We're just working on theories about immense fields of energy in space that can be tapped for anti-gravity, identity exchange control—all that. They use it already! Derek, we've got to get this back to the Federation."

"But the way they live?" Siryl protested.

"Why not?" Derek asked. "With power like that, they don't need the usual heavy science and gadgetry. There's no reason not to live the simple life."

Kayel was pacing about, sucking on an empty pipe, and wearing a flush of excitement. Normally, it was easy to overlook his mental powers, but a good physicist had to have mental flexibility; he was supposed to be one of the best. "We can't conquer them—not when one man can handle a fleet. But we look enough like them to pass among them, once we know what to expect. We'll drop a few small fliers into the wastelands. With any luck, they'll find the god machine. Derek, do you think they'll still let us work on the *Sépelora,* now that you know?"

It had been bothering the captain. He shrugged uncertainly.

"I told you not to break their taboos!" Siryl reminded them. "I also told you this had to be a homogenous culture! Now maybe you'll listen to me. They have to have *some* neuroses; any isolated group has. What we've got to do is to find their weakness. Kayel, they think you're smarter than they are. Let's . . ."

Derek had heard enough. She still had a genius for remembering only when she'd been right and assuming she always would be infallible. He turned toward the door. "Coming, Kayel?"

The little man hesitated, obviously swayed by the chance to work closely with her. Then he smiled apologetically at her and followed Derek.

She sat in offended dignity through breakfast. Luckily, Wolm was there and Lari kept up a steady stream of talk, trying to get Ferad to join the boy in some project or other. Nothing was noticed by the two natives. And nobody tried to stop the two men as they headed toward the ship.

Michla was busy seeding something on the harrowed field. He'd already added nitrates and other fertilizer— probably from the same planet as the water, carefully selected and dissolved in it. He called out a greeting as they passed, and they waved back. It was all friendly and normal. Derek breathed a sigh of relief as they swung around a pile of boulders.

Where the space ship had rested there was nothing but a depression in the ground. And coming toward them from that was the greybearded priest, the serape over his shoulders whipping about him in the breeze that was blowing. His face was serious as he drew near them.

Derek stepped toward him, trying to force anger to replace the fear that was thick in him. "Where's our ship, Skora?"

"Safe. Up there." The old man pointed toward the sky above them. "In an orbit around Vanir."

"So we're prisoners?"

Skora sighed, and he seemed embarrassed. "Not exactly. We feel obligated to you for bungling the way we handled the return of your ship to Sirius, Derek, and we'd like to return you. But that must wait for further study. You have full freedom here, though. And if you are permitted to leave, the ship will be ready."

"And I suppose you'll make up all the time when we should be repairing it?" Derek asked grimly.

"We have already done that. We repaired it last night, before we sent it up. Not the space-denial generators— that is beyond our understanding. But from god we learned how to use what was there to set up the much better time-negation drive that was used before your Collapse."

"But—time-negation . . ." Kayel swallowed, stumbling. Derek hadn't known that the little man understood Classic. From the accent, he must have only a reading and weak hearing knowledge of it. But he obviously had understood enough.

"Yes, time-negation works." Skora smiled at the man's amazement. "It's simpler in application, but much more difficult in theory, I believe, than space-denial. It was discovered by accident when our common ancestors had no right to find it. Fortunately, god knew how it worked. And your ship will be ready for you if we find we can let you return."

He was heading back to the village, and they were following without thought. Kayel caught Derek's arm, pulling him back out of earshot. He spoke in hasty Universal. "We've got to forget the ship. Now it's up to god and his charms. Derek, I've got to see how those amulets are made."

"But they were nothing but baked clay. We took one apart," Derek protested.

The physicist shrugged. "A transistor works because of a few parts per millions of impurities. A detector works because of its crystalline structure. Take his job!"

Skora had noticed that they weren't with him and had slowed his steps. Derek caught up, trying to look somewhat cheerful. "I guess we'll have to get ourselves a house of our own and stop bothering Lari until you decide, then. And since we can't use the power of your god, we'd make pretty poor farmers around here. Is the job in your kiln still open?"

"Is it?" The old man chuckled. "Do you think I like

71

doing it by myself? And since we'd have to feed you and care for you even if you did no work, your help will be pure profit to me."

Derek had little hope for any great revelation from the work. Either there wasn't much of a secret to the tools, or there was something so tricky that they felt sure Kayel and he couldn't discover it.

The work seemed to confirm his doubts. Any child could have handled it, with no more than five minutes of instruction. Skora had teleported in a big tub of soft white clay from a bank of the stuff beyond the village. They had to pack this inside metal molds, press them down firmly and let them rough-dry until they would hold their shape. Then they went into the kiln to be baked. Finally, Skora inspected them, throwing out the defective ones along with his own hand-formed failures.

The priest answered Kayel's stumbling questions without any hesitation. The material wasn't important, so long as the final product had the right shape and the markings on it were clear. They had a few metal tools, but these were rare and too heavy for normal use.

"You can think of them as instructions," he suggested. "There is too much to remember easily, and these help. They—well, they describe a stress in space, more or less."

"Then plastics would work? Because if they would, there are a thousand pounds of thermoplastic in the ship's stores, and we'd save a lot of time here," Kayel suggested.

Skora apparently thought it was a fine idea. He questioned the physicist about what to look for, and the stock of plastic was suddenly in front of them. They began boring small holes in the molds for pouring the plastic to make unbreakable amulets, and the work went faster after that.

On the way back to Lari's that night, Kayel shook his head positively. "Nothing, Derek! Nothing can be concealed in our own plastic. The secret has to be in their god."

A god who wasn't immortal, though he had lived for at least twelve hundred years; a god who taught the children somehow though he had been dead for a hundred years. A god who could fling a seventy-thousand ton ship quadrillions of miles instantly!

Derek lingered after the second day of work. He took the bottle of beer from the priest and dropped to a seat. "Skora, I'm still curious about your god. And this time, I'll try to behave myself. How long did he live?"

"Since before the sun exploded. Let's see." The priest tipped the capped bottle up without thinking. Beer seemed to appear just beyond the seal and run into his mouth. "He was about sixty of your years old then. He came here to see us about five years before the trouble, I think. I could find out, if you like."

Derek took his eyes off the other's drinking habits and swallowed his own drink, trying to find some point of exploration. "I haven't heard any stories about his creating the world or your people, at that. No legends of that?"

"Of course not. We evolved on Terra, like your people; and this planet grew from the usual space whorl." The old man chuckled. "This isn't a religion—though I'm afraid sometimes it's beginning to degenerate. God had some strange ideas that are getting distorted lately. Many of us have a belief in some divine spirit, Derek, but we try not to confuse that with god. He was just a man. Kayel knows more than he did, though not the same— and all of us are stronger than he was."

"He didn't teach you to worship him, then?"

"He didn't know." Skora shook his head sadly. "He thought we would mostly be dead. He didn't care and couldn't know what happened to us. He was unconscious. And when he revived, he was sure we were dead. With his stores all ruined and nobody to save him, he went crazy. He began blasting his way out and brought down a rock on his skull. Naturally, with his medulla crushed, he

73

died. It was just as well. He couldn't move the rocks to get out and he'd have been afraid of the world we'd made."

It made no sense at all. Their god couldn't even move rocks out of his own way. Yet the rains fell, in spite of the fact that the amulets were nothing but symbols. The power had to come from some source. "So he was destroyed. Yet you say he still is!"

"He's there, and the young learn from him still. We had to find out how to build the time-negation drive from him since you came." Skora found another beer, remembering to open this one. He was mellowing from the liquor. "Derek, I don't know. He's dead and he's deteriorating—slowly, but the changes are there. We've always been in danger of becoming superstitiously dependent on him without realizing how much so we are. But now, some of us are worried. As he deteriorates, he may warp our children. Sometimes I've thought of digging him up and destroying him."

"Why don't you?" Derek suggested softly.

"I've thought of it. As senior priest for Vanir, I could. But it's hard . . . Emotional attachment, I suppose. And fear of what would happen."

Derek frowned. "Suppose I were to destroy him?"

The old priest looked up, studying him, resolution coming slowly. "You could! Of course, *you* could! Derek, one more beer! Then go home. And be back here early. We'll do it!"

Skora's hands were trembling as he reached for the bottles.

6

Siryl would have none of it.

"Nonsense," she told them after she had heard the story, along with Kayel. "Primitive cultures don't breed agnostics. Skora was just drunk or testing you! Probably saving face by trying not to act superstitious. Derek, if you break any more taboos—"

"They aren't primitive! Damn it, Siryl, if you can't get that much through your pathological skull, go outside and watch it rain for a while!"

She stiffened and then cloaked herself in professional calm. "A culture," she recited, almost by rote, "observed *in situ* may have certain apparently inconsistent developments, usually as a result of some isolated individual genius or accidental discovery. These, however, do not violate the fundamental attitudes and emphases, the cultural gestalt, but are inevitably assimilated emotionally. That means, Derek, that they can have a machine left over from pre-Collapse days that makes miracles—but they still think it's magic. If you'll drop your persecution complex and listen to—"

He grimaced, and then grinned slowly. "My hairy-chested persecution complex, you undefiled prude!"

She drew in her breath harshly and marched out of the room, white to her lips. Kayel looked sick, starting after her and turning back. "You shouldn't have done that, Derek!" he protested. He sighed, shook his head, and sat down slowly, reaching for his pipe. "I wonder what we'll find—and whether Skora will do it?"

Derek had his own doubts, but they found the old man ready the next morning, with Wolm behind him, carrying a supply of amulets and two battery torches he must have pulled from the *Sépelora*. The priest looked as if he had been unable to sleep, and the porch where the school was usually held was locked up tightly.

He saluted them, his eyes still troubled, but with no doubt in his voice. "The place is on the other side of Vanir, deep in a cave our ancestors built. He expected the explosion toward the last and had the one of them who could use his power dig two such caves—one for him, one for us. He had a machine . . . We almost starved and died of asphyxiation, until that one who

75

could use the power found from god how to bring food and keep fresh air coming from another world."

He sighed, and his eyes ran across the landscape and the growing fields. "When we came out years later, the world was a cinder, and god had to teach us to restore it and to farm it. At first, we thought of moving to another world. Even the air here had to be brought in. But we stayed near god. Well, let's go!"

There was an abrupt, sickening shift of scenery and they were standing at the base of a mountain that stretched up as one of a huge chain, barren and forbidding. Only a few stunted plants existed there, and the sun was purpling the sky in the west. Ahead of them was a cliff that stretched up nearly half a mile, and there were two rubble-filled holes in it, near them.

The priest motioned to one of them, and Wolm moved ahead. He had what seemed to be a huge umbrella without covering. He pointed the ribs toward the fallen rocks, twisting it slowly and feeling the swivelled handle of clay. He came to the stones and continued walking. The rock seemed to flow away from the device, compacting itself against the walls of the older passage that was there.

"This is the way he taught Moskez, the only one of us who could learn the power," Skora explained. "God came across space from Terra to study us with other scientists. When the enemy began exploding suns, he stole us to help him, taking all the supplies he could carry. We built this cave for him, and the one beyond for ourselves. Fortunately, the sun's explosion was a weak one."

He was worried, but oddly determined. They were moving downward and forward. Then they hit a clear passage that wound down and down. It must have taken a great depth to protect them from the solar blowup. Other people had tried it, without this digging device, and had failed.

They reached a long section where the passage was clear, and foul air rushed out at them. Skora reached for an amulet and cold, clear atmosphere blew in rapidly.

Derek wondered why the old man didn't simply teleport them into the cave where their god lay, but decided to let the question go. It was probably only a means of delaying the accomplishment. His legs ached, and Kayel was panting, but they went steadily down.

Finally it flattened out and another five minutes of walking brought them into a partially clear chamber. There was a great radium motor on one side, whirring softly. In the center stood a huge glass case, covered with thick layers of ice from the ages of slow atmospheric seepage. Oxygen tanks were beside it and stores of food and equipment lay about, all rotted and useless now. Wolm scraped off the ice at a gesture from the priest, and Derek stared into the tank.

Doubled up on the floor of the case was an old man, his face hidden by one arm, his neck bent at an impossible angle. He was naked and fat, with the waxy color of frozen flesh. One hand lay near a heavy notebook and the other clutched an archaic type of heat-projecting rifle. A rock lay near the wound on the back of his neck, and another had wedged itself into the hole at the top of the case, sealing it with the layer of ice around it. From the breakage inside the case, it was obvious that he had gone mad, to wind up shooting at the ceiling above him. The cooling system must have been cut off before he revived, but it had somehow gotten turned on again during his insane frenzy.

"Suspended animation!" Kayel said. "There were accounts that it had been developed. But no details on the cooling, chemicals in the blood, the irradiation frequencies. Skora, was he a biologist or biophysicist?"

"No, he stole the parts from the place where our people were studied," the priest said. "Another man meant to use it, but god took it. And he didn't adjust it right. He wanted to wait fifty years, but it was twelve hundred before it released him. We left him because we needed him and he was preserved in this."

Wolm had drawn closer to the case, trembling. Now he bent his white face down and stared into the case. Skora stood beside the boy, indecision working on him.

"What do we do now?" Derek asked, as gently as he could.

The old man sighed. "I don't know. The enzymes of his body are bringing a slow decay, despite the cold. And things go wrong with the teaching of the young . . . but without him, god is gone and Vanir may have no power. If I could only be sure—"

He waited, while Derek stared at the case and its machinery. At first, he had wondered if it might not conceal the great machine that could perform the miracles he had seen. But Kayel had looked it over at once and had shaken his head. It seemed to be no more than it was supposed to be. And that left only their god—a fat, dead god who had gone insane because of his weakness and his fear.

"No!" Wolm broke. The boy's shoulders heaved. He buried his face against the case, shouting and clawing at the ice. "No! Skora, you can't. He is all we have. He's holy! Don't touch him! God will come again! I saw it. It is *his* thought! You can't—"

Skora's fingers moved on the amulet savagely. Wolm's body snapped out of existence, while flakes of ice trickled down where he had been.

The priest looked sicker than before. "I sent him home," he said. "Derek, that is what our youngsters learn now. There is decay, and distinctions are going. The old emotional superstitions are stronger than later logic, and all children used to have them. Now they creep through into the minds of our young. A decaying mind and an insane one—and our children absorb *that* knowledge."

He sighed heavily. "And I—even I must have absorbed some of it. I can't destroy him! It's—horror! Derek, it's up to you. Do what you will. I'll wait fifteen minutes for you and keep the air pure here for you. But I can't even watch!"

He was suddenly gone, too.

Kayel swallowed thickly, his neck bobbing against tight muscles. He reached for his pipe, then stuffed it back. "But if he loses his power when the body is destroyed, he can't keep air for us or get us out?"

Derek kicked at the glass case. Kayel hesitated, and then joined him. It broke finally, and they waited while the blast of freezing air wheezed out, foul and miasmic. Derek reached for the weapon, but it was too cold to touch. He kicked it around with his foot until he could point it toward the corpse, while he found a bit of cloth he could use to cover the trigger.

Kayel knocked his arm aside before he could fire. The little man pointed toward the notebook and began hastily ripping off his shirt. He scooped up the book and spread it out on a low couch, ripping off the thin plastic that protected it. "We still have fourteen minutes, Derek. And this may be our only chance to find the secret."

The captain stepped back, feeling relief wash over him. He had been bracing himself to take the chance, but the excuse to delay it was welcome. If burning the body destroyed the power of god, Vanir would be just another primitive world—and they would almost certainly die before they could get out. If the power remained, there would still be the need to warn the Federation of the menace here—and no clue on which to operate.

Kayel flipped the cover back and skimmed through a few pages as quickly as he could turn them. It was obviously written in Classic, heavily interspersed with strange mathematics like none Derek had ever seen. From Kayel's puzzled glance, they were equally strange to him. He turned to the front again. Then he pointed. "Aevan—god is Aevan!"

The book was described on the first page grandiloquently as the diary and records of A. Evan, the discoverer of metadynamics, the only true science of all time—the full and final work, from which the notes the world had been unready for had been extracted.

The body of the book began with the man's need for people with unusually developed "ability" for his experiments, and his discovery of the border world of Vanir, where scientists had bred small groups for special abilities and were studying them.

In one of those little colleges, he had found the children he needed, and one child had proved capable of manipulating space as Aevan had been sure was possible. Moskez had even been able to force a few of the other children to bridge the difficult gap and begin work on it. There were long experiments and formulae for levitation, teleportation, penetrability, and other things. It ended on a note of self-adulation for his own success, in spite of the poor material he'd had with which to work.

Derek frowned and went back carefully, looking for the missing factor. The mathematics looked good, and in time Kayel could probably figure them out. But Aevan had been unable to make them work himself. It had taken some other ability.

He found it finally, in a footnote he'd skipped. It was telepathy. Aevan had known that the mental power needed was related to telepathy, and had been forced to find a group which had been bred for that. The boys on Vanir who succeeded had had more than eleven generations in which to build up such power.

Telepathy! And since the Collapse, while Vanir went on with its exclusive breed of telepaths, the rest of the worlds had had no such power—the psychologists had proved that it had been bred out of humanity, if it had ever existed. Yet without it, the mathematics would be useless. Only Vanir could have infinite power.

There the children had been forced to use it to survive. The single advanced one had somehow taught the others, and they had stolen their ideas for survival from the mind of Aevan. In suspended animation, his thoughts were nearly still, but his memories remained, and they could be tapped. Even dead, the memory cells were preserved for a time, though now they were deteriorating at last.

The amulets were only traditions to help them—they had used them as children, probably, to remember and feel the complex mathematical formulae, and the use of the tools had become so closely associated with the power that nobody questioned it now.

Derek tossed the book to Kayel and reached for the trigger. Nothing visible came from the weapon, but the body of the god—or Aevan—charred and began to vanish, along with most of the wall of the case behind it. Fourteen minutes had gone by.

He began to tense as the seconds drifted by, picturing Skora standing up there without the symbol of the power he had used, uncertain of his own powers, afraid to try them! If the man couldn't work without the familiar—

Abruptly, they were back at the foot of the mountain, outside the tunnel they had cleared. Skora stood there, his face strained and white and his hands shaking; but his eyes were burning with the end of more than a thousand years of slavery to a useless custom and the fear of its loss.

"It worked—the tools still have power!" His voice was hoarse, as if he had been shouting.

Derek had one final test. He turned toward the priest, keeping his lips sealed and trying to throw the words silently out of his mind toward the other. *"Not the tools, Skora. They were only memory aids. All you need is the knowledge and power that you have in your own mind. You were bound to a superstition!"*

Skora smiled wearily, his eyes moving toward the book Kayel still held. He nodded thoughtfully. "Superstition? I suppose you're right," he admitted. "Or conditioned reflexes of thought. Until about the age of nine, it was easier for a young telepath to explore the passive, unresisting mind of god than that of a busy adult. Eventually, it became the only way for them to learn in our culture. Now I suppose we'll have to train teachers for the children."

Kayel was staring at them, his mind busily adjusting to the new conditions. "Telepathy!" he said, without fear,

81

but with a growing sense of wonder, as he knitted his brows and stood silently while Skora seemed to listen. Derek wondered why his own mind wasn't curling up in horror at being read. But what difference would it make? He'd helped Vanir, but the Federation could never use the secret.

Skora sighed at last. "Sanity, new morals, many other things, Kayel. We only deceived you about our ability to read minds, and that for your own good. We were afraid it might be too disturbing. And we're doubly grateful now. If there is anything we can do . . ."

"Send us home on the *Sépelora,*" Derek suggested.

"The affairs of the rest of the universe are not ours, Derek," the old man answered, and he seemed genuinely sorry. "We can't risk having them brought to us by returning you. The decision of the majority went against me. Now all I can do is make you welcome here on Vanir."

Derek stared up at the sky where the *Sépelora* lay out of reach but ready to carry them home. He let his eyes fall again to the planet that was to be their prison. He had come to like the people and to feel more at ease among them in many ways than among his own race. But there had been hope, until now.

"All right," he said at last. "Keep your world, Skora. Live on it comfortably while the rest of the human race nearly kill themselves in another war. You'll be safe. Dredge up a few more tricks from Aevan's notes. You like being alone—most provincials do. And it won't matter in your time. But when the children of my people find mechanical ways of doing what you do with your minds—when they sweep in here with ten battleships for each that your people can handle—remember that you could have joined us and saved us from the enemy that burned this planet once already. When that happens, cry for the brotherhood of men. See what they think of a single planet that kept its secrets to itself. Oh, damn it, send us back to Lari's and let us alone!"

Skora reached for the amulet. Then he threw it away

and stared at them, frowning in concentration without the help of tools. His hands clenched at his side.

They stood in Derek's bedroom.

7

Derek lay wearily on the bed while Kayel's low voice went on explaining things to Siryl. The woman had resented their going off without her, even though she had wanted no part of the trip. But now her hurt scorn had cooled down to an unbelieving interest. In a way, the captain thought, she had been right all along. But she didn't seem to be enjoying it. He started to turn over.

Siryl screamed thinly. By the time he could look, she was throwing Aevan's notebook away and whimpering. "No!" Her voice was low now, but rising slowly toward hysteria as Derek got off the bed. "No. No! It *can't* be telepathy!"

"It is," Derek assured her. "I tested it. So did Kayel."

Her face contorted, and she swung toward him, groping for support. She found his shoulder and buried her face in it, clinging to him, her nails digging into his back as she strained closer. "Take me away! Derek, take me away. I can't stand having them read my mind—every thought I ever had, every wish ... *Derek!*"

He reached up to disentangle the hands that were trying to dig through his backbone. "Siryl—" he began.

She flung herself from him and groped toward the door. But Kayel was there, his tortured face sympathetic. The little man caught her, and she dragged herself against him. He drew her closer while she sobbed, standing the pain of her hysteria as if he were being knighted.

"I'll protect you, Siryl. Some way I'll protect you. They aren't going to read your mind. I won't let them." He was scowling furiously with some effort as he tried to comfort her. His eyes turned toward Derek. "Maybe if they know about their god now, they're upset! Maybe they won't think too well. Get Lari, Derek—she's not very suspicious, I hope. And don't think about anything except that Siryl's sick."

The woman had whimpered at the mention of Lari's name. Kayel drew her down beside him, rubbing her hair gently. "There, there, baby. Nobody is going to read your mind now."

Derek found Lari in the kitchen, naturally, and brought her back with him. She was wearing her big apron with the amulet pockets, and moved ahead of him with the bowl in her hands clattering against one of them while she went on stirring—the picture of a quiet housewife, Derek thought bitterly. With the power of a god!

"Lari," Kayel told her, "Siryl's sick. We're not just like you. We're neurotics—we have been since the Collapse. We need things you don't have which are on the *Sépelora* —Ferad will need them, too. Can you send Siryl and Derek up for them? They'll know where to find the drugs."

Derek started to protest. But this was more important to the physicist than escape. He was being the space knight who could slay monsters for his lady. The captain glanced at Lari, trying to keep his thoughts down. She puzzled over it, but seemed completely unsuspicious. It must have been a hard day for her already, and her mind wasn't on the request.

"I guess so," she answered. "If I sort of pretend god is still there and use the amulet. I'll have to concentrate. You stir this till I work it." She handed the bowl to Kayel, who took it quickly, keeping the swirling bubbles in the mixture going.

Lari pulled out the amulet and clutched it firmly. She bent over it, hesitated, and looked up. "No sense in two of you going for a few drugs," she commented, and clenched her hand.

Derek found himself in the control room of the *Sépelora*, beside a new bank of instruments. He let out a yell of protests at the miscarriage of Kayel's plans, but his finger hit the red button that was still marked Firing Pin. There was no way he could go back for them, nothing he could do to help. And he was still captain of the ship, in the service of the Federation, with a job to do.

The *Sépelora* came to life. There was no blanking out of the ports, but the stars began rushing by at an incredible rate, while the radar checked them and threw the ship about to avoid a direct hit. They were making better than a thousand light years an hour!

Derek found the instructions beside the new panel and began setting their course for Sirius. He had no idea of how the machines worked, but that would be for experts if he got back; and it was something to aid the Federation, at least.

He could feel the breath of fear blowing down his neck as he worked frantically. Lari might not be able to handle a time-negation field. She might have to waste time in hunting for Skora. Or perhaps none of them could work through this. Perhaps there was no way to locate him. He could be sure of nothing, except that each thousand light years gave him a slight added reason for hope—but sure that it wasn't enough reason, even so.

He wondered about Siryl and Kayel. She might be sick at their failure, but she was probably female enough to appreciate the attempt Kayel had made more than the fact that he hadn't delivered. And she'd been rocked by telepathy enough to seek comfort where she could find it and in the strongest manner.

Then he went back to worrying, staring back in the direction of Vanir. He had no idea of how far they could reach. Maybe they could throw things further than they could suck them in. The *Waroak* had been tossed two hundred thousand light years. But the people of Vanir had gone out only a few light years to bring supplies. Maybe he was already safe.

He began to think so as the hours drifted by. And he began to appreciate the time-negation field more as he saw the simplicity of the generators. He could already construct another set from memory, if he had to. With this, the Federation still might win.

Worry over pursuit kept him from sleeping until fatigue finally took over. That day and the next went by. Then the next.

He went to bed with more confidence. He'd underestimated the speed of the new drive and was already half the distance back to Sirius—they should have stopped him before that, since he was now near some of the outer fringes of the Federation. He considered landing on one, but decided against it. The further he went, the better. And the new drive should be taken directly to headquarters.

In the so-called morning, his head was aching as if the back of his skull were about to split, and the worry had returned. There was no reason for it, except the jinx that had become such a part of him. He swallowed anodynes and fought off some of the pain, but it kept coming back, as if something were busting inside.

He made his way up to the control room, while the feeling that he had lost grew stronger and stronger inside him. He should have remembered that the anodyne was a depressant. It wouldn't do to go into a fit of depression now, while he was nearing home.

He opened the door to the precabin, strode through it, and into the cabin beyond. Then he stopped.

Skora sat in a seat there, staring at the great spread of stars that streaked across the ports. This time there were no pants of homespun and no serape over the old shoulders. The beard was still there, but shortened and trimmed. It projected over the collar of a Federation Fleet uniform —and on the side of the collar was pinned the double cluster of a Galaxy Commander!

The old man saluted crisply, smiling in amusement at the gesture, and waited while Derek's arm automatically returned the honor. "As you were, Captain!" Then he sobered. "As you can see, Derek, your words made an impression on me. Vanir couldn't stand in a backwater, hoping that men would never catch up. Nor could we forget that we belonged to the race of mankind and were all brothers. Telepaths are unusually sensitive to that argument, once it's pointed out to them. I couldn't convince enough of our council. But after I teleported myself to Sirius and convinced your command there, it was too late for Vanir to retrench. We aren't limited to one planet now, clinging to the memory of a decaying god. Now there are two millions of us being fitted for your uniforms —enough to win your war without having to destroy the enemy we both fought once before."

"And I suppose headquarters took one look at what you could do and made you all officers," Derek said bitterly, remembering the years he'd spent fighting for a mere Sector Commander's rating.

The pain in his head broke over him again, and he doubled over. Skora seemed not to notice.

"It wasn't hard, Derek. They were paralyzed with fear of new weapons until they were beginning to lose the battle. Your command had its own superstitions. And reading their minds helped me to find ways of convincing them. Then, when I could, I came to take you back. I've been waiting here for you for hours—though not idly."

The pain hit a sharp peak and faded somewhat. Skora was staring at him intently, and he covered the remaining pain under automatic questions. "How's Siryl? And I suppose Kayel is happy working out more of the mathematics for you?"

"Siryl—" Skora paused and shrugged. "Kayel had her promise to marry him, of course, and is a new man. She is recovering, we hope, since he made her a metal net and told her it would keep us from reading her mind. It won't, if we try, but she needs her little superstition, if she's to stop hating us."

Derek stared out at the stars rushing by, knowing he

had won what he had been sent to win—and had lost the Federation. His jinx had outgrown him, and had spread to the whole race.

Now Siryl hated and feared the men of Vanir for their power to see the things which a prude must conceal within her own mind. She might get over that; perhaps she could learn to accept their power. But in time, all the women on Federation planets would have to hate the telepaths—not for themselves, but for the sake of the children who should never be born into the life that must come.

Skora had spent a few days gaining himself the coveted rank of Galaxy Commander, while Derek had never dared to hope he could rise that high in a lifetime. And Skora's people could have everything they wanted for the asking.

Monsters were loose on the world. Until power could corrupt them, they might be kind monsters. But they were worse than any enemy defeat could have been. They would save the Federation, but after the triumph, those most fit would own it. The men who had built the starships would never control the future—that would be left for the conquering march of the men who had done nothing, but had simply been given a power denied to the rest of the race.

"There was an old legend," Skora said suddenly. "About a boy who lived with some kind of animals. When men discovered him at the age of twelve, he was a savage. He was unable to talk—and nobody learned how to teach him. Yet his powers of speech were latently as good as those of any man."

The pain had lashed out again at the man's words. Derek let them slip over his mind without trying to understand. Skora was reading his mind, but it didn't matter. He went on thinking, forced to recognize that he had brought total defeat to all non-telepathic men. If there had been any hope . . .

But the psychologists and geneticists had looked for

the power of telepathy in the current race, and had found none.

Skora stirred impatiently. "Telepathy never occurred strongly in men more than once in perhaps a billion births. Even in the group at the place where god found us, only Moskez had any great power, after all the careful breeding for it. He had to teach it to the others, so that they would not be wolf-boys in the world which the explosion left them. And Lari and Ferad are having a child —who will learn, like all the rest of us, even though Ferad is its father."

Derek groped for the hope, and then shrugged. It was a good line for the rest of the worlds. It would give them faith in their future, while Vanir replaced them. They could believe that with a little more work and time, they would slowly develop the power—and their "teachers" would find ways of convincing them they were succeeding. Maybe they needed that faith, no matter how wrong it was. They would forget the legends that spoke of a time when the strange *psi* factor was bred out of the race—for the benefit of a few, as he now knew. They would pretend there was only one race, instead of the two into which it had been split.

The pain caught him again, and Skora got up sympathetically to rub the back of his neck. It helped. "Men," the old man told him, "have been finding ways to claim they are not all one race since there first were human beings. But it's still wrong. And science has made mistakes, while legends are only superstitions."

The old fingers found the spot of greatest anguish and began rubbing it out. Derek looked up, grateful in spite of his bitterness against what had been done. "The advantage of being a telepath," he admitted. "You know where the pain is. Thanks, Skora."

"It always hurts at first," Skora's voice said softly.

His lips had been tightly shut, and he was smiling. Derek felt his body tauten, and his eyes froze on the unmoving lips, while the voice continued quietly somewhere in his mind.

"It takes time," Skora's voice went on, with a warmth that had always been lacking in it before. *"And it hurts. So does the loss of some of the things we believe—that we are persecuted, that we must depend on god, that incomplete knowledge and old legends can tell us everything, or that we are more than one race. Telepathy is never easy for an adult, Derek. But with it, we can unite our whole race—perhaps even the ones we call an enemy!"*

The pain was gone now, leaving only a strange sense of completion behind it. Derek stumbled to his feet, choking over words that would not come.

The old man caught his mind, smiling, and led him to the viewing port.

"Sector Commander Derek," he said aloud, while the warm soft echo of the words came into the former captain's mind, "out there is man's kingdom. All of space! But there's no room there for any more of the superstitions we've all had too long."

Derek looked out through the ports toward the stars that rushed by the *Sépelora,* while the ship carried the two men into their future.

There was no jinx reflected in the port glass. There were only the images of two faces, smiling back at him.

LIFE WATCH

1

Norden could feel fear knot his mind as he watched the tiny blue speck against the black sky. It was a senseless, unnatural fear, and he knew it. The searing blue point of flame meant that the ship up there was powered by atomic rockets—but the Aliens drove their ships in some mysterious manner without any kind of reaction motor. The object coming down toward the tiny asteroid could only be a human device.

Yet the fear grew worse. He shook his head, wondering again how close to insanity he had drifted. His eyes darted sideways, scanning the wreckage that had been the laboratory, then back to the approaching ship. Mercifully, he couldn't remember most of what had happened, but it had been enough to drive any human close to the brink of madness. It would have been bad enough to be left here for days in a wrecked and airless dome while the oxygen tanks were used up, one by one. But to have seen Hardwick's fate when the Aliens caught him . . .

He tried to stop thinking of it. The Aliens were only vague shadows in his mind now—the picture of what must have happened had been washed out completely, along with most of the memories of the period of struggling free from the wreckage.

Somehow, he'd survived, undetected by the Aliens. He'd dug out the emergency transmitter and tried signalling for help with it. Now, apparently, before the last

91

tank of oxygen on his back was exhausted, rescue had come. He should have been ecstatic with relief.

The fear remained, some twisted reaction left over from the days of terror and hopelessness. He lifted his hands and studied them. They were steady enough; the fear was having no outward effect.

Already the ship was close enough for Norden to see glints of weak sunlight reflecting from the metal hull. The pilot must have been one of the best; there was no wavering or side-jetting to correct the course. It was coming straight down, slowing to a drift. The exhaust hit the jagged surface of the asteroid and splashed out. Suddenly it cut off, and the ship dropped slowly the few remaining feet, to come to rest less than half a mile away.

Norden knew he should start running toward it, and stood up. But he couldn't give the order to his legs. He stared toward the ship, then back at the ruins. Maybe there was something he should take with him. He had air enough for another hour. There was no need to rush things; men would be coming here for him. And it wouldn't do any harm to put off meeting them a little longer. He didn't want to be subjected to their questions yet.

He started hesitantly toward the ship, trying to force himself to move. Men began to emerge from the ship and head toward him. He dropped onto a mess that had been a superspeed-tape instrument recorder and waited.

His mind was running a rat-race inside his head, and there was a growing tension. He cleared his throat and reached for the switch on his suit radio. The men were almost up to him. He got to his feet again, fumbling with the little switch.

Then the harsh beam of a flashlight picked him out, and a gruff voice sounded in his headphones. "Dr. William Norden?"

He nodded, and rehearsed words stumbled onto his lips. "Thank God, you got here! I was afraid the transmitter wouldn't work!"

There was a hint of something like kindness in the voice. "Take it easy, Dr. Norden! It did work, and we're here. What happened to Hardwick?"

"Dead, I hope," Norden answered. "The Aliens got him!" He shuddered, glancing at the spot where it had happened.

The man wearing colonel's comets nodded, while sickness spread over his face. He motioned to one of the others. "Get the pics of this wreck, and collect any records you can. The rest of you give Dr. Norden a hand. And make it snappy! They may have spotted us already!"

The man with the camera went to work, flashing his shots with a strobe light that blinked twenty-four times a second. Two others began unrolling a stretcher. Norden shook his head. "I can walk. And I've already collected Hardwick's notebooks."

They set a pace closer to a run than a walk, bouncing ludicrously in the slight gravity of the asteroid. Norden kept up with them easily enough, trying to make sense of his reactions. Most of the fear and tension was gone, as if he'd passed over some hurdle. Maybe the presence of military efficiency was restoring his confidence; maybe he hadn't believed in his rescue until now. But he felt better, though his eyes went on studying the others cautiously, as if looking for any reaction that would somehow betray them.

They reached the ship and began pulling themselves through its flexible hatch. The colonel jerked off his helmet and suit, showing iron-grey hair that contrasted with an almost youthful face; it was the face of a man who hadn't grown soft during the years before the Aliens came. He swung toward Norden.

"How much gravity can you take, Dr. Norden. Six g's?"

"In a hammock, for a few minutes," Norden answered.

They were already heading up the ladder toward the nose of the ship. The colonel ripped a sling out of its case when they reached the control cabin. He snapped it to its

93

lugs, motioned Norden onto it, and bound him in place in less time than he could have ordered the job done. Then he dropped to his own control seat. "Six g's for five minutes, then hold her at four till I order. Up ship!"

Norden didn't black out during the first five minutes, though the pressure was enough to drive the sling to its bottom mark and make its cables groan in protest. As they switched from six to four gravities, the pressure eased a little. An hour crept by, and another. When the colonel finally ordered the drive cut, Norden estimated that they had been under acceleration for nearly five hours and were doing about two million miles an hour. Either the colonel was crazy, or the ship must have been stocked to the last bin with fuel. They were making more than five times the normal emergency speed.

Then the leader shoved back and began releasing Norden. "Sorry to give you such a beating after what you've been through, Dr. Norden. But we'll still be lucky if we have enough speed to slip past their detectors before they can trace our orbit and overhaul us. They've been getting worse lately."

He sighed, and his lips thinned. Then he managed a smile. "But you can hear all that later. You need food. And I guess the doctor and psychiatrist they shipped along will be biting their nails to give you the works. Oh, I'm Armsworth."

Norden felt the chill hit his mind again. He'd expected a doctor and had been bracing himself for one. But a psychiatrist . . . He forced calmness into his voice and tried to grin. "I could eat a horse!"

"You probably will," Colonel Armsworth told him with automatic humor. "This is the Space Service!"

The little cabin to which Armsworth took him was crowded already. There were the two men waiting for him, and their equipment. In addition, there was the bulk of a large recording machine ready to take down every word. He acknowledged the introductions and downed a glass of some oversweetened fruit juice the doctor held out.

"It'll get you ready for some real food," the physician told him. "Like to clean up while I look you over, before the main course comes?"

Norden grabbed the chance. It would give him something to do besides worrying, and it was obvious he needed grooming. His dark hair was matted, his face marked with dirt that had sunk into every wrinkle and line, and there was a thick growth of stubble on his skin. It was a thin, fairly good-looking face, as unfamiliar as if he'd only seen it in a photograph. He seemed to have forgotten himself, even.

While he washed and shaved, the doctor was busy. But the examination was less detailed than he had expected, and finally the man stood back, nodding.

"For someone nearing forty, you're in good shape, Dr. Norden. You had a rough time of it, but nothing serious. I was sure of that when I heard you hadn't blacked out under high acceleration. Okay, go ahead and eat." He moved toward the door, out of the way, but showed no sign of leaving until his curiosity could be satisfied.

Norden fell to on the food, forcing himself to eat ravenously, though he had no apparent appetite. The psychiatrist leaned forward casually, watching him. "Want to tell us about it, Dr. Norden? What happened to Hardwick?"

Norden shook his head, while the tension increased again. The man would be watching for every hidden meaning in his words, and he wasn't ready for that. But he couldn't put it off. "I'm not sure I can tell much. I—well, everything's pretty foggy. A lot of it I can't remember at all."

"Partial amnesia is fairly common," the psychiatrist said quietly. "In fact, everyone has touches of it. Try going back a ways—say to your childhood—to give you a running start. We've got plenty of time."

Gods and Golems

Norden had little interest in his childhood, and he skimmed it with a few words. He'd done nothing unusual until he drifted into the new investigation of radiation outside the electromagnetic spectrum in his post-graduate college work. Then he'd suddenly developed. He was the first man ever to prove there was more than theory involved. He'd been called to Mars for the interplanetary award for his demonstration of proto-gravity after floating two ounces of lead with a hundred thousand dollars worth of equipment that used twenty kilowatts of power. In fifteen years at Mars Institute, he'd discovered four new types of extra-spectral radiation, become a full professor, and had almost discovered how to harness nuclear binding energy.

Then the Aliens had come. They had appeared abruptly near Pluto, apparently coming at a speed greater than light, in strange globular ships that defied radar detection. Without provocation or mercy, they had sought out and destroyed every settlement beyond Saturn and had begun moving inward, systematically destroying all life. Nobody had ever seen an Alien—they invariably exploded to dust before they could be captured—but the horror of their senseless brutality showed up in the hideous corpses they left behind them.

Norden had been drafted while there was still optimism. Men could build a hundred ships to the Aliens' one, equally radar-proof, free from danger of magnetic or electronic detection, and nearly invisible in space. In anything like an even battle, men were sure to win. But they soon discovered it wasn't an even battle. The Aliens had some means of detecting human ships accurately at distances of millions of miles, and blasting them with self-guided torpedoes, while remaining undetected. And behind the torpedoes would come the dark globular ships to spray the wreckage with some force that left every cell utterly lifeless. Then Norden had been assigned to test Hardwick's hypothesis.

Hardwick had been a quasi-scientist mixed up with certain weird cults who maintained a private so-called laboratory on an asteroid near Jupiter's orbit. And in the desperation that followed the first foolish optimism, his theory that the Aliens could detect life itself, or the presence of the fabulous mitogenetic rays that were supposed to radiate from nerve endings, was actually taken seriously. Surprisingly, the tests indicated that remote-controlled ships which had been completely sterilized went undetected, while ships carrying rats or other life were blasted. Norden, as the expert on all strange radiation, had been sent to the asteroid to work with Hardwick in attempting to devise a screen for the hypothetical life radiation.

He never learned whether Hardwick was a wild genius or an even wilder lunatic. While he was wearing Hardwick's improvised shield during one of the attempts to test it, the Aliens had landed and broken in.

"What did they look like?" the psychiatrist asked casually—too casually, Norden felt.

"Sort of . . ." He frowned, trying to remember, but a clamp came down over his mind, freezing it. "I—I can't remember. And they did—something—to Hardwick. I—I . . ."

Colonel Armsworth brushed the other questions aside. "Never mind. You were wearing Hardwick's shield. Didn't they notice you?"

Norden shook his head doubtfully. "No, I don't think so. It's all blurred. I think I jumped for the spacesuit locker when they breeched the airlock on the dome. I must have gotten into a suit and been hidden by the locker door. And I must have run out after they—took Hardwick—away."

At least he hadn't been hurt when the Alien bomb ruined the dome. He'd dug out the transmitter, sent the message, and then spent the agony of waiting in trying to decipher the cryptic code in Hardwick's notebooks.

They went over it several times, but he could tell them little more. Then there were tests, some of which he could understand and answer without trouble, while others left

97

him taut with uncertainty and etched worried lines into the face of the psychiatrist. But at least the man nodded doubtfully.

"I think he'll do," he reported hesitantly to Armsworth. "A traumatic experience always leaves scars, but . . ."

"But or no but, he'd better do," Armsworth said gruffly. "No wonder they ordered us out to pick him up . . . Within fifty feet of the Aliens, and they didn't locate him! Dr. Norden, if that shield works and you can duplicate it, you're the most valuable man alive!"

"And the tiredest and sleepiest," Norden suggested. His eyes narrowed and his mind darted about, seeking some sign of the wrong reaction. Then he relaxed as the doctor and psychiatrist picked up their equipment and went out with advice he hardly heard. Armsworth lingered, and Norden hunted for and found what seemed to be a safe question. "How long until we reach Mars, Colonel?"

"We don't!" Armsworth's voice was suddenly thick and bitter. "We've abandoned Mars. The Aliens have moved inward. We—oh, hell, we'll reach our new laboratory on the Moon base in about four days! And you'd better start praying that shield works, or . . ."

He shrugged abruptly and left, closing the cabin door. Norden slumped onto the bed, not bothering to remove his clothes.

Automatically, he lifted his arms until his hands were both pressing against the nape of his neck, settled into a comfortable position against the automatic straps, and began reviewing all the events of his rescue carefully. And bit by bit, the worry in his head quieted. He'd gotten away with it. What "it" was, he didn't know, but the horrible tension was gone.

2

The tension returned briefly when he reached the base on the ` Moon where the frenzied activity of the new laboratories went on. The taped interviews had been signalled ahead, together with Hardwick's notebooks and Norden's suggested list of equipment. Apparently, the information on him hadn't been satisfactory. He was rushed through an airlock and into a room where three men mumbled and muttered unhappily as he was given tests that served no purpose he could see. And finally, he was forced to sit in another room for nearly an hour while the three conferred, before he was given an envelope of papers and led through a tunnel to the office of General Miles, head of the whole Moon base.

Miles skimmed through the reports and reached for the hushed phone. He was a man of indeterminate age, with a young voice and old eyes. There was a curious grace to his gaunt body, and a friendly smile on his rough-hewn face, in spite of the marks of exhaustion. Norden watched him tensely, but could read no reaction to whatever was told him.

Then Miles turned back and stuck out a hand. "You're in, Dr. Norden, though you should be sent for six months' rest cure. You've had a devil of a time of it, and you show it. But we can't afford to let you go. Anyhow, you're probably no more psychotic than I am, since you're able to work. And we need your work. The last settlement on Mars was wiped out just before we could evacuate it. Hardwick's notes are pure gobbledegook, and we have to depend on your help. Come on."

He stood up and led Norden through a narrow door and into a tunnel that connected GHQ with a large Quonset-type building to the south. "We've got everything we could for you. We even got you an assistant, in spite of your idea that nobody could help, and the exclusive use of one of our computers." He threw open the door to the laboratory, and gestured. "It's all yours. I'll be around from time to time, but if you need anything, holler for it. You have star priority here."

Norden closed the door behind him as the general left. He studied the equipment—more than he'd dreamed they could provide. To them, he was probably off balance; but at the moment, they might have given top priority to a man who could do the Indian rope trick. It seemed like a sloppy way of running things, particularly since they hadn't put a guard over him or suggested a penalty for failure.

He moved back through the laboratory, examining its capabilities. Again, there was the disturbing sense that his experience had blanked out whole sections of his mind, until he had to puzzle out apparatus he must have used a thousand times. But it was still obvious that the laboratory had everything he could possibly want, and more.

He wandered back and around a big computer and almost bumped into a small, brown-haired girl in a lab smock that showed a well-formed body beneath. She stared up at him from her work at the keyboard, and her face broke into a slow smile. "Dr. Norden? I'm Pat Miles, your assistant. And don't let the general's being my father fool you. I had three years of extraspectral math and paraphysics at Chitec and I'm a registered computer operator, grade one. I only got assigned here when they couldn't find anyone else available."

It was obvious, of course, that she was the guard placed over him—a direct source of information for her father on his progress. But a known factor was always better than an unknown. He stuck out his hand, and she took it quickly. "Glad to have you, Pat. But until I can decode Hardwick's notes from what little I learned of them, there won't be much to do."

He'd decided during his examination of the laboratory that this was a reasonable job, and one which would take

100

up enough time for him to orient himself. After that . . . his mind skidded off the subject.

She pointed to the worktable by the machine where the notes lay spread out. "I've been programming it already. If you can supply half a dozen keys, the computer should be able to translate the rest."

It rocked him for a second. He hadn't thought of the possibility, and it meant an end to stalling long before he could be ready. But there was nothing to do about it. He picked up the notes and began pointing out the few phrases he had learned, together with the only clear memory he seemed to have of his time with Hardwick. "The last page covers the final test. Hardwick had some cockroaches and mosquitoes left over from an experiment with various vermin, and he put them in a glass case. I stood at one side with the screen he'd made on me, and he stood on the other. Apparently he figured the things could sense the human aura, and the roaches should move toward my absence of one, the mosquitoes toward him for food. But there was no statistical evidence of its success."

She began feeding information to the machine, and reeling out the results, checking with him. At first, he begrudged the work, but then he found his interest quickening in the puzzle and its untangling. She was good at the work, though she found it hard to believe that the cult-inspired nonsense could be a correct translation. He began trying to anticipate the problems of her programming, and to scan the results, cross-checking to reduce errors from his own confusion.

Finally she nodded. "That's it, Bill. The computer can cross-check the rest itself. All I've got to do is cut the notes on a tape and feed them in. And you'd better go to lunch while I'm doing it—you're already five minutes overdue by the clock. Dad has you scheduled for his table, down in the GHQ basement cafeteria."

"What about you?" he asked.

She shook her head. "I want to finish this. I'll grab a bite later. Go on, don't keep Dad waiting."

Norden found most of the seats filled, but Miles spotted him and waved him over. There was a round of introductions to names that were tops in their fields—famous enough for even him to recognize, though he'd stuck closely to his own specialty.

As he waited to be served, Norden watched the men around him with surprise that grew into a sense of shock. There was none of the serious discussion to be expected of leading scientists and engineers. Instead, one group was undulging in some kind of horseplay that seemed to involve spilling ketchup over their plates, while another group was teasing one of the waiters about a large boil on his nose.

"How's it shaping up?" Miles wanted to know.

"We should have the notes decoded tonight," Norden told him. "After that, it's a matter of how useful they are."

Miles grunted unhappily. "They'd better offer a more promising lead than most of the others we've had. And soon! At this rate, in two more weeks, the Aliens will be taking over the Moon—and when that happens, we might as well stay here waiting for them." He turned to the head psychologist, while Norden was still hunting for the meaning of the implied threat there. "Jim, what about Enfield?"

"No dice," the psychologist answered. "He's obsessed with xenophobia—he hates the Aliens for breakfast, lunch and between meals. I can't treat him here. Of course, after what happened to his wife . . ."

Miles put his fork down and faced the group, but his eyes were on Norden. His words had the ring of an often-delivered but still fresh lecture. "Damn it, we can't afford hatred. Maybe the mobs need it to keep them going, but we have serious things to do that take sound judgment. Why not hate disease germs or any other natural enemy? The Aliens aren't horrible monsters, out for the pure love of evil. They're intelligent beings, doing what they think has to be done. I think they're wrong, and I can't under-

102

stand them—though I wish I could. I consider poisoning bedbugs a wise move, though no intelligent bedbug would agree or understand. This expedition of theirs would be a major job for any race, and they're going at it as if it's serious business, just as we had to exterminate the boll weevil. Emotions haven't a thing to do with it. We're in a battle for raw survival, and we haven't got the time for indulging in our animal emotions. This is a scientific problem that has to be solved for our lives—like a plague. Let it stand that way!"

Norden added that to the puzzles; either Miles. was setting another trap for him, or it was hard to understand how he'd gotten the five stars in his ears. An enemy was an enemy! He decided on silence as the best course, and was glad when the others began to leave. He watched them moving out, shocked again at the horseplay that was going on. Did they really think war to the death was a game?

He started to follow, then hesitated. But it could do no harm. He located one of the waiters and asked for a package of food to take to Pat. With relief, he saw no surprise, and he soon had a bag in his hand.

Pat was still sitting at the machine, but nearly done. She took the food with a pleased smile that told him he'd done the right thing, studying his face. "Why so glum?"

"Puzzled," he told her. On a sudden impulse, he mentioned the lecture and the horseplay of the men.

"Dad!" She snorted, but she was pleased. "He always gives that lecture in front of a new man. Bill, did you ever see a little boy fighting a bigger one, wading in, crying, whimpering, but so mad he couldn't stop—couldn't even see where he was hitting? That's hate-fighting. And it's senseless, because the other side may be just as right as you are. Professional fighters don't really hate—they simply do everything they can to win, coldly and coolly, because that's best. As to the teasing—where've you been? Didn't they do that on Mars? You can't keep the whole world dead serious—if they didn't relax by playing like kids now and then, they'd go crazy with the pressure here. Loosen up! You act as if we couldn't win."

"Does it look like it?"

"The computer thinks so. I tried it. And we'll win because we aren't dead serious and totally efficient. We'll haggle and fuss and do all the wrong things, because we don't have a set pattern—because we've kept individuality. But those Aliens act like a pre-set machine. Like a crew killing pests. Start at the outside of a circle and exterminate inwards, planet by planet! Phooey. They should have hit Earth at once, even if they had to retrace their steps a few times. But they aren't investigating whether we act like the enemy they planned on. No—what's the proper way is the only proper way. A lot of our nations tried such predetermined, inflexible, fanatical tactics once—and look where they are now."

He shook his head, not believing her, but it left him uncertain and disturbed. The fact was that the enemy was closing the net—closing it so fast that he had only two weeks to live, if he couldn't find the solution. As to hatred and horseplay . . .

He shook his head and went into his office. There were copies of his own published works there, as well as the magazines he hadn't yet seen. He dropped down to fill in the holes his memory had developed.

Paraphysics was tricky stuff, being so new. For a long time men had known no other spectrum than the electromagnetic one, running from heat up through cosmic rays; when atomic particles moved from one energy level to another, they produced quanta of energy in that spectrum, which was limited to the speed of light. The kinetogravitic spectrum began with gravity and moved up through nuclear binding force toward some unknown band; apparently it was the product of the behavior of some sub-particle finer than any known, and its speed of propagation was practically infinite. Other spectra were being considered, but no order or logic had fitted yet.

104

Life Watch

He found an article by a Japanese scientist that suggested there might be a spectrum related to the behavior of atoms in the molecule—with crystals in some cases acting on one level due to the electron drift and on another due to atomic strains within the molecule. Colloids, polymers and even the encephalograph waves were dragged in, but the mathematics seemed sound enough. Norden caught his breath, and began digging into the equations. The third manipulation suggested that magnetism might somehow be involved, and that would mean . . .

He couldn't dig the idea out. Just when it was about to open before him, his mind seemed to shy away and drift off to other things. He was still working on it when Pat came in and dropped a sheaf of papers onto the table. Strips of tape had been pasted up to form a crude book. "The whole thing," she reported. "But most of it's nonsense about some secret asteroid where the survivors of the fifth planet are waiting for men to mature before bringing the Great Millennium—or pages where he worked on the numerology of your name before he discovered your middle name had no H in it—or little notes to himself about buying a gross of Martian sand lizards. I had the machine go through it and strike out all completely meaningless matter, and came up with this."

It was a clip of five sheets. Norden skimmed through them and groaned. The shield he had tested for Hardwick had been made of genuine mummy cloth, ground mandrake and a glue filled with bat blood.

"Yet you did live," Pat pointed out. "And he was right about their being able to detect life—we sent out sterile neoprene balloons loaded with live rabbits and others with completely dead rabbits. Every one with the live rabbits was blasted—and none with the dead ones. We could use the same test to find out whether any one of those things worked—or any combination of them."

"We'll have to," he decided. "And then it may have been the closet instead of the shield—or an accident to

105

their detector that saved me. Pat, have they got some kind of library here?"

It was already quitting time, but she went with him while he persuaded the library attendant to let him in, before the next shift came on. Mummy cloth, it seemed, might become infused with a number of aromatic preservatives, products from the mummy, and such. It was ridiculous—but hardly more ridiculous than using the byproducts of mold to cure disease must have seemed. Anything dealing with life was slightly implausible. And when he called in the order for the materials to Miles, there were no questions.

"Thanks, Pat," he told her after she'd shown him where his sleeping quarters were.

She shrugged. "Why? If we don't find the answer, I'll be as dead as you in a few weeks."

He shuddered, and then shoved it out of his mind. Worrying about death wasn't decent, somehow. He found his bunk, stretched out with his hands behind his neck, and tried to review the serious events of the day—without the matter of hatred, horseplay, overefficiency, or Pat and her father. He saved those to worry about after he rolled over on his side and gave up all ideas of sleeping.

Then abruptly there was a yell from down the hall, and lights snapped on. Norden sprang out with the others, to see the outer lock click shut. Through it, in the glare of the overhead lights, he could see a figure running desperately for the edge of a further Quonset—running in the airlessness of the exposed surface without a spacesuit!

More lights snapped on, and a guard in a suit came around the corner, throwing up a rifle. There was a tiny spurt of flame from the muzzle, and the running man pitched forward. The guard started toward him just as a few men began to dart out of the huts in hastily donned spacesuits.

A greenish-yellow flame bloomed shockingly where the runner had fallen, and the floor shook under Norden. The guard was thrown backwards, and the others stumbled. When the explosion was over there was no sign of the men who had run.

"Alien!" somebody muttered. "A damned Alien! They always blow up like that before you can get near them! I've seen it out in space!"

And Norden remembered the bomb that had wrecked the dome on the asteroid—a bomb that had flared up with the same greenish-yellow color. He slipped into a vacuum suit and went out, but there was nothing to see.

Guards came up to drive the men back to their huts, but Norden seemed to have high enough rating to stay for a while. He learned that one of the workers was missing, and that it had been his badge which the Alien had worn to enter the sleeping sections. Either the Alien had killed and destroyed the worker for his clothing or else he had been the worker!

And he had been discovered forcing the lock on the sub-section of the hut where Norden had been sleeping!

3

The invasion of the base by the Alien had shocked them all, and few people had slept during the night. On his way to breakfast, Norden could feel the attention that was riveted on him. To the others, he was probably one of the most likely targets for whatever attack had been intended. He'd wondered about it himself, sick with a feeling of close disaster; but he could find no logical basis for the fear.

Miles waited until they had finished picking at their food, his own face a study in worry. Then he stood up and faced them. "No work this morning," he announced. "There's going to be a fluoroscopic test of every person on the base!"

Norden felt a wrench at his mind that left his thoughts

spinning. He caught himself, just as he heard a gasp from Colonel Armsworth, a few places down. But Miles went on as if nothing had been unusual.

"The guards have already been checked. They'll lead us all down to the explosive-test chamber. There we'll go in, one at a time, and stand on a marked square. The fluoroscope results will show on a television screen where all can see. If you pass, you'll go across the chamber to the cleared rooms beyond. Any man resisting or proven non-human will be shot at once. The Alien last night looked human, but he didn't breathe oxygen, so his internal structure must be different. However, if anyone wants to declare that he's an Alien, he'll be treated as a prisoner of war instead of a spy."

Nobody made such a declaration, and Miles nodded to the guards who had filed in, while fear-ridden faces were still staring at their neighbors. Norden wondered how long a confessed Alien would last before the men tore him to bits. Discounting hate was fine at long range—but not when the danger was at your elbow.

Miles and Pat went into the chamber first, with the expected human skeletons and shadowy organs showing up on the screen. Norden stared at it in fascination, while fear built up inside him. Armsworth passed in and found his position, with a face that was somehow both taut and frozen. The guards took a look at the screen and waved him on. He half staggered to the exit, his face filled with an emotion that was unreadable.

Norden tried to fight down his own panic. Damn it, he knew he was human! But a doubt began to throb in his mind. He couldn't remember so much. He'd thought the Aliens had never found him. But if they had taken him, tampered with his mind, and turned him back, would he know it? He'd still pass this test, though. Suppose he was an Alien—one given a spurious, hypnotic belief that he was Norden until the right signal to become himself again . . .

It was ridiculous, absurd! But the speculations ran on in

108

his mind. He didn't belong here. Men apparently took it for granted that a confessed spy could keep his life—and Norden took it equally for granted that death was the only answer. He didn't think like the rest of them. There'd been a week on the asteroid. His memories were spotty ...

"Dr. William Norden!" the speaker announced.

He jerked. Then he caught himself and forced his unwilling legs to move. The door shut behind him, and ahead lay the white outlines on which he was to stand. He drew up to the place automatically, aiming himself to face straight ahead toward the fluoroscope screen.

Now! It was almost a physical voice in his head. And his mind seemed to shift, and to shout something down. *Not yet! Look!*

"Okay, Dr. Norden," the speaker said. His eyes flicked to the screen, where a human skeleton showed dimly.

Crazy, he told himself. Hag-ridden with fears no sane human mind could have held. No wonder the psychologists had been uncertain about him. Crazy—but human!

Pat smiled weakly at him as he entered the room beyond to join the ranks of the elect. Then they watched as their group passed successfully, to give place to men from the freight gang.

The sixth one came through the door boldly enough—and suddenly leaped toward the side of the chamber where another door was. His hands were jolting at the locked barrier when the rifles sounded. A violent blast of greenish-white explosion rocked the chamber and shook the floors beyond. When it cleared, the Alien was dust and vapor, with nothing that could be studied for evidence.

Two workers who had been standing in line in a building beyond broke through the seal together, without waiting their turn, and headed for the shelter of a near barracks. A rifle bullet hit one, and both exploded.

By the time the rest had been proved safe, it was time for lunch—a quiet lunch at first. Then one of the men caught sight of a neighbor busily shaking his fork and looking sideways to emphasize some point. A tiny gadget appeared and was slid under the steak on the man's plate. Ten seconds later, when the man cut into the meat there was the bellow of a frightened cow and the meat leaped six inches up and two feet sideways. There was a shout of laughter that grew into a roar, and everything was suddenly normal again.

Norden shook his head. Fluoroscope or not, something was wrong with him; he couldn't have been so different from other men before the time on Hardwick's asteroid. That ruined steak had cost a small fortune in transportation from Earth, and the man would lose valuable time while waiting for another to be cooked. And yet, Norden could see that somehow it had been effective therapy, and he even felt somewhat better himself.

They spent the afternoon sending out the test "balloon" rockets with the various elements of Hardwick's screen. On the way back to the barracks, Norden noticed that there were now six guards about the laboratory, two of whom fell into step behind him. And he had been shifted to the dormitory over the Headquarters building, where he would be in the least danger—and also have the least freedom from observation!

But he forgot it the next day as the results of their tests came in. The shields had been completely ineffective. Dead rabbits still were unmolested, but live ones were picked off in everything they had sent out. Miles accepted the result with a tired shrug, but Pat was hit hard by it. None of the other research teams seemed to be getting anywhere. There was no way to detect Aliens and no way to screen humans.

On the fourth day, when the last possible variation of Hardwick's formula had proved useless and the Aliens had moved their lines up to fifty million miles from Earth's orbit, Pat was down early, rechecking the translation the computer had made. Norden came in, saw the results, and swore. For three hours he pored over the paper with the Japanese scientist's mathematics—and as before, he found his mind reaching for something, only to begin some useless side speculation that threw him off. It was as if he had a censor in his mind telling him he could go no further. He considered the prospect of ten days or more of life for himself and the men here, until the lunch signal sounded.

Somebody had put a new glue on the handle of his knife and fork, and it was fifteen minutes before he could locate a solvent that removed it. Pat howled at his plight along with the others. He checked his anger, swallowed it —and suddenly realized that, in a strange way, the practical joke was a mark of acceptance. He went back to the laboratory trying to think of something both mean and acceptable enough to live up to their queer code. An idea that had nagged him tantalizingly, just below consciousness, nibbled at his mind, but he let it go. If he could fit a protogravity generator under a plate . . .

And abruptly, he was digging for the complete set of Hardwick's notes and scanning the nonsense that the computer had declared meaningless. He picked up the telephone and called the library. "Give me what you've got on Martian sand lizards!"

Most of it was useless. They were typical low-grade Martian life, tiny things covered with fur, but vaguely lizard-like. Then the significant part came. "The females demonstrate a remarkable ability to locate the rare males at extreme distances. Janiekowski found that a female with all sense organs removed could locate a male at a distance of five kilometers, even when the male was enclosed in an airtight box of laminated copper and soundboard. No satisfactory explanation is known."

It *had* to be some form of telepathy or sensitivity to the life forces of the male! He went over the work done with the creatures a dozen times and could find no other explanation. And his mind was milling about, trying to slide away from it again. "Taboo!" he said. "Damn the taboo!" It was too late for it to operate now, whatever the reasons behind it; and judging by his growing certainty that some-

111

thing had been done to him, it only served to confirm the fact that he was on the right track.

Pat listened to his summary of what he'd found, and nodded quick agreement. "A quick test! It's what we need, all right. We still may not find the insulator for the shield, but we can run tests fast enough to have a chance. Metals first, then the other broad classifications, until something shows a sign. Bill, I guess this makes me and the computer look pretty silly. And after all the yelling I've done about flexibility being needed, too. I hope some place on Earth has a collection of the little beasts."

It turned out that Harvard was well stocked as a result of someone preparing to rework Janiekowski's experiments. In less then three hours, twelve females and two rare males were lying in front of Norden. They looked like small lizards covered with chinchilla hair and possessing eight legs apiece. The females were busily trying to break down the wall that kept them from the males.

Pat had already installed three television pickups and cages at various distant points, doing the work herself to insure secrecy, and picking the places most difficult to break into. Now she came back to move the females to their new homes, where they immediately began trying to crawl toward the torpid males, as shown by the television screens. The walls of their cages were equipped with pressure-measuring devices to test the strength of their efforts.

The mummy cloth drew a complete blank, as did the bat's blood. But the ground mandrake set the males to pawing at their cage with their triple tongues out, trying to reach it, while the distant females went berserk. Pat took the stuff away, snorting at them. "They'll die of frustration in another minute. To them an active male seems to be a combination billionaire, video star, and grand master in the art of love. I guess I know how they feel."

He was getting better at reading her glances, and he frowned as her eyes flickered toward him. He liked Pat, but . . .

She laughed. "Forget it, Bill. I was only ribbing you. You have about as much sex appeal to me as my grandfather."

It was ten minutes later before he realized what a typical masculine human reaction to such a remark would have been. He frowned, while his mind chilled at the implications. There wasn't much doubt now that the Aliens had caught him and done something to him—something drastic. He wasn't quite human, in spite of what the bones of his body indicated.

And that could only mean that Hardwick's shield had never worked. He stopped short, and then reconsidered. The difficulty he had forcing his mind to think about tests for the lizards still spelled a taboo in his mind—and that indicated there might be a shield. It left him exactly where he was, except for the question of what the Aliens wanted. If he could find that and defeat it . . .

Nothing they tried gave any positive result, though Pat thought that the variation in the female activity had been slightly more than normal when they'd tried the potassium salt solution around the males. They gave up late, and Norden went back to his bunk, and to the familiar pattern of lulling himself into a semi-conscious condition by the ritual of reviewing the day with his hands behind his head.

Then he swore. It was a pointless habit. He put his arms at his sides and held them, while his head squirmed uncertainly. Habits could be broken—and any compulsion he had as a result of whatever had happened was a luxury he couldn't permit himself. There would be no recovery until he had overcome them all and filled all the gaps in his mind with useful things. Perhaps the Aliens had already succeeded; they might have decided somehow that he was the man who *could* solve the problem, and had tampered just enough to make sure he failed, while keeping him able enough to insure that no other man would replace him.

He yanked his arms down again, and started to turn

over. Fifteen minutes later he came out of complete blackout with his hands at the back of his neck and a queer feeling that his mind had remained active, with only his memory of it missing. His glance darted to the door, but it was still locked, and his clothes lay on the floor where he'd kicked them. Apparently he hadn't done anything while he was short-circuited from his memory, at least.

He thrust himself up from the bed in disgust, yanked on his clothes, and headed down the hall, back towards the laboratory. He passed the cubicle where General Miles should have been sleeping and noticed a trace of light shining under the door. For a second, he remembered the man's words—a spy who confessed would be treated as an honorable prisoner of war. Only, damn it, he wasn't a spy, whatever else he was. And there was no time left to find someone to solve the problem that had been dumped into his lap. He couldn't turn himself in while that was still hanging.

Inside his mind was a slowly growing hatred of the Aliens, and he clung to it. They'd denied him his right to be a normal human being—and while their imposed attitudes made it impossible for him to understand the absurd conduct of men, he was beginning to assume that the fault was with him, and not the rest of humanity.

Fresh guards had replaced the other couple, but they swung in behind him, and then stopped at the entrance of the laboratory. He'd insisted that they stay out, since he wanted no one to know what went on with the lizards. Complete ignorance of events was the only sure protection against spies.

He headed around the computer by letting his feet guide him, and reached for the switch. It clicked, just as a voice sounded in front of him.

"Norden, you damned fool! Leave those lights off!"

But they were already on, showing the figure of Colonel Armsworth standing before the cage of the lizards with a knife in his hand.

114

4

Norden felt a wave of hate boil up, then checked it coldly, his mind reacting to the situation before he could realize more than a few of the implications. Obviously, Armsworth was a spy who knew of the work here and had come to wreck things. With his rank, it would be easy enough to get in. Also, the man stood there with none of the fear he should have shown on being discovered, and Norden felt the sick confirmation of his being a pawn for the Aliens.

But the fact gave him some chance. He lifted his arm to the switch and then dropped it. "The guards would suspect something if I cut it off now. Any suggestions?"

"I could kill the lizards and let you discover me and chase me out to explode," Armsworth said thoughtfully, without any emotional color to the suggestion. He shook his head. "I don't know. It's funny they can't trust you to stall off the Miles girl and have to send me here. With replacements tough, I'd hate to blow up unless it's necessary." Then his eyes narrowed suddenly. "Hey, wait a minute. You weren't supposed to know . . ."

Norden's hand swept up and hit the light switch. His other arm jerked out for the big tongs he had spotted. He heard the spy leap and slipped backwards, just in time to avoid the rush. His arm came down with the instrument, and there was a solid thud. When he turned the lights on again, Armsworth lay on the floor with a groove running across his head deep enough to bury three fingers in.

Then slowly the corpse sat up and began hitching along the floor toward the cage of lizards.

Norden grabbed up the little cage and swung towards the door. He took one step, stopped abruptly, and reached down. His hand gripped the collar of the thing on the floor and he heaved it up against the light gravity of the

Moon. The thing sailed across the laboratory, heading toward the rear of the heavy protogravity generator. Norden cushioned the cage of lizards against his chest and dropped to the floor in the shelter of the computer.

There was a blast that nearly ruptured his eardrums and the glare of greenish-yellow cut through his closed lids. The floor heaved and shook, while sections of the curved roof began falling. The air gushed upwards, the floor jarred again as the automatic airseal dropped, cutting off other sections.

Norden jumped toward a plainly marked closet and threw it open. He yanked down one of the spacesuits stored there for emergencies, thrust the lizard cage inside, and turned on the oxygen. Adapted to the thin air of Mars, they should be safe enough after so short an exposure here. He groped about until he found another suit that would fit, cursed as he found it zipped closed, and finally worked it open. Once in, he sealed it, and headed toward the lock on the big emergency airseal.

He got through just as the guards were about to enter in their own spacesuits, dragging rescue equipment. Miles was with them, waiting impatiently while Norden slipped his helmet off. "Who was it?"

"Armsworth," Norden told him. "And he passed the fluoroscope test!"

Miles sighed, but there was no surprise. "Damn! I should have had him checked when he came back from inspecting the far side. They must have had a spy all ready to make the switch as soon as they got him. Or maybe the test doesn't mean anything. How much damage?"

The guards had come back. One of them began to report what they had seen into a recorder. Most of the damage had been confined to the roof of the building and to the big protogravity generator. It seemed to have shielded the rest of the equipment. Norden and Pat, who had finally been called, went inside in their suits to supervise clearing away the debris. Outside, a crew was al-

116

ready erecting a new roof on the laboratory, using prefab sheets. Aside from the generator they had never used, nothing irreplaceable was hurt. And the two little male lizards were doing well enough. Inside of two hours the laboratory was back in business.

By common consent, Pat and Norden abandoned all idea of sleeping. He started to draw up a list of new tests, and then went back to the potassium shield. It seemed to produce a very slight quantitative difference in the reaction of the females. He consulted the vague speculations in his own works on possible other spectra, and came back. The trouble was that he wasn't working with any natural phenomenon, but with life. He grimaced at the twist of his logic, but the sense remained. Something came into the back of his mind from a phrase in Hardwick's notes. It teased him, until his mind almost had it, and then another taboo clamped down on his thoughts.

He fought it out, standing still while Pat stared at him doubtfully. Twice he could feel himself almost black out, but he tracked the taboo down in his mind, chased it into its lair, and strangled it. It died hard, but left his answer available.

"K-40," he said. His voice was steady, and Pat relaxed, unable to see the complete fatigue inside him. Disciplining himself seemed to be the hardest possible task. "Radioactive potassium isotope. It's supposed to be mixed up somehow with the life processes."

She reached for the phone, and spoke into it briefly. Then there was a wait before she handed it over, and a voice came on. "This is General Dawes at Oak Ridge. Who's calling?"

"William Norden, Project A-sub-zero, Moon base. I want five pounds of K-40 up here in four hours. Use my top priority and mark the shipment for delivery to me only."

There was the usual few seconds waiting while the message travelled to Earth and back. "Five *pounds?*" the voice asked.

117

"Five pounds! And I may want more as fast as it can be gathered."

Pat was on another phone. Before Earth could answer again there was a click, and General Miles' voice broke in. "This is Miles, Dawes. Give Norden what he wants."

A sputter of protest began, and ended abruptly as Miles' voice reached Earth. The silence was broken with a sigh. "Okay, Norden, we'll get it to you by then, somehow."

It arrived in less time, and the two of them began the tricky job of getting the highly active element into a container both chemically and radioactively safe. They clamped it over the cage at last, and watched the pressure on the female cages. The results weren't spectacular, but they were unquestionable. And later, when they had reduced the amount of K-40 to a thin coating, it still worked. The quantity made very little difference beyond a certain minimum.

The effects still weren't good enough. They tried painting various substances with the chloride of the potassium, with equally good results and much greater ease of handling. The nitrate was even better to work with. But it took them until late that night before they learned that coating the nitrate onto cleaned iron was a major step forward. It had been all hit and miss, except for vague directional hunches, up until then.

Norden looked at Pat, who seemed ready to drop. "Better go back for some rest," he suggested. She shook her head, but did agree to lie down while he began formularizing their results to date. Their best efforts had quieted the excitement of the females by no more than ten percent. He reduced everything he could to a consistent basis and added other formulae which might apply from the incomplete relationship tables that strove to reconcile the two recognized spectra. Those might also indicate something about any third spectrum. Either his memory was coming back or his reading of the books and articles was beginning to take effect, he was pleased to notice.

Pat was busy at the computer, which had fortunately

suffered only minor damages and had been repaired. From the computations, they made the indicated experiments, and fed the results into the machine. This time, it gave only seven suggested answers, with a rough weighing of them. The second one called for one of several organic substances soaked in potassium ferrocyanide and grounded. While they waited for the chemistry shed to handle that with due precautions on the radioactive isotope, they tried the others. One gave a better than fifty percent reduction, which meant that the females were only mildly crazy.

"Don't they ever relax?" Pat wondered, nibbling at one of the sandwiches Miles had ordered sent in to them.

The female sand lizard's libido mattered less than nothing to Norden at the moment. He was staring at the work he had done in relating hints and fragments of information with pure hunches to get new facts, and realizing that he could never have done that even before the Aliens had tampered with him. Either he was mysteriously more capable now that he'd managed to overcome a few of the taboos in his mind, or else the loss of so much of his memory had left his thoughts freer to operate.

"We'll call this the Hardwick spectrum," he decided aloud. "The man was a crackpot cultist, but he was a genius, all the same. And with this, we'll pay those damned Aliens back for what they did to him."

"We wouldn't be able to if you hadn't had time to get the males and yourself into oxygen suits before Armsworth exploded," Pat told him. "They're the only males left alive, now that Mars has been scoured by the Aliens."

He swung around in surprise. "I never . . ."

The phone saved him from finishing. He hadn't had time to get the spacesuit first. He'd spent probably five minutes fumbling around after the blast before he was in one. And he'd arrived outside the lock without ever having felt discomfort from living in a vacuum that long!

His self-satisfaction vanished, and revulsion replaced it. He stared at his body in horror. No human body could

119

ever stand such punishment, but he had taken it without noticing it!

Pat came back at a run. "Come on, Bill. A messenger just came up from Earth with five hundred pounds of K-40!"

"Five hundred?" He jolted out of his thoughts, into a memory of the amazed voice of General Dawes when he had asked for the fabulous quantity of a mere five pounds of the single isotope. Pat's face confirmed his suspicions. Earth couldn't have separated any five hundred pounds by now.

They found the guards already waiting to take them to where Miles was, and followed them down to the entrance of the explosion-testing chamber. There Miles was smiling and chatting with a man who appeared to be a perfectly normal rocket pilot, and who seemed bored until he spotted Norden. He consulted a picture on some kind of manifesto, and stepped forward.

"Orders are that I have to deliver the K-40 to you, Dr. Norden," he said. "But it's pretty bulky in its containers. If you'll come out to the ship and okay it . . ."

Miles cut in blandly. "I've been explaining the new regulations, Dr. Norden." He winked slightly with a faint motion toward the chamber.

"Go ahead and clear through," Norden told the pilot. "I'll wait, and then we can look at your cargo. It's a damned nuisance having to hold things up while everyone is X-rayed, but that's regulations now." He caught Miles' look of approval and knew he'd reacted correctly.

The pilot shrugged. "Why not? Let me know if you find any dangerous diseases." He chuckled and stepped through the entrance, and out toward the fluroscope set-up.

The picture on the screen was perfect, and the guards started to relax from the slits where their guns projected into the chamber. Miles glanced at them, and his voice was low and commanding. "Shoot to miss. And keep getting closer."

Another screen showed the pilot turning back, just as the first bullet hit the floor three feet from his boots. He jumped and yelled something. Another bullet came closer, and a third just missed. Shock hit his face, and vanished as he turned into a bright splash of greenish-yellow light.

"They overestimated our production and underestimated our ability to bluff," Miles said. "Good shooting, men. I'm glad he decided he'd failed the test before you had to shave it closer."

Norden stood staring at the blasted area and back toward the screen that had shown the picture of a normal human before a fluoroscope. Breathing vacuum for five minutes hadn't hit him as hard; subconsciously, he'd counted on the fluoroscopic evidence—and it had proved to be a lie.

"He couldn't have been an Alien with that kind of a skeleton!"

Miles shook his head. "He wasn't. As near as our cyberneticists could gather, he was some kind of a robot, designed to mix with us. We've caught a few telephotos of the Aliens, and they look a little like octopi on stubby legs. Nothing could make them look human."

"But a robot with a human skeleton?" Pat asked.

"It's possible, with enough advanced development. Hide the metal works in the so-called bones and skull, and shape everything else to the right form and transparency. Hughes swears that any race capable of developing such an advanced cybernetic brain could handle the rest—down to letting him get his energy out of our food." Miles' face was more fatigued than ever, but he found enough strength for a smile. "Thanks for playing along with me, Bill. Now get back to work, if you can stand it. The chem lab delivered your stuff while you were coming here."

The stuff from the chemists looked like wool, impregnated with the K-40 salt. Pat slashed off a yard of the coarse cloth and draped it around the cage, after a quick check with the Geiger-Mueller counter. She formed a

121

rope of it and connected the cage-cover to the nearest pipe.

And the images of the females in the screens were suddenly still, as if all of them had gone to sleep at once. Pat yanked the cover off and instantly the females were dashing at the gates of their cages again.

Pat let out a yell and grabbed for the phone. Norden tried to echo her enthusiasm, but there was no resiliency left in him. He stared at the answer to their problems, while part of his mind estimated that the pilots could stand the radioactivity from suits of such cloth for long enough if an undersuit of lead-cloth were also worn.

But the rest of his mind was in the depths of his own private hell. Robot, it shouted at him—robot and spy! It was plain enough now that his periods of "relaxation" and review of the day had been the leak of information to the Aliens. His rebellious attempt to end it had been the signal to send Armsworth against the male lizards. Hands-behind-the-head-Norden, he thought—the robot too dumb to recognize the working of an automatic transmitter switch.

He fondled the cloth slowly, tasting the anticipation of revenge. The Aliens had taken a man named William Jon Norden from a lonely asteroid and had drained him of his life history and knowledge. They'd built a poor dupe of a robot and had sent it out to spy for them, and to believe for a while that it was real and alive. Now let them feel the defeat they'd earned when they built their robot too close to the original in abilities!

Then he considered the thin thread on which his hopes rested. He had something that stopped some form of energy from being detected by the lizards—an unknown bandwidth of an unknown spectrum which might not even be the right one.

He swung around to check Pat's call, but it was too late. The word had already spread, judging by the whoops coming from beyond the laboratory.

5

Norden broke away from the men, who refused to listen to his warnings, as quickly as possible. Pat had already gone to her bunk, worn out completely by the brief burst of hope, and he headed for his own cubicle. There was no physical fatigue—how could there be in a robot? But his mind was dulled with too many shocks. He dropped to the bunk, and his arms came up automatically.

He forced them down, and this time he was ready when his brain tried to black out on him. The compulsions that acted on him to make him pass on his information to the Aliens was partly under his control. He managed to side-track his thoughts before blacking out, and to keep his arms down. He lay there, cursing himself and the things which had created him, fighting his battle silently, until he knew he had won.

His legs were unsteady when he finally stood up. The effort of will had shocked even his motor control impulses, but the damage was not permanent, and by the time he passed Miles' darkened doorway he was moving smoothly enough again. He saw surprised looks exchanged by his guards as they followed him back to the laboratory.

"You might as well come in," he told them. "I'll be here all night, and there's nothing secret about my work now. I think there's a deck of cards in the desk over there."

One of them looked and came back, holding the deck and grinning. "Thanks, Doc," he said. "You're all right."

For a second, Norden savored the words as he turned into his office. He'd learned in the days he was here. He could find some acceptance among men now. Then he grimaced bitterly, as he realized what they'd think of him if they knew what he was. It was one thing to ape humanity, and another to belong.

123

The article on speculative spectra by the Japanese was still there, and he began poring over it. Almost at once his mind jerked away on a flight of curiosity about the card game the men were playing. He pulled it back, and it turned to hatred of the Aliens. He fought against that, tempting as it was. He'd licked the compulsion to communicate with them in two hours. There was hope that he could lick the taboo against investigating into this forbidden field. And the fact that it was forbidden made it doubly worth studying.

Bit by bit he traced down the mathematics, but in the end the taboo threw him. It required all the effort he could bring to the problem to follow the tricky formulae, and it couldn't be done while fighting the treachery of his own mind. He gave up in disgust and turned to the computer.

He'd seen Pat use it often enough, and apparently his robot mind was good at memorizing. He searched through the available tapes of information until he came to one marked as covering Einstein's unified field theory. He fed it in, and began adding the spectra-relation data from the books, storing them in the memory circuits of the machine. The mathematics of the article went in next. He made sure the material they had used to find the screen was still active, and brought it up to date. Finally he set the machine to deriving all possible extensions of the mathematics he couldn't handle himself.

When that was finished, there was no longer any need to worry about the taboo. The computer had done what he had tried, and more. He stared at the sheaf of papers. There was enough material here for years of work on extraspectral radiation. And his suspicion that magnetism was the common link seemed to be confirmed. It seemed to be something of a universal transformer, when properly handled.

But the machine couldn't tell him what section of the Hardwick spectrum would involve life. The field used by

the lizards to locate each other lay well up in it, somewhat analogous to the X-rays of the normal spectrum. But
if that failed, there was no clue to what would work. In
any new field, one fresh fact could open up tremendous
stores of knowledge—but there would always be even
greater ones not revealed.

He put in a call to the library for more material on
Janiekowski's work with the lizards and was told that
they'd have to secure a tape from Earth. Earth promised
a ship with the material and other things he requested
within three hours; there was no questioning of his pri-
orities this time.

Then he glanced at the clock and was shocked to find it
already past noon. He got up impatiently, heading toward the lunchroom. It was strange that Pat hadn't come.

He found her and Miles coming toward the laboratory,
and one look was enough. Miles motioned Norden to follow him and led to his office. There he closed the door
and threw the decoded dispatches down for the other to
see.

"The Aliens have cut the distance to ten million miles
from Earth," he said wearily. "We've been holding out by
sheer numbers of ships. Send out a hundred near each
other, and the Aliens can't handle them all at once. If
they're lucky and spot the first torpedoes, they can trace
them back and a few ships may survive long enough to
send visual-pattern-seeking atomic torpedoes toward the
Alien ship. But we can't get closer than a few hundred
thousand miles with any life aboard a ship, because that
radiation—or whatever it is—that they use is fatal closer,
so long as they can detect us. You can see why Command rushed through all the screen suits they could and
struck with them this morning. They had to."

Norden picked up the dispatches and scanned them.
Seven hundred pilots out of twice that many thousand had
been screened. A third of the total number had returned
—but none who had been theoretically protected. The

Aliens had apparently not only spotted them all, but had concentrated their torpedo fire on those ships. It had been a complete failure!

There was no use in reminding them that he'd tried to warn them. Earth hadn't been able to heed such warnings. He handed the papers back, and his thoughts were filled with the picture of seven hundred men—men probably like the guards who'd called him all right—who had lost all their marginal chance to live because a robot had failed. It was nonsense, his mind told him; soldiers were meant to die. But the picture remained. "So what happens to me now?"

"So you try again, of course," Miles answered, apparently surprised at the question. "At least the fact that they worked that hard to eliminate the ships with the screen indicates you're on the right track."

"Tracing a single drop of water in the ocean. Looking for a trace of life that can be detected for millions of miles when we're in the middle of millions of living creatures. I've been working on that already. And the only reason we could detect and screen the lizard signals was because they were unique. Hardwick was right about that, too—you have to look for life forces where they're unique. I need isolation from people, animals—even from germs and viri, probably."

Pat gestured to a map on the wall. "There are the mine installations on the far side of the Moon. Would they do?"

He had no idea, but it was the best he could hope for. He nodded slowly, and she turned towards the door.

"Then what are we waiting for? We've got too little time now."

"You're not going, Pat," he told her. "Nobody is. I need isolation from life, remember! Besides, if there's any means of communication between here and there, I'll need you here to work the communicator."

There was a line that was still useful, as a quick check showed. And there were ships to carry all the equipment he needed, including two rabbits, and a male and female

126

sand lizard in little airtight cages where oxygen could be supplied from tanks. He had no idea of what he would need, and had to take everything he could imagine as being useful. But three hours later he stood alone in a building that had served as a barracks for a mine crew. He watched the rockets leave, and began opening the air-locks to space. Any bacteria left by the former men would be killed by that, he hoped.

He had no belief in success yet. He might be keeping a death watch over the human race as the Aliens moved in —or a life watch, since he was seeking life while they were heading toward the end of it. But he, at least, was no living thing, and the life detectors of the Aliens should miss him. Somehow, he'd learn enough to seek vengeance among them.

They'd made a mistake in creating him with all the ability of the original William Norden and the thinking speed of a robot. They'd made a bigger mistake in thinking that a robot capable of understanding humans was only a robot, and that orders in the form of compulsions would be followed without question. And for their mistakes, they'd pay. He had twenty-four hours out of each day for work, until they caught him, to learn their further weaknesses.

He flooded the front entrance, where the television link to Moon base was, with air to make speech possible, and rigged up a flexible seal to the rest of the building.

Janiekowski had dissected countless sand lizards, and the pictures were included in the reel of tape from Earth. He studied them, digging into what the calculator had supplied him about radiation and its behavior in the third spectrum. He found, as he had expected, that a tiny bit of radioactive material lay at the base of the microscopic receptor in the female, and that the same was to be found in the organ the male used to generate the force. And there was a tiny helix of superfine, wirelike material around it. He had no idea of what the conductor was composed of, or how the animals generated the faint cur-

127

rents of electricity they'd need, but he was sure the helix was a tiny-electromagnet.

He built a model as best he could, and tried to find some sign that it picked up a signal from the male. And finally he was forced to anesthetize the female and remove her receptor for examination under the portable electron microscope.

It took eleven tries before he was able to detect anything, and then the result surprised him. The faint, almost invisible glow from the radioactive disintegration in his device abruptly faded. He had been expecting it to increase, but whatever force the male broadcast acted to decrease the "unchangeable" rate of decay of a bit of K-40.

He called Pat, asking for information. Her face was haggard with worry and her attempt to be awake whenever he might call, but she wrote down his questions and cut off without wasting time. Half an hour later, she called back.

"You're right. Uranium-bearing ores from out in space contain much less uranium in proportion to lead than those on Earth. Geologists say this is because either those space-borne rocks are older or because cosmic radiation acts on them more."

"They'll have to change that," he said flatly. "It's because radioactivity is inhibited by the life processes. And I don't know how. I know I need that data fed into the computer, though."

It meant that they'd have to revise all their figures about the age of the Earth, and that since life began on Earth and Mars, no radioactive half-life had been natural. Probably the rate of decay had varied slightly with each century, as the amount of life changed.

He fed her a list of calculations, and waited while the machine ground out its answers. Pat came back to the screen while it worked on automatically. "They're bombing the base now," she reported dully. "We've been able to miss being hit by keeping a cover of volunteers up to attract the seeking units before they reach us. And the

Aliens are within three million miles. We can't hold out much longer."

"Don't forget your optimism," he said. He'd meant it for reassurance, but she stared back as if he'd slapped her. "I mean your computer calculations on victory for Earth. How come they moved in so quickly?"

"It's been three days," she told him. "Don't you know how long you've been out there?"

He hadn't kept track. But the cluck of the computer ending its work interrupted them, and she held the results up to the screen for him to copy with the camera at his end.

He studied the formulae for long, wasted minutes before he could accept them. Then he sighed, and went on to other work.

There was no shield possible for any object bigger than about twice the size of the cage they had used. There could never be any way to protect a man from the Aliens. It was to be a death watch he kept apparently. And Pat must have known it when she saw the formulae, since she had picked up the basic knowledge to read it.

He stood staring up at the space above him, letting the hate harden inside him, while he pictured the base in the hands of the invaders! The men there were beyond saving, according to the figures he had now. But it was still not too late for vengeance, or for them to strike back at the Aliens, perhaps.

This time he deliberately searched through all the taboos in his mind to find the answers he needed. It was still painful and difficult work, but he seemed to be gaining skill at overcoming his compulsions. At last he found the information he wanted in those areas of forbidden knowledge.

The Aliens were not life as men knew it. All protoplasmic life was imbued with and radiated the mysterious, extraspectral life forces he had discovered. Tiny—incredibly weak—as the energy of those life forces was, it could seriously inhibit the rate of radioactive decay for hundreds of millions of miles around it. Alien existence was a pseudo-life based on the rapid breakdown of radioactive isotopes. To the Invaders, protoplasmic life was a fatal poison; they had no choice but to accept extinction or wipe out all living things around them.

Understanding of the weapon used to eliminate every living cell was buried in Norden's head, but he disregarded it now. His interest centered on their means of detecting life. It had evolved from an inherent ability, but was now mechanically strengthened and refined far beyond any human theory of extraspectral forces and their control. And with knowledge of that, he hoped, would be the fuller knowledge needed to control and project such forces against the Aliens.

He found what he wanted, finally. The theory was difficult, but the application was within his means. And fortunately, only tiny amounts of power would be needed.

He drew up the plans this time with sureness. He was no longer amazed at the progress he'd made in understanding extraspectral phenomena. It might very well represent the work of generations of scientists, but he was a robot designed to gain understanding of human science from the few smatterings the Aliens had been able to learn when he was created. His mind had to be programmed for speed and adaptability.

He finished the designs, wrote down the proper formulae, and stuck the papers in front of the television pick-up, pressing the call button. Without waiting for an answer, he went back into the workshop and began assembling the tiny, radioactive strontium batteries and tubes of protein plastic wound with layers of iron wire. He had enough for what he needed.

The device was set to work both as a detector and a generator of the radiation involved. He tuned one, setting it to receive. It took a few minutes to replace the antenna of the small radar set he'd brought with the hastily constructed new device, and he forced himself to work faster by the sheer drive of his will. Then he stepped back, letting the new antenna revolve on the antenna mount. He began increasing the current that controlled the degree of electromagnetism in the wire, which served to tune the device.

A pip appeared on the screen, pointing toward the cage where the male and crippled female lay peacefully together. Norden raised the frequency until another pip appeared, this time pointing to the rabbits. He adjusted it for maximum brightness. In the section which should cover the direction of Moon base below him, a brilliant glow sprang up, indicating radiation that cut straight through all the layers of the Moon. Then he found the exact frequency, and the whole screen blazed, blanked out by overloading of the amplifier. Apparently all life of Earth stock radiated at the same frequency. He cranked up the frequency control, expecting nothing more. Then he bent forward sharply as other pips appeared, indicating objects out in space!

. The Aliens also radiated in the same spectrum—but at such a high frequency that no atomic nucleus was small enough to be affected by the radiation.

As he watched, the central pip suddenly began to grow brighter, holding its position in a way that indicated a straight descent toward his detector!

They also had detectors for that frequency, and his detector was sloppy enough to radiate a faint trace of its own. He'd been spotted, and the exterminating force was on the way.

6

Norden grimaced at his own stupidity, and estimated the time it would take. If they decided to come in to spray this area with their own force, or to capture it, he had several minutes. If they sent one of their superspeed torpedoes, he was already on borrowed time.

With a few minutes to spare, he could tune the tube to make it function as a weapon and spray them with that. Its straight-line efficiency should be enough to make sure no dangerous amount of its radiation reached the men two thousand miles away. Vengeance was his for the taking.

He reached for the other tube, hesitated, and grabbed up a piece of paper and a pencil. The men at the base had the working plans of his device by now. They had to be warned of the danger of not making absolutely sure their radiation generators or detectors couldn't spill dangerous radiation among them, and that the Aliens could detect an inefficient search ray.

Norden headed for the flexible seal at a full run, while his rock-steady hands pencilled the final information on the radiation frequencies needed. He broke through into the air of the entrance, yanked the diagrams off the pickup rack, and snapped in the new piece of paper. He turned with a single motion and headed for the workroom again. And stopped!

Beyond the entrance, the fins of a rocket were visible. And the red light on the airlock indicated that someone was using it. As his eyes focussed, he saw the inner lock open, and Miles and Pat stepped through it.

They started to say something, but he cut them off. "For God's sake, stay here. There's no air beyond. Alien ship!"

He jumped through the seal. His hands swept up the tube that was to be a weapon, and his eyes darted to the screen. The pip was bigger now, and at maximum brightness. The Alien ship must be only tens of thousands of miles above, braking down to spray the moonscape here.

And less than a hundred feet away, the two humans waited, subject to any energy that might spill from his weapon. It would have to be a perfect piece of workmanship, with all its radiation directed in a straight line.

The formulae of its propagation seemed like an endless belt in his mind. He tightened the helix of wires about it, trying to be sure they were even. With time, there were a·

number of things he could do, but he had no time to spare. This might harm Miles and Pat—but the Alien beam would leave nothing to chance.

The thought of them jolted through his mind in a delayed reaction. They'd seen him come into this airless space without a helmet. They knew he wasn't human! Discovered! *Explode!*

"No!" he shouted silently into the airless room. He had to get the Alien first!

He had no idea of the time left as he snapped fresh batteries into place and tried to line the weapon into resonance with the detector settings. He lifted his eyes, to stare up through the open roof of the building. There must be a faint black dot in the sky, but he couldn't see it against the blackness of space. He lifted the weapon, pointed it toward where the Aliens should be, and depressed the little trigger, moving the rheostat back and forth to be sure he had covered the lethal frequency.

He felt a tremor on the floor, and his eyes caught a glimpse of Pat beside him before he could force his gaze toward space again. She was shouting something inside her helmet.

Then he caught the first visible sign of the Alien ship, already within miles of the building, and big enough to show in the sidelight of the sun. It came rushing down in an unchecked plunge, apparently heading straight for him! He strained his eyes, tracing its path. Then he relaxed. It was moving sideways and would land a mile away. The weapon had worked. No ship would have that speed so near the surface if the pilot were not destroyed.

He grabbed for Pat and dragged her to the floor, away from anything that could fall on them. There was no sound, but a tremendous jolt rocked the floor of the building, and the ground around seemed to dance madly. A shaft of greenish-yellow sprang up, mixed with a glaring red from the distance. The ship had struck at a terrific speed—fast enough to reduce everything in it to pulp. Then the ground was quiet, and Norden sprang to his feet.

133

Now!

He caught the thought in time. He couldn't let himself explode here. He had to get outside, away from the two humans. The compulsion squeezed and writhed in his mind, but he held it. It was tenfold as strong as the others —and the need to overcome it until they could be safe was a hundred times as great.

He stumbled toward the seal as Pat stood up. His body slipped through the seal and almost bumped into Miles, who was apparently waiting for him. Norden had no spare effort for speech or thought. He headed dumbly for the airlock that would lead outside.

"Norden!" The general had grabbed his arm and was following. "Norden, if you go out there, I'm going with you. And whatever happens will happen to me, too. You've got to listen!"

He tried to bull his way ahead, shaking his arm to free it. The other arm was also carrying a dead weight, and he could see Pat's face beside his own.

She was screaming at him over the suit radio. "Bill! Bill, we knew it all along! We *knew* you were a robot! It doesn't matter. If you explode, you'll take us with you!"

He hit the lock with them still on his arms, and the words froze meaninglessly in his ear as he held back the driving urge until he could escape from them.

Miles clung grimly. "It's the Aliens, Bill! It's their idea for you to explode. The damned Aliens who want to kill you! Do you love them so much you'll kill us all? Or do you hate them?"

It penetrated slowly. The Aliens wanted to kill him. And he hated them. They'd played with him, had made him a monster to do their dirty work. They'd given him nothing. And now they wanted everything. They wanted to kill him and his friends. He hated them.

The hate washed through him—the cold, hard hate that had the greater strength for its lack of endocrines or other emotions. He'd be damned if he'd let the Aliens force him to kill himself!

"I'm all right," he said slowly. "You're safe. You can go back to the base."

Miles stared down at him with the smile growing stronger on his lips, though his eyes were sick with worry and strain. "We did know about you, Bill. That business about being the only undetected human out there on the asteroid looked suspicious, and the psychologists weren't fools. We were gambling on a chance to get some information on their detector out of you before you could do anything. Norden was the only man who could have known enough to have any chance; with him dead, we had to hope they'd give you information enough to act in his place. Pat volunteered to watch you. And we had ultra-violet sensitive cameras in every room where you ever were, watching you every second."

He paused, but Norden could think of nothing to say. He looked at Pat for confirmation, and she nodded. "We set the whole thing up for you, Bill. But we found we were wrong. The Aliens had done too good a job on you for their own good. They made you too human—so human that you had to begin thinking our way. After that business with Armsworth, we stopped worrying."

"But you came out here . . ." he began.

"Not to spy on you, Bill," Miles told him. "Earth's evacuating the Moon, now that you found us weapons to handle the Aliens. We're needed to supervise things back at the factories. Pat and I just came to pick you up, when you wouldn't answer your calls. We're taking you home."

He stared at them silently, and there was a complex of feelings in his mind that made thinking almost impossible. But bitterness was heavier than anything else. "That's fine for someone who won't hate an enemy—though you're quick enough to use hate when it's useful. What about the rest of the world? Will they want a bomb-carrying monster as a pet?"

Miles put his hands on Norden's shoulders, while Pat went back into the workroom. "Sit down on the desk, Bill. The only people who know are the two of us and Jim—the psychologist who predicted exactly how you'd react from the beginning. He also gave you one test that first day that involved our top-grade X-ray machine—not one of these fluoroscope toys. It's a good thing you've got your brains all through you, because when I get done, you'll be literally empty-headed."

Pat came back with a collection of equipment. Norden squirmed, trying to sit up. "You damned crazy fools! Do you want to be killed if I blow? Are all humans crazy?"

Miles chuckled. "Hold still. It shouldn't hurt—I don't think they put pain centers back there. We're going to leave the communication gadget in there, Bill—it may be useful, later. But that bomb's gotta come out." He chuckled again. "As to humans—well, you should know."

7

It was only three days later when Bill Norden took his hands from the back of his neck and sat up. He joined Miles and Pat at the screen of the big life-force "radar." Far out in space, a group of objects were drawing together, according to the pips that showed there. They formed up into clusters and began heading outwards.

The pips grew dimmer almost instantly, though they should have lost half their brightness only after a billion miles of travelling.

"Obviously faster than light, and heading straight toward Sirius," Miles said slowly. "The poor devils! Until some darned fool from Earth goes there some day to try to make peace, they're going to live every day of their life in the horrible certainty that we can wipe them out any year we choose—and that the best their race could do was a total failure. They'll probably have sunk back to

136

being scared, unhappy savages before we reach them."

Norden thought of the charts that had been shown him while he lay in the communicating position. Earth had enough life-force projectors to sweep the skies with lethal radiation already, and she had just begun to tool up. The Aliens had guessed wrongly about every step—they'd followed a logical pattern against a race that defied logic.

And somehow, now, all Norden's hatred was gone. "You'll have the superlight drive next year, probably," he guessed. "There are enough of their ships now with Aliens who died before they could set off their bombs for you to figure that out. Earth will be sending a ship to Sirius before they can sink very far into fear-driven savagery."

"And I suppose you want to be on it?" Pat asked. She looked at her father, smiling thoughtfully as he nodded at her lifted eyebrow. "I reckon the three of us could swing permission, at that."

Norden nodded. He'd planned it all out. He'd have to go back to university work, pretending to explore the new trails of science that had opened with the discovery of Hardwick's spectrum. The notes he had made had been destroyed on the Moon, but he could always remember enough to keep up with the eager young men who would go plunging into the field. He'd have to avoid revealing too much too soon. Maybe, that way, by the time the probable levels of telepathy and other psi-phenomena were discovered, the world would be ready for them. He had no intention of acting as a superbrain, however well equipped he might be. With the emergency over, the human race could discover enough by itself.

Miles and his daughter would be busy with the long and difficult job of trying to resettle the planets that the Aliens had slaughtered and despoiled. But all three of them would be ready when the first ship capable of reaching the stars was built.

"Yes," he said. "Yes, I guess I want to be on it. I helped teach the Aliens enough about human beings as enemies. Now I'd like to teach them about us as friends."

FOR I AM A JEALOUS PEOPLE!

1

*... the keepers of the house shall tremble, and the strong
men shall bow themselves , ... and the doors shall be shut in
the streets, when the sound of the grinding is low ... they
shall be afraid of that which is high, and fears shall be in the
way, and the almond tree shall flourish ... because man goeth
to his long home, and the mourners go about the streets ...*

Ecclesiastes, XII, 3-5.
THE BOOK OF THE JEWS

There was the continuous shrieking thunder of an alien
rocket overhead as the Reverend Amos Strong stepped
back into the pulpit. He straightened his square, thin
shoulders slightly, and the gaunt hollows in his cheeks
deepened. For a moment he hesitated, while his dark
eyes turned upwards under bushy, grizzled brows. Then
he moved forward, placing the torn envelope and telegram on the lectern with his notes. The blue-veined hand
and knobby wrist that projected from the shiny black
serge of his sleeve hardly trembled.

Unconsciously, his eyes turned toward the pew where
his wife should be, before he remembered that Ruth would
not be there this time. She had been delayed by the arrival
of the message and had read it before sending it on to
him. Now she could not be expected. It seemed strange to
him. She hadn't missed service since Richard was born
nearly thirty years ago.

139

The sound of the rocket hissed its way into silence over the horizon, and Amos stepped forward, gripping the dusty surface of the rickety lectern with both hands. He straightened and forced his throat into the pattern that would give his voice the resonance and calm it needed.

"I have just received final confirmation that my son was killed in the battle of the moon," he told the puzzled congregation, which had been rustling uncertainly since he was first interrupted. He lifted his voice, and the resonance in it deepened. "I had asked, if it were possible, that this cup might pass from me. Nevertheless, not as I will, Lord, but as Thou wilt."

He turned from their shocked faces, closing his ears to the sympathetic cries of others who had suffered. The church had been built when Wesley was twice its present size, but the troubles that had hit the people had driven them into the worn old building until it was nearly filled. He pulled his notes to him, forcing his mind from his own loss to the work that had filled his life.

"The text today is drawn from Genesis," he told them. "Chapter seventeen, seventh verse; and chapter twenty-six, fourth verse. The promise which God made to Abraham and again to Isaac." He read from the Bible before him, turning to the pages unerringly at the first try. "And I will establish my covenant between me and thee, and thy seed after thee, in their generations, for an everlasting covenant, to be a God unto thee, and to thy seed after thee.

"And I will make thy seed to multiply as the stars of heaven, and will give unto thy seed all these countries: and in thy seed shall all the nations of the earth be blessed."

He had memorized most of his sermon, no longer counting on inspiration to guide him as it had once done. He began smoothly, hearing his own words in snatches as he drew the obvious and comforting answer to their uncertainty. God had promised man the earth as an everlasting covenant. Why then should men be afraid or lose

140

faith because alien monsters had swarmed down out of the emptiness between the stars to try man's faith? As in the days of bondage in Egypt or captivity in Babylon, there would always be trials and times when the faint-hearted should waver, but the eventual outcome was clearly promised.

He had delivered a sermon from the same text in his former parish of Clyde when the government had first begun building its base on the moon, drawing heavily in that case from the reference to the stars of heaven to quiet the doubts of those who felt that man had no business in space. It was then that Richard had announced his commission in the lunar colony, using Amos' own words to defend his refusal to enter the ministry. It was the last he saw of the boy.

He had used the text one other time, over forty years before, but the reason was lost, together with the passion that had won him fame as a boy evangelist. He could remember the sermon only because of the shock on the bearded face of his father when he had misquoted a phrase. It was one of his few clear memories of the period before his voice changed and his evangelism came to an abrupt end.

He had tried to recapture his inspiration after ordination, bitterly resenting the countless intrusions of marriage and fatherhood on his spiritual forces. But at last he had recognized that God no longer intended him to be a modern Peter the Hermit, and resigned himself to the work he could do. Now he was back in the parish where he had first begun; and if he could no longer fire the souls of his flock, he could at least help somewhat with his memorized rationalizations for the horror of the alien invasion.

Another ship thundered overhead, nearly drowning his words. Six months before, the great ships had exploded out of nothing in space and had fallen carefully to the moon, to attack the forces there. In another month they had begun a few forays against Earth itself. And now, while the world haggled and struggled to unite against

141

them, they were establishing bases all over and apparently setting out to conquer the world mile by mile.

Amos saw the faces below him turn up, hate-filled and uncertain. He raised his voice over the thunder, and finished hastily, moving quickly through the end of the service.

He hesitated as the congregation stirred. The ritual was over and his words were said, but there had been no real service. Slowly, as if by themselves, his lips opened, and he heard his voice quoting the Twenty-Seventh Psalm. "The Lord is my light and my salvation; whom shall I fear?"

His voice was soft, but he could feel the reaction of the congregation as the surprisingly timely words registered. "Though an host should encamp against me, my heart shall not fear; though war should rise against me, in this will I be confident." The air seemed to quiver, as it had done long ago when God had seemed to hold direct communion with him, and there was no sound from the pews when he finished. "Wait on the Lord: be of good courage, and he shall strengthen thine heart; wait, I say, on the Lord."

The warmth of that mystic glow lingered as he stepped quietly from the pulpit. Then there was the sound of motorcycles outside, and a pounding on the door. The feeling vanished.

Someone stood up and sudden light began pouring in from outdoors. There was a breath of the hot, droughty physical world with its warning of another dust-storm, and a scattering of grasshoppers on the steps to remind the people of the earlier damage to their crops. Amos could see the bitterness flood back over them in tangible waves, even before they noticed the short, plump figure of Dr. Alan Miller.

"Amos! Did you hear?" He was wheezing as if he had been running. "Just came over the radio while you were in here gabbling."

He was cut off by the sound of more motorcycles.

They swept down the single main street of Wesley, heading west. The riders were all in military uniform, carrying weapons and going at the top speed of their machines. Dust erupted behind them, and Doc began coughing and swearing. In the last few years, he had grown more and more outspoken about his atheism; when Amos had first known him, during the earlier pastorate in Wesley, the man had at least shown some respect for the religion of others.

"All right," Amos said sharply. "You're in the house of God, Doc. What came over the radio?"

Doc caught himself and choked back his coughing fit. "Sorry. But damn it, man, the aliens have landed in Clyde, only fifty miles away. They've set up a base there! That's what all those rockets going over meant."

There was a sick gasp from the people who had heard, and a buzz as the news was passed back to others. Faces greyed. Some dropped back to the hard seats, while others pressed forward, trying to reach Doc, shouting questions at him.

Amos let himself be shoved aside, hardly noticing the reaction of his flock. It was Clyde where he had served before coming here again. He was trying to picture the alien ships dropping down, scouring the town ahead of them with gas and bullets. The grocer on the corner with his nine children, the lame deacon who had served there, the two Aimes sisters with their horde of dogs and cats and their constant crusade against younger sinners. He tried to picture the green-skinned, humanoid aliens moving through the town, invading the church, desecrating the altar! And there was Anne Seyton, who had been Richard's sweetheart, though of another faith ...

"What about the garrison nearby?" a heavy farmer yelled over the crowd. "I had a boy there, and he told me they could handle any ships when they were landing! Shell their tubes when they were coming down ..."

Doc shook his head. "Half an hour before the landing, there was a cyclone up there. It took the roof off the main building and wrecked the whole training garrison."

143

"Jim!" The big man screamed out the name, and began dragging his frail wife behind him, out toward his car. "If they got Jim . . ."

Others started to rush after him, but another procession of motorcycles stopped them. This time they were travelling slower, and a group of tanks were rolling behind them. The rear tank drew abreast, slowed, and stopped, while a dirty-faced man in a major's untidy uniform stuck his head out.

"You folks get under cover! Ain't you heard the news? Go home and stick to your radios, before a snake plane starts potshooting the bunch of you for fun. The snakes'll be heading straight over this town if they're after Topeka, like it looks!" He jerked back down and began swearing at someone inside. The tank jerked to a start and began heading away toward Clyde.

There had been enough news of the sport of the alien planes in the papers. The people melted from the church. Amos tried to stop them for at least a short prayer and to give them time to collect their thoughts, but gave up after most of the people began moving away. A minute later, he was standing alone with Doc Miller.

"Better get home, Amos," Doc suggested. "My car's half a block down. Suppose I give you a lift?"

Amos nodded wearily. His bones felt dry and brittle, and there was a dust in his mouth thicker than that in the air. He felt old, and for the first time, almost useless. He followed the doctor quietly, welcoming the chance to ride the six short blocks to the little house the parish furnished him.

A car of ancient age and worse repair rattled toward them as they reached Doc's auto. It stopped, and a man in dirty overalls leaned out, his face working jerkily. "Are you prepared, brothers? Are you saved? Armageddon has come, as the Book foretold. Get right with God, brothers! The end of the world as foretold is at hand, amen!"

"Where does the Bible foretell alien races around other suns?" Doc shot at him.

144

The man blinked, frowned, and yelled something about sinners burning forever in hell before he started his rickety car again. Amos sighed. Now, with the rise of their troubles, fanatics would spring up to cry doom and false gospel more than ever, to the harm of all honest religion. He had never decided whether they were somehow useful to God or whether they were inspired by the forces of Satan.

"In my Father's house are many mansions," he quoted to Doc as they started up the street. "It's quite possibly an allegorical reference to other worlds in the heavens."

Doc grimaced, and shrugged. Then he sighed and dropped one hand from the wheel onto Amos' knee. "I heard about Dick, Amos. I'm sorry. The first baby I ever delivered—and the best-looking!" He sighed again, staring toward Clyde as Amos found no words to answer. "I don't get it. Why don't we ever drop atom bombs on them? Why didn't the moon base use their missiles?"

Amos had no answer to that, either. There was a rumor that all the major powers had sent their whole supply of atomic explosives up to the moon base early in the invasion, and that a huge meteorite had buried the stockpile under tons of debris, where there had been no chance to excavate it. It matched the other cases of accidents that had beset all human resistance.

He got out at the unpainted house where he lived, taking Doc's hand silently and nodding his thanks.

He would have to organize his thoughts this afternoon. When night fell and the people could move about without the danger of being shot at by chance alien planes, the church bell would summon them, and they would need spiritual guidance. If he could help them to stop trying to understand God, and to accept Him . . .

There had been that moment in the church when God had seemed to enfold him and the congregation in warmth —the old feeling of true fulfillment. Maybe, now in the hour of its greatest need, some measure of inspiration had returned.

He found Ruth setting the table. Her small, quiet body moved as efficiently as ever, though her face was puffy and her eyes were red. "I'm sorry I couldn't make it, Amos. But right after the telegram, Anne Seyton came. She'd heard—before we did. And . . ."

The television set was on, showing headlines from the *Kansas City Star,* and he saw there was no need to tell her the news. He put a hand on one of hers. "God has only taken what he gave, Ruth. We were blessed with Richard for thirty years."

"I'm all right." She pulled away and picked up a pot, turning toward the kitchen, her back frozen in a line of taut misery. "Didn't you hear what I said? Anne's here. Dick's wife! They were married before he left, secretly— right after you talked with him about the difference in religion. You'd better see her, Amos. She knows about her people in Clyde."

He watched his wife move from the room, his heart heavy with her grief, while the words penetrated. He'd never forbidden marriage, he had only warned the boy, who had been so much like Ruth. He hesitated, and finally turned toward the tiny second bedroom. There was a muffled answer to his knock, and the lock clicked rustily.

"Anne?" he said. The room was darkened, but he could see her blonde head and the thin, almost unfeminine lines of her figure. He put out a hand and felt her slim fingers in his palm. As she turned toward the weak light, he saw no sign of tears, but her hand shook with her dry shudders. "Anne, Ruth has just told me that God has given us a daughter . . ."

"God!" She spat the word out harshly, while the hand jerked back. "God, Reverend Strong? Whose God? The one who sends meteorites against Dick's base, plagues of insects and drought against our farms? The God who uses tornadoes to make it easy for the snakes to land? That God, Reverend Strong? *Dick* gave you a daughter, and he's dead! Dead! Dead!"

146

For I Am a Jealous People!

Amos backed out of the room. He had learned to stand the faint mockery with which Doc pronounced the name of the Lord, but this was something that set his skin into goosepimples and caught at his throat. Anne had been of a different faith, but she had always seemed religious before.

It was probably only hysteria. He turned toward the kitchen to find Ruth and send her in to the girl.

Overhead, the staccato bleating of a ramjet cut through the air in a sound he had never heard. But the radio description fitted it perfectly. It could be no Earth ship with such a noise!

Then there was another and another, until they blended together into a steady drone.

And over it came the sudden firing of a heavy gun, while a series of rapid thuds came from the garden behind the house. Rover let out two loud barks, and then screamed in animal agony!

Amos stumbled toward the back door, but Ruth was already ahead of him. "Dick's dog! Now they've got his dog!" she cried out.

Before Amos could stop her, she threw back the door and darted out. There was another burst of shots and a sick cry. Ruth was crumpling before he could get to the doorway.

2

My God, my God, why hast thou forsaken me? . . . I am poured out like water, and all my bones are out of joint: my heart is like wax; it is melted in the midst of my bowels. My strength is dried up like a potsherd; and my tongue cleaveth to my jaws; and thou has brought me into the dust of death.
Psalms, XXII, 1, 14, 15.
THE BOOK OF THE JEWS

There were no more shots as he ran to her and gathered her into his arms. The last of the alien delta planes had

147

gone over, heading for Topeka or whatever city they were attacking.

Ruth was still alive. One of the ugly slugs had caught her in the abdomen, ripping away part of her side, and the wound was bleeding horribly. But he felt her heart still beating, and she moaned faintly when he lifted her. Then, as he put her on the couch, she opened her eyes briefly, saw him, and tried to smile. Her lips moved, and he dropped his head to hear.

"I'm sorry, Amos. Foolish. Nuisance. Sorry."

Her eyes closed, but she smiled again after he bent to kiss her lips. "Glad now. Waited so long."

Anne stood in the doorway, staring unbelievingly. But as Amos stood up, she unfroze and darted to the medicine cabinet, to come back and begin snipping away the ruined dress and trying to staunch the flow of blood.

Amos reached for the phone, unable to see it clearly. He mumbled something to the operator, and a minute later to Doc Miller. He'd been afraid that the doctor would still be out. He had a feeling that Doc had promised to come, but could remember no words.

The flow of blood outside the wound had been stopped, but Ruth was white, even to her lips. Anne forced him back to a chair, her fingers gentle on his arm.

"I'm sorry, Father Strong. I—I . . ."

He stood up after a few minutes and went over to stand beside Ruth, letting his eyes turn toward the half-set table. There was a smell of scorching food in the air, and he went out to the old wood-burning stove to pull the pans off and drop them into the sink. Anne followed, but he hardly saw her, until he heard her begin to cry softly. There were tears this time.

"The ways of God are not the ways of man, Anne," he said, and the words released a flood of his own emotions. He sank tiredly onto a stool, his hands falling limply onto his lap. He dropped his head against the table, feeling the weakness and uncertainty of age. "We love the carnal form and our hearts are broken when it is gone. Only

God can know all of any of us or count the tangled threads of our lives. It isn't good to hate God!"

She moved beside him as he rose and returned to the living room. "I don't, Father Strong. I never did." He couldn't be sure of the honesty of it, but he made no effort to question her, and she sighed. "Mother Ruth isn't dead yet!"

He was saved from any answer by the door being slammed open as Doc Miller came rushing in. The plump little man took one quick look at Ruth and was beside her, reaching for plasma and his equipment. He handed the plasma bottle to Anne, and began working carefully.

"There's a chance," he said finally. "If she were younger or stronger, I'd say there was an excellent chance. But now, since you believe in it, you'd better do some fancy praying."

"I've been praying," Amos told him, realizing that it was true. The prayers had begun inside his head before she was outside the door, and they had never ceased.

They moved her gently, couch and all, into the bedroom, where the blinds could be drawn, and where the other sounds of the house couldn't reach her. Doc gave Anne a shot of something and sent her into the other bedroom. He turned to Amos, but didn't insist when the minister shook his head.

"I'll stay here, Amos," Doc said. "With you. As long as I can until I get another emergency call. The switchboard girl knows where I am."

He went back into the bedroom without closing the door. Amos stood in the center of the living room, his head bowed, for long minutes.

It was a whining sound that finally called him back to the world around him. He went to the back door and stared out. The Scotty was still alive, pulling its little body along the dirt of the garden toward the house. The whole hind section was paralyzed, and the animal must have been in agony from the horrible wound on its back. But it saw him and whined again, struggling toward him.

He went out automatically. He had never been fond of the dog, nor it of him. But now there was an understanding between them. "Shh, Rover," he told the dog. "Quiet, boy. The mistress is all right."

Rover whined again, and a wet tongue caressed Amos' hand. He bent as gently as he could to examine the wound. Then he stood up, trying to reassure the animal.

He found Richard's hunting rifle in one of the trunks and made sure it was unrusted. He loaded it carefully, feeling his skin crawl at the touch of the gun. It seemed strange to use the weapon on Rover when the dog and Richard had both found such pleasure in hunting with this same gun. But he couldn't see the animal suffering.

Rover looked up and tried to bark as he saw the gun. Amos dropped beside him, feeling that the dog knew what he meant to do. The eyes looked up at him with a curious understanding as he placed the muzzle near the animal's head. Amos stopped, wondering. The wound was a horrible thing—but Doc might be able to save the animal, even though he was no veterinarian. If it had been a wounded human, the attempt would have to be made.

Rover drew back his lips, and Amos stopped, expecting a growl. He even reached out to put the gun away. But the wet tongue came out again, brushing across his hand, accepting the fate intended, and blessing him for it. He patted the dog's head, closed his eyes, and pulled the trigger. It was merciful. There wasn't even time for a cry of pain.

If the dog had fought him, if it had struggled against its fate in a final desire to live . . . But it had submitted to what it considered a superior being. Only man could defy a Higher Will. Rover had accepted . . . and Rover was dead. He buried the small body in the soft dirt of the garden.

Doc stood in the doorway when he started back for the house. "I heard the shot and thought you were trying something foolish," the doctor said. "I should have known better, I guess, with your beliefs. Then I waited here, listening for a snake plane, ready to pull you back. According to the television, they must be returning by now."

Amos nodded. He found Ruth still in a coma, with nothing he could do. Then he remembered the planes and turned to watch the television. Topeka was off the air, but another station was showing news films.

Hospitals, schools and similar places seemed to have been the chief targets of the aliens. Gas had accounted for a number of deaths, though those could have been prevented if instructions had been followed. But the incendiaries had caused the greatest damage.

And the aliens had gotten at least as rough treatment as they had meted out. Of the forty that had been counted, twenty-nine were certainly down.

"I wonder if they're saying prayers to God for their dead?" Doc asked. "Or doesn't your God extend his mercy to races other than man?"

Amos shook his head slowly. It was a new question to him. But there could be only one answer. "God rules the entire universe, Doc. But these evil beings surely offer him no worship!"

"Are you sure? They're pretty human!"

Amos looked back to the screen, where one of the alien corpses could be seen briefly. They did look almost human, though squat and heavily muscled. Their skin was green, and they wore no clothes. There was no nose, aside from two orifices under their curiously flat ears that quivered as if in breathing. But they were human enough to have passed for deformed men, if they had been worked on by good make-up men.

They were creatures of God, just as he was! And as such, could he deny them? Then his mind recoiled, remembering the atrocities they had committed, the tortures that had been reported, and the utter savageness so out of keeping with their inconceivably advanced ships. They were things of evil who had denied their birthright as part of God's domain. For evil, there could be only hatred.

151

And from evil, how could there be worship of anything but the powers of darkness?

The thought of worship triggered his mind into an awareness of his need to prepare a sermon for the evening. It would have to be something simple; both he and his congregation were in no mood for rationalizations. Tonight he would have to serve God through their emotions. The thought frightened him. He tried to cling for strength to the brief moment of glory he had felt in the morning, but even that seemed far away.

There was the wail of a siren outside, rising to an ear-shattering crescendo, and the muffled sound of a loudspeaker with its amplifier driven to high distortion levels.

He stood up at last and moved out onto the porch with Doc as the tank came by. It was limping on treads that seemed to be about to fall apart, and the amplifier and speaker were mounted crudely on top. It pushed down the street, repeating its message over and over.

"Get out of town! Everybody clear out! This is an order to evacuate! The snakes are coming! Human forces have been forced to retreat to regroup. The snakes are heading this way, heading toward Topeka. They are looting and killing as they go. Get out of town! Everybody clear out!"

It paused, and another voice blared out, sounding like that of the major who had warned the town earlier. "Get the hell out, all of you! Get out while you've still got your skins outside of you. We've been licked. Shut up, Blake! We've had the holy living pants beat off us, and we're going back to momma. Get out, scram, vamoose! The snakes are coming! Beat it!"

It staggered down the street, rumbling its message, and now other stragglers began following it—men in trucks, piled together like cattle; men in ancient cars of every description. Then another amplifier sounded from one of the trucks.

"Stay under cover until night! Then get out! The snakes won't be here at once. Keep cool. Evacuate in order, and under cover of darkness. We're holing up ourselves when we get to a safe place. This is your last warning. Stay under cover now, and evacuate as soon as it's dark."

There was a scream from the sky, and alien planes began dipping down. Doc pulled Amos back into the house, but not before he saw men being cut to ribbons by missiles that seemed to fume and burst into fire as they hit. Some of the men on the retreat made cover. When the planes were gone, they came out and began regrouping, leaving the dead and hauling the wounded with them.

"Those men need me!" Amos protested.

"So does Ruth," Doc told him. "Besides, we're too old, Amos. We'd only get in the way. They have their own doctors and chaplains, probably. Those poor devils are risking their lives to save us, damn it. The Army must have piled all its movable wounded together and sent them to warn us and to decoy the planes away from the rest who are probably sneaking back through the woods and fields. They're heroes, Amos, and they'd hate your guts for wasting what they're trying to do. I've been listening to one of the local stations, and they've already been through hell."

He turned on his heel and went back to the bedroom. The television program tardily began issuing evacuation orders to all citizens along the road from Clyde to Topeka, together with instructions. For some reason, the aliens seemed not to spot anything smaller than a tank in movement at night, and all orders were to wait until then.

Doc came out again, and Amos looked up at him, feeling his head bursting, but with one clear idea fixed in it. "Ruth can't be moved, can she, Doc?"

"No, Amos." Doc sighed. "But it won't matter. You'd better go in to her now. She seems to be coming to. I'll wake the girl and get her ready."

Amos went into the bedroom as quietly as he could, but there was no need for silence. Ruth was conscious, as if some awareness of her approaching death had forced her

153

to make the most of these last few minutes of her life. She put out a frail hand timidly to him. Her voice was weak, but clear.

"Amos, I know. And I don't mind now, except for you. But there's something I had to ask you. Amos, do you . . .?"

He dropped beside her when her voice faltered, wanting to bury his head against her, but not daring to lose the few remaining moments of her sight. He fought the words out of the depths of his mind, and then realized it would take more than words. He bent over and kissed her again, as he had first kissed her so many years ago.

"I've always loved you, Ruth," he said. "I still do love you."

She sighed and relaxed. "Then I won't be jealous of God anymore, Amos. I had to know."

Her hand reached up weakly, to find his hair and to run her fingers through it. She smiled, the worn lines of her face softening. Her voice was content and almost young. "And forsaking all others, cleave only unto thee . . ."

The last syllable whispered out, and the hand fell.

Amos dropped his head at last, and a single sob choked out of him. He folded her hands tenderly, with the worn, cheap wedding ring uppermost, and arose slowly with his head bowed.

"Then shall the dust return to the earth as it was; and the spirit shall return unto God who gave it. Father, I thank thee for this moment with her. Bless her, O Lord, and keep her for me."

He nodded to Doc and Anne. The girl looked sick and sat staring at him with eyes that mixed shock and pity.

"You'll need some money, Anne," he said. "I don't have much, but there's a little . . ."

She drew back and shook her head. "I've got enough, Reverend Strong. I'll make out. Doctor Miller has told me to take his car. But what about you?"

"There's still work to be done," he said. "I haven't even written my sermon. And the people who are giving up their homes will need comfort. In such hours as these, we all need God to sustain us."

She stumbled to her feet and into her bedroom. Amos opened his old desk and reached for pencil and paper.

3

The wicked have drawn out the sword, and have bent their bow, to cast down the poor and needy, and to slay such as be of upright conversation.

I have seen the wicked in great power, and spreading himself like a green bay tree.

Psalms, XXXVII, 14, 35.
THE BOOK OF THE JEWS

Darkness was just beginning to fall when they helped Anne out into the doctor's car, making sure that the tank was full. She was quiet, and had recovered herself, but she avoided Amos whenever possible. She turned at last to Doc Miller.

"What are you going to do? I should have asked before, but . . ."

"Don't worry about me, girl," he told her, his voice as hearty as when he was telling an old man he still had forty years to live. "I've got other ways. The switchboard girl is going to be one of the last to leave, and I'm driving her in her car. You go ahead, the way we mapped it out. And pick up anyone else you find on the way. It's safe; it's still too early for men to start turning to looting, rape or robbery. They'll think of that after the shock of this wears off a little."

She held out a hand to him, and climbed in. At the last minute, she pressed Amos' hand briefly. Then she stepped on the accelerator and the car took off down the street at top speed.

"She hates me," Amos said. "She loves other men too much and God too little to understand."

"And maybe you love your God too much to under- stand that you love men, Amos. Don't worry, she'll figure it out. The next time you see her, she'll feel different. Look, I really do have to see that Nellie gets off the switchboard and into a car. I'll see you later."

Doc swung off toward the telephone office, carrying his bag. Amos watched him, puzzled as always at anyone who could so fervently deny God and yet could live up to every commandment of the Lord except worship. They had been friends for a long time, while the parish stopped fretting about the friendship and took it for granted, yet the riddle of what they found in common was no nearer solution.

There was the distant sound of a great rocket landing, and the smaller stutterings of the peculiar alien ramjets. The ships passed directly overhead, yet there was no shooting this time.

For a moment, Amos faced the bedroom window where Ruth lay, and then he turned toward the church. He opened it, throwing the doors wide. There was no sign of the sexton, but he had rung the bell in the tower often enough before. He took off his worn coat and grabbed the rope.

It was hard work, and his hands were soft. Once it had been a pleasure, but now his blood seemed too thin to suck up the needed oxygen. The shirt stuck wetly to his back, and he felt giddy when he finished.

Almost at once, the telephone in his little office began jangling nervously. He staggered to it, panting as he lifted the receiver, to hear the voice of Nellie, shrill with fright. "Reverend, what's up? Why's the bell ringing?"

"For prayer meeting, of course," he told her. "What else?"

"Tonight? Well, I'll be—" She hung up.

He lighted a few candles and put them on the altar, where their glow could be seen from the dark street, but where no light would shine upwards for alien eyes. Then he sat down to wait, wondering what was keeping the organist.

There were hushed calls from the street and nervous cries. A car started, to be followed by another. Then a group took off at once. He went to the door, partly for the slightly cooler air. All along the street, men were moving out their possessions and loading up, while others took off. They waved to him, but hurried on by. He heard telephones begin to ring, but if Nellie was passing on some urgent word, she had forgotten him.

He turned back to the altar, kneeling before it. There was no articulate prayer in his mind. He simply clasped his gnarled fingers together and rested on his knee, looking up at the outward symbol of his life. Outside, the sounds went on, blending together. It did not matter whether anyone chose to use the church tonight. It was open, as the house of God must always be in times of stress. He had long since stopped trying to force religion on those not ready for it.

And slowly, the strains of the day began to weave themselves into the pattern of his life. He had learned to accept; from the death of his baby daughter on, he had found no way to end the pain that seemed so much a part of life. But he could bury it behind the world of his devotion, and meet whatever his lot was to be without anger at the will of the Lord. Now, again, he accepted things as they were ordered.

There was a step behind him. He turned, not bothering to rise, and saw the dressmaker, Angela Anduccini, hesitating at the door. She had never entered, though she had lived in Wesley since she was eighteen. She crossed herself doubtfully, and waited.

He stood up. "Come in, Angela. This is the house of God, and all His daughters are welcome."

There was a dark, tight fear in her eyes as she glanced back to the street. "I thought—maybe the organ . . ."

He opened it for her and found the switch. He started

157

to explain the controls, but the smile on her lips warned him that it was unnecessary. Her calloused fingers ran over the stops, and she began playing, softly as if to herself. He went back to one of the pews, listening. For two years he had blamed the organ, but now he knew that there was no fault with the instrument, but only with its player before. The music was sometimes strange for his church, but he liked it.

A couple who had moved into the old Surrey farm beyond the town came in, holding hands, as if holding each other up. And a minute later, Buzz Williams stumbled in and tried to tip-toe down the aisle to where Amos sat. Since his parents had died, he'd been the town problem Now he was half-drunk, though without his usual boisterousness.

"I ain't got no car and I been drinking," he whispered. "Can I stay here till maybe somebody comes or something?"

Amos sighed, motioning Buzz to a seat where the boy's eyes had centered. Somewhere, there must be a car for the four waifs who had remembered God when everything else had failed them. If one of the young couple could drive, and he could locate some kind of a vehicle, it was his duty to see that they were sent to safety.

Abruptly, the haven of the church and the music came to an end, leaving him back in the real world—a curiously unreal world now.

He was heading down the steps, trying to remember whether the Jameson boy had taken his rebuilt flivver when a panel truck pulled up in front of the church. Doc Miller got out, wheezing as he squeezed through the door.

He took in the situation at a glance. "Only four strays, Amos? I thought we might have to pack them in." He headed for Buzz. "I've got a car outside, Buzz. Gather up the rest of this flock and get going!"

"I been drinking," Buzz said, his face reddening hotly.

"Okay, you've been drinking. At least you know it, and there's no traffic problem. Head for Salina and hold your speed under forty and you'll be all right." Doc swept little Angela Anduccini from the organ and herded her out, while Buzz collected the couple. "Get going, all of you!"

They got, with Buzz enthroned behind the wheel and Angela beside him. The town was dead. Amos closed the organ and began shutting the doors to the church.

"I've got a farm tractor up the street for us, Amos," Doc said at last. "I almost ran out of tricks. There were more fools than you'd think who thought they could hide it out right here. At that, I probably missed some. Well, the tractor's nothing elegant, but it can take back roads no car would handle. We'd better get going. Nellie has already gone, with a full load."

Amos shook his head. He had never thought it out, but the decision had been in his mind from the beginning. Ruth still lay waiting a decent burial. He could no more leave her now than when she was alive. "You'll have to go alone, Doc."

"I figured." The doctor sighed, wiping the sweat from his forehead. "I'd remember to my dying day that believers have more courage than an atheist! Nope, we're in this together. It isn't sensible, but that's how I feel. We'd better put out the candles, I guess."

Amos snuffed them reluctantly, wondering how he could persuade the other to leave. His ears had already caught the faint sounds of shooting, indicating that the aliens were on their way.

The uncertain thumping of a laboring motor sounded from the street, then wheezed to silence. There was a shout, a pause, and the motor caught again. It seemed to run for ten seconds before it backfired, and was still.

Doc opened one of the doors. In the middle of the street, a man was pushing an ancient car while his wife steered. But it refused to start again. He grabbed for tools, threw up the hood, and began a frantic search for the trouble.

"If you can drive a tractor, there's one half a block down," Doc called out.

The man looked up, snapped one quick glance behind him, and pulled the woman hastily out of the car. In almost no time, the heavy roar of the tractor sounded. The man revved it up to full throttle and tore off down the road, leaving Doc and Amos stranded. The sound of the aliens was clearer now, and there was some light coming from beyond the bend of the street.

There was no place to hide, except in the church. They found a window where the paint on the imitation stained glass was loose and peeled it back enough for a peephole. The advance scouts of the aliens were already within view. They were dashing from house to house. Behind them, they left something that sent up clouds of glowing smoke that seemed to have no fire connected to its brilliance. At least, no buildings were burning.

Just as the main group of aliens came into view, the door of one house burst open. A scrawny man leaped out, with his fat wife and fatter daughter behind him. They raced up the street, tearing at their clothes and scratching frantically at their reddened skin.

Shouts sounded. All three jerked, but went racing on. More shots sounded. At first, Amos thought it was incredibly bad shooting. Then he realized that it was even more unbelievably good marksmanship. The aliens were shooting at the hands first, then moving up the arms methodically, wasting no chance for torture.

For the first time in years, Amos felt fear and anger curdle solidly in his stomach. He stood up, feeling his shoulders square back and his head come up as he moved toward the door. His lips were moving in words that he only half understood. "Arise, O Lord; O God, lift up Thine hand; forget not the humble. Wherefore doth the wicked contemn God? He hath said in his heart, Thou wilt not requite it. Thou hast seen it, for Thou beholdest mischief and spite, to requite it with Thy hand: the poor committeth himself unto Thee; Thou art the helper of the fatherless. Break Thou the arm of the wicked and the evil

160

ones; seek out their wickedness till Thou find none . . ."

"Stop it, Amos!" Doc's voice rasped harshly in his ear. "Don't be a fool! And you're misquoting that last verse!"

It cut through the fog of his anger. He knew that Doc had deliberately reminded him of his father, but the trick worked, and the memory of his father's anger at misquotations replaced his cold fury. "We can't let that go on!"

Then he saw it was over. The aliens had used up their targets. But there was the sight of another wretch, unrecognizable in half of his skin . . .

Doc's voice was as sick as Amos felt. "We can't do anything. I can't understand a race smart enough to build star ships and still stupid enough for this. But it's good for our side, in the long run. While our armies are organizing, the snakes are wasting time on this. And it makes our resistance get tougher, too."

The aliens didn't confine their sport to humans. They worked just as busily on a huge old tomcat they found. And all the corpses were being loaded onto a big wagon pulled by twenty of the creatures.

The aliens obviously had some knowledge of human behavior. At first they had passed up all stores and had concentrated on living quarters. The scouts had passed on by the church without a second glance. But they moved into a butcher shop at once, to come out again carrying meat, which was piled on the wagon with the corpses.

Now a group was assembling before the church, pointing up toward the steeple where the bell was. Two of them shoved up a mortar of some sort. It was pointed quickly and a load was dropped in. There was a muffled explosion, and the bell rang sharply, its pieces rattling down the roof and into the yard below.

Another shoved the mortar into a new position, aiming it straight for the door of the church. Doc yanked Amos down between two pews. "They don't like churches, damn it! A fine spot we picked. Watch out for splinters!"

161

The door smashed in and a heavy object struck the altar, ruining it. Amos groaned at the shattering sound it made.

There was no further activity when they slipped back to their peepholes. The aliens were on the march again, moving along slowly. In spite of the delta planes, they seemed to have no motorized ground vehicles, and the wagon moved on under the power of the twenty green-skinned things, coming directly in front of the church.

Amos stared at it in the flickering light from the big torches burning in the hands of some of the aliens. Most of the corpses were strangers to him. A few he knew. And then his eyes picked out the twisted, distorted upper part of Ruth's body, her face empty in death's relaxation.

He stood up wearily, and this time Doc made no effort to stop him. He walked down a line of pews and around the wreck of one of the doors. Outside the church, the air was still hot and dry, but he drew a long breath into his lungs. The front of the church was in the shadows, and no aliens seemed to be watching him.

He moved down the stone steps. His legs were firm now. His heart was pounding heavily, but the clot of feelings that rested leadenly in his stomach had no fear left in it. Nor was there any anger left, nor any purpose.

He saw the aliens stop and stare at him, while a jabbering began among them.

He moved forward with the measured tread that had led him down the aisle when he married Ruth. He came to the wagon and put his hand out, lifting one of Ruth's dead-limp arms back across her body.

"This is my wife," he told the staring aliens quietly. "I am taking her home with me."

He reached up and began trying to move the other bodies away from her. Without surprise, he saw Doc's arms moving up to help him, while a steady stream of whispered profanity came from the doctor's lips.

Amos hadn't expected to succeed. He had expected nothing.

162

Abruptly, a dozen of the aliens leaped for the two men. Amos let them overpower him without resistance. For a second, Doc struggled; then he too relaxed while the aliens bound them and tossed them onto the wagon.

4

He hath bent his bow like an enemy: he stood with his right hand as an adversary, and slew all that were pleasant to the eye in the tabernacle of the daughter of Zion: he poured out his fury like fire.

The Lord was as an enemy: he hath swallowed up Israel, he hath swallowed up all her palaces: he hath destroyed his strong holds, and hath increased in the daughter of Judah mourning and lamentation.

The Lord hath cast off his altar, he hath abhorred his sanctuary, he hath given up into the hand of the enemy the walls of her palaces; they have made a noise in the house of the Lord, as in the day of a solemn feast.

Lamentations, II, 4, 5, 7.
THE BOOK OF THE JEWS

Amos' first reaction was one of dismay at the ruin of his only good suit. He struggled briefly on the substance under him, trying to find a better spot. A minister's suit might be old, but he could never profane the altar with such stains as these. Then some sense of the ridiculousness of his worry reached his mind, and he relaxed as best he could.

He had done what he had to do, and it was too late to regret it. He could only accept the consequences of it now, as he had learned to accept everything else God had seen fit to send him. He had never been a man of courage, but the strength of God had sustained him through as much as most men had to bear. It would sustain him further.

Doc was facing him, having flopped around to lie near

163

him. Now the doctor's lips twisted into a crooked grin. "I guess we're in for it now. But it won't last forever, and maybe we're old enough to die fast. At least, once we're dead, we won't know it, so there's no sense being afraid of dying."

If it were meant to provoke him into argument, it failed. Amos considered it a completely hopeless philosophy, but it was better than none, probably. His own faith in the hereafter left something to be desired; he was sure of immortality and the existence of heaven and hell, but he had never been able to picture either to his own satisfaction.

The wagon had been swung around and was now being pulled up the street, back toward Clyde. Amos tried to take his mind off the physical discomforts of the ride by watching the houses, counting them to his own. They drew near it finally, but it was Doc who spotted the important fact. He groaned. "My car!"

Amos strained his eyes, staring into the shadows through the glare of the torches. Doc's car stood at the side of the house, with its left front door open! Someone must have told Anne that he hadn't left, and she'd forgotten her anger with him to swing back around the alien horde to save him!

He began a prayer that they might pass on without the car being noticed, and it seemed at first that they would. Then there was a sudden cry from the house, and he saw her face briefly at a front window. She must have seen Doc and himself lying on the wagon!

He opened his mouth to risk a warning, but it was too late. The door of the house swung back, and she was standing on the front steps, lifting Richard's rifle to her shoulder. Amos' heart seemed to hesitate with the tension of his body. The aliens still hadn't noticed. If she'd only wait . . .

The rifle cracked. Either by luck or some skill he hadn't suspected, one of the aliens dropped. She was running forward now, throwing another cartridge into the barrel.

For I Am a Jealous People!

The gun barked again, and an alien fell to the ground, bleating horribly.

There was no attempt at torture this time, at least. The leading alien finally jerked out a tube-like affair from a scabbard at his side and a single sharp explosion sounded. Anne jerked backward as the heavy slug hit her forehead, the rifle spinning from her dead hands.

The wounded alien was trying frantically to crawl away. Two of his fellows began working on him mercilessly, with as little feeling as if he had been a human. His body followed that of Anne toward the front of the wagon, just beyond Amos' limited view.

She hadn't seemed hysterical this time, Amos thought wearily. It had been her tendency to near-hysteria that had led to his advising Richard to wait, not the difference in faith. Now he was sorry he'd had no chance to understand her better.

Doc sighed, and there was a peculiar pride under the thickness of his voice. "Man," he said, "has one virtue which is impossible to any omnipotent force like your God. He can be brave. He can be brave beyond sanity for another man or for an idea. Amos, I pity your God if man ever makes war on Him!"

Amos flinched, but the blasphemy aroused only a shadow of his normal reaction. His mind seemed numbed. He lay back, watching black clouds scudding across the sky almost too rapidly. It looked unnatural, and he remembered how often the accounts had mentioned a tremendous storm that had wrecked or hampered the efforts of human troops. Maybe a counterattack had begun, and this was part of the alien defense. If they had some method of weather control, it was probable. The moonlight was already blotted out by the clouds.

Half a mile further on, there was a shout from the aliens, and a big tractor chugged into view, badly driven by one of the aliens who had obviously only partly mastered the human machine. With a great deal of trial and error, it was backed into position and coupled to the wagon. Then it began churning along at nearly thirty miles an hour, while the big wagon bucked and bounced behind. From then on, the ride was a physical hell. Even Doc groaned at some of the bumps, though his bones had three times more padding than Amos could boast.

Mercifully, they slowed when they reached Clyde. Amos wiped the blood off his bitten lip and managed to wriggle to a position where most of the bruises were on his upper side. Beyond the town there was a flood of brilliant lights where the alien rockets stood, and he could see a group of strange machines driven by non-human creatures busy unloading the great ships. But the drivers of the machines looked totally unlike the other aliens.

One of the alien trucks swung past them, and he had a clear view of the creature steering it. It bore no resemblance to humanity. There was a cone-like torso, covered with a fine white down, ending in four thick stalks to serve as legs. From its broadest point, four sinuous limbs spread out to the truck controls. There was no head, but only eight small tentacles waving above it.

He saw a few others, always in control of machines, and no machines being handled by the green-skinned people, as they passed through the ghost city that had been Clyde. Apparently there were two races allied against humanity, which explained why such barbarians could come in space ships. The green ones must be simply the fighters, while the downy cones were the technicians. From their behavior, though, the pilots of the planes must be recruited from the fighters.

Clyde had grown since he had been there, unlike most of the towns about. There was a new supermarket just down the street from Amos' former church, and the tractor jolted to a stop in front of it. Aliens swarmed out and began carrying the dead loot from the wagon into big food lockers, while two others lifted Doc and Amos.

But they weren't destined for the comparatively merciful death of freezing in the lockers. The aliens threw them into a little cell that had once apparently been a

166

cashier's cage, barred from floor to ceiling. It made a fairly efficient jail, and the lock that clicked shut as the door closed behind them was too heavy to be broken.

There was already one occupant—a medium-built young man whom Amos finally recognized as Smithton, the Clyde dentist. His shoulders were shaking with sporadic sobs as he sat huddled in one corner. He looked at the two arrivals without seeing them. "But I surrendered," he whispered to himself. "I'm a prisoner of war. They can't do it. I surrendered . . ."

A fatter-than-usual alien, wearing the only clothes Amos had seen on any of them, came waddling up to the cage, staring in at them, and the dentist wailed off into silence. The alien drew up his robe about his chest and scratched his rump against a counter without taking his eyes off them. "Humans," he said in a grating voice, but without an accent, "are peculiar. No standardization."

"I'll be damned!" Doc swore. "English!"

The alien studied them with what might have been surprise, lifting his ears. "Is the gift of tongues so unusual, then? Many of the priests of the Lord God Almighty speak all the human languages. It's a common miracle, not like levitation."

"Fine. Then maybe you'll tell us what we're being held for?" Doc suggested.

The priest shrugged. "Food, of course. The *grethi* eat any kind of meat—even our people—but we have to examine the laws to find whether you're permitted. If you are, we'll need freshly killed specimens to sample, so we're waiting with you."

"You mean you're attacking us for *food?*"

The priest grunted harshly. "No! We're on a holy mission to exterminate you. The Lord Almighty commanded us to go down to Earth where abominations existed and to leave no living creature under your sun."

He turned and waddled out of the store, taking the single remaining torch with him, leaving only the dim light of the moon and reflections from further away.

Amos dropped onto a stool inside the cage. "They had to lock us in a new building instead of one I know," he said. "If it had been the church, we might have had a chance."

"How?" Doc asked sharply.

Amos tried to describe the passage through the big unfinished basement under the church, reached through a trapdoor. Years before, a group of teen-agers had built a sixty-foot tunnel into it and had used it for a private club until the passage had been discovered and bricked over from outside. The earth would be soft around the bricks, however. Beyond, the outer end of the tunnel opened in a wooded section, which led to a drainage ditch that in turn connected with the Republican River. From the church, they could move to the stream and slip down that without being seen. There was even an alley—or had been one—behind the store that would take them to the shadow of the trees around the church.

Doc's fingers were fumbling with the lock as Amos finished. He grunted and reached for his pocket, taking out a few coins. "They don't know much about us, Amos, if they expect to hold us here, where the lock is fastened from the inside. Feel those screws."

Amos fumbled over the lock surface. There were four large screws on the back of the lock, holding it to the door. The cashier's cage had been designed to keep others out, not to serve as a jail. As best, he thought, it was a poor chance. Yet was it merely chance? It seemed more like the hand of God to him.

"More like the stupidity of the aliens, to my mind," Doc objected. He was testing the screws with a quarter now. He nodded in some satisfaction, then swore. "Damn it, the quarter fits the slot, but I can't get enough leverage to turn the screw. Hey, Smithton or whatever your name is, pull out that money drawer and knock the bottom out. I need a couple of narrow slats."

Smithton had been praying miserably—a childhood

prayer for laying himself down to sleep. But he succeeding in kicking out splinters from the drawer bottom.

Doc selected two and clamped them around the quarter, trying to hold them in place while he turned them. It was rough going, but the screws turned. Three came loose finally, and the lock rotated on the fourth until they could force the cage open.

Doc stopped and pulled Smithton to him. "Follow me, and do what I do. No talking, no making a separate jump, or I'll break your neck. All right!"

The back door was locked, but from the inside. They opened it to a backyard filled with garbage. The alley wasn't as dark as it should have been, since open lots beyond let some light come through. They hugged what shadows they could until they reached the church hedge. There they groped along, lining themselves up with the side office door. There was no sign of aliens.

Amos broke ahead of the others, being more familiar with the church. It wasn't until he had reached the door that he realized it could have been locked; it had been kept that way part of the time. He grabbed the handle and forced it back—to find it unlatched.

For a second, he stopped to thank the Lord for their luck. Then the others were with him, crowding into the little kitchen where social suppers were prepared. He'd always hated those functions, but now he blessed them for providing a hiding place that gave them time to find their way.

There were sounds in the church, and odors, but none that seemed familiar to Amos. Something made the back hairs of his neck prickle. He took off his shoes and tied them around his neck, and the others followed suit.

The way to the trapdoor lay down a small hall, across in front of the altar, and into the private office on the other side.

They were safer together than separated, particularly since Smithton was with them. Amos leaned back against the kitchen wall to catch his breath. His heart seemed to have a ring of needled pain around it, and his throat was so dry that he had to fight desperately against gagging. There was water here, but he couldn't risk rummaging across the room to the sink.

He was praying for strength, less for himself than for the others. Long since, he had resigned himself to die. If God willed his death, he was ready; all he had were dead and probably mutilated, and he had succeeded only in dragging those who tried to help him into mortal danger. He was old, and his body was already treading its way to death. He could live for probably twenty more years, but aside from his work, there was nothing to live for—and even in that, he had been only a mediocre failure. But he was still responsible for Doc Miller, and even for Smithton now.

He squeezed his eyes together and squinted around the doorway. There was some light in the hall that led toward the altar, but he could see no one, and there were drapes that gave a shadow from which they could spy the rest of their way. He moved to it softly, and felt the others come up behind him.

He bent forward, parting the drapes a trifle. They were perhaps twenty feet in front of the altar, on the right side. He spotted the wreckage that had once stood as an altar. Then he frowned as he saw evidence of earth piled up into a mound of odd shape.

He threw the cloth back further, surprised at the curiosity in him, as he had been surprised repeatedly by the changes taking place in himself.

There were two elaborately-robed priests kneeling in the center of the chapel. But his eye barely noticed them before it was attracted to what stood in front of the new altar.

A box of wood rested on an earthenware platform. On it were four marks, which his eyes recognized as unfamiliar, but which his mind twisted into a sequence from no alphabet he had learned; yet in them was always more

170

than they were. And above the box was a veil, behind which Something shone brightly without light.

In his mind, a surge of power pulsed, making something that might almost have been words through his thoughts.

"I AM THAT I AM, who brought those out of bondage from Egypt and who wrote upon the wall before Belshazzar, MENE, MENE, TEKEL, UPHARSIN, as it shall be writ large upon the Earth, from this day forth. For I have said unto the seed of Mikhtchah, thou art my chosen people and I shall exalt thee above all the races under the heavens!"

5

And it was given unto him to make war with the saints, and to overcome them: and power was given him over all kindreds, and tongues, and nations.

He that leadeth into captivity shall go into captivity: he that killeth with the sword must be killed with the sword.
                                        Revelations, XIII, 7, 10.
                                        THE BOOK OF THE CHRISTIANS

The seed of Mikhtchah. The seed that was the aliens . . .

There was no time and all time, then. Amos felt his heart stop, but the blood pounded through his arteries with a vigor it had lacked for decades. He felt Ruth's hand in his, stirring with returning life, and knew she had never existed. Beside him, he saw Doc Miller's hair turn snow white and knew that it was so, though there was no way he could see Doc from his position.

He felt the wrath of the Presence rest upon him, weighing his every thought from his birth to his certain death, where he ceased completely and went on forever, and yet he knew that the Light behind the veil was unaware of him, but was receptive only to the two Mikhtchah priests who knelt unaware.

171

All of that was with but a portion of his mind so small that he could not locate it, though his total mind encompassed all time and space, and that which was neither; yet each part of his perceptions occupied all of his mind that had been or ever could be, save only the present, which somehow was a concept not yet solved by the One before him.

He saw a strange man on a low mountain, receiving tablets of stone that weighed only a pennyweight, engraved with a script that all could read. And he knew the man, but refused to believe it, since the garments were not those of his mental image, and the clean-cut face fitted better with the strange Egyptian headpiece than with the language being spoken.

Amos saw every prayer of his life tabulated. But nowhere was there the mantel of divine warmth which he had felt as a boy and had almost felt again the morning before. And there was a stirring of unease at his thought, mixed with wrath; yet while the thought was in his mind, nothing could touch him.

Yet each of those things was untrue, because he could find no understanding of that which was true.

It ended as abruptly as it had begun, either a microsecond or a million subjective years after. It left him numbed, but newly alive. And it left him dead as no man had ever been hopelessly dead before.

He knew only that before him was the Lord God Almighty, who had made a covenant with Abraham, with Isaac, and with Jacob, and with their seed; and that mankind had been rejected, while God now was on the side of the enemies of Abraham's seed, and all the nations of earth.

Even that was too much for a human mind no longer in touch with the Presence, and only a shadow of it remained.

Beside him, Amos heard Doc Miller begin breathing again, brushing the white hair back from his forehead wonderingly as he muttered a single word. "God!"

One of the Mikhtchah priests looked up, his eyes turning about; there was a glazed look on his face, but it was leaving.

Then Smithton screamed! His open mouth poured out a steady, unwavering screaming, while his lungs panted in and out. His eyes opened, staring horribly. Like a wooden doll on strings, the man stood up and walked forward. He avoided the draperies and headed for the Light behind the veil. Abruptly, the Light was gone, but Smithton walked toward it as steadily as before. He stopped before the falling veil, and the scream cut off sharply.

Doc had jerked silently to his feet, tugging Amos up behind him. The minister lifted himself, but he knew there was no place to go. It was up to the will of God now . . . Or . . .

Smithton turned on one heel precisely. His face was rigid and without expression, yet completely mad. He walked mechanically forward toward the two priests. They sprawled aside at the last second, holding two obviously human-made automatics, but making no effort to use them. Smithton walked on toward the open door at the front of the church.

He reached the steps, with the two priests staring after him. His feet lifted from the first step to the second and then he was on the sidewalk.

The two priests fired!

Smithton jerked, halted, and suddenly cried out in a voice of normal, rational agony. His legs kicked frantically under him and he ducked out of the sight of the doorway, his faltering steps sounding further and further away. He was dead—the Mikhtchah marksmanship had been as good as it seemed always to be—but still moving, though slower and slower, as if some extra charge of life were draining out like a battery running down.

The priests exchanged quick glances and then darted after him, crying out as they dashed around the door into the night. Abruptly, a single head and hand appeared again, to snap a shot at the draperies from which Smithton

173

had come. Amos forced himself to stand still, while his imagination supplied the jolt of lead in his stomach. The bullet hit the draperies, and something else.

The priest hesitated, and was gone again.

Amos broke into a run across the chapel and into the hall at the other side of the altar. He heard the faint sound of Doc's feet behind him.

The trapdoor was still there, unintentionally concealed under carpeting. He forced it up and dropped through it into the four-foot depth of the incompleted basement, making room for Doc. They crouched together as he lowered the trap and began feeling his way through the blackness toward the other end of the basement. It had been five years since he had been down there, and then only once for a quick inspection of the work of the boys who had dug the tunnel.

He thought he had missed it at first, and began groping for the small entrance. It might have caved in, for that matter. Then, two feet away, his hand found the hole and he drew Doc after him.

It was cramped, and bits of dirt had fallen in places and had to be dug out of the way. Part of the distance was on their stomachs. They found the bricked-up wall ahead of them and began digging around it with their bare hands. It took another ten minutes, while distant sounds of wild yelling from the Mikhtchah reached them faintly. They broke through at last with bleeding hands, not bothering to check for aliens near. They reached a safer distance in the woods, caught their breaths and went on.

The biggest danger lay in the drainage trench, which was low in several places. But luck was with them, and those spots lay in shadow.

Then the little Republican River lay in front of them, and there was a flatbottom boat nearby.

Moments later they were floating down the stream, resting their aching lungs, while the boat needed only a trifling guidance. It was still night, with only the light from the moon, and there was little danger of pursuit by

174

the alien planes. Amos could just see Doc's face as the man fumbled for a cigarette.

He lighted it and exhaled deeply. "All right, Amos— you were right, and God exists. But damn it, I don't feel any better for knowing that. I can't see how God helps me—nor even how He's doing the Mikhtchah much good. What do they get out of it, beyond a few miracles with the weather? They're just doing God's dirty work."

"They get the Earth, I suppose—if they want it," Amos said doubtfully. He wasn't sure they did. Nor could he see how the other aliens tied into the scheme; if he had known the answers, they were gone now. "Doc, you're still an atheist, though you now know God is."

The plump man chuckled bitterly. "I'm afraid you're right. But at least I'm myself. You can't be, Amos. You've spent your whole life on the gamble that God is right and that you must serve Him—when the only way you could serve was to help mankind. What do you do now? God is automatically right—but everything you've ever believed makes Him completely wrong, and you can only serve Him by betraying your people. What kind of ethics will work for you now?"

Amos shook his head wearily, hiding his face in his hands. The same problem had been fighting its way through his own thoughts. His first reaction had been to acknowledge his allegiance to God without question; sixty years of conditioned thought lay behind that. Yet now he could not accept such a decision. As a man, he could not bow to what he believed completely evil, and the Mikh- tchah were evil by every definition he knew.

Could he tell people the facts, and take away what faith they had in any purpose in life? Could he go over to the enemy, who didn't even want him except for their feeding experiments? Or could he encourage people to fight, with the old words that God was with them—when he knew the words were false? Yet their resistance might doom them to eternal hellfire for opposing God.

It hit him then that he could remember nothing clearly

about the case of a hereafter—either for or against it. What happened to a people when God deserted them? Were they only deserted in their physical form, and still free to win their spiritual salvation? Or were they completely lost? Did they cease to have souls that could survive? Or were those souls automatically consigned to hell, however noble they might be?

No question had been answered for him. He knew that God existed, but he had known that before. He knew nothing now beyond that. He did not even know when God had placed the Mikhtchah before humanity. It seemed unlikely that it was as recent as his own youth. Otherwise, how could he account for the strange spiritual glow he had felt as an evangelist?

"There's only one rational answer," he said at last. "It doesn't make any difference what I decide! I'm only one man."

"So was Columbus when he swore the world was round. And he didn't have the look on his face you've had since we saw God, Amos! I know now what the Bible means when it says Moses' face shone after he came down from the mountain, until he had to cover it with a veil. If I'm right, there's little help for mankind if you decide wrong!"

Doc tossed the cigarette over the side and lit another, and Amos was shocked to see that the man's hands were shaking. The doctor shrugged, and his tone fell back to normal. "I wish we knew more. You've always thought almost exclusively in terms of the Old Testament and a few snatches of Revelations—like a lot of men who became evangelists. I've never really thought about God—I couldn't accept Him, so I dismissed Him. Maybe that's why we got the view of Him we did. I wish I knew where Jesus fits in, for instance. There's too much missing. Too many imponderables and hiatuses. We have only two facts, and we can't understand either. There is a manifestation of God which has touched both, Mikhtchah and

176

mankind; and He has stated now that He plans to wipe out mankind. We'll have to stick to that."

Amos made one more attempt to deny the problem that was facing him. "Suppose God is only testing man again, as He did so often before?"

"Testing?" Doc rolled the word on his tongue, and seemed to spit it out. The strange white hair seemed to make him older, and the absence of mockery in his voice left him almost a stranger. "Amos, the Hebrews worked like the devil to get Canaan; after forty years of wandering around a few square miles, God suddenly told them this was the land—and then they had to take it by the same methods men have always used to conquer a country. The miracles didn't really decide anything. They got out of Babylon because the old prophets were slaving night and day to hold them together as one people, and because they managed to sweat it out until they finally got a break. In our own time, they've done the same things to get Israel, and with no miracles! It seems to me God always took it away, but they had to get it back by themselves. I don't think much of that kind of a test in this case."

Amos could feel all his values slipping and spinning. He realized that he was holding himself together only because of Doc; otherwise, his mind would have reached for madness, like any intelligence forced to solve the insoluble. He could no longer comprehend himself, let alone God. And the feeling crept into his thoughts that God couldn't wholly understand him, either.

"Can a creation defy anything great enough to create it, Doc? And should it, if it can?"

"Most kids have to," Doc said. He shook his head. "It's your problem. All I can do is point a few things out. And maybe it won't matter, at that. We're still a long ways inside Mikhtchah territory, and it's getting along toward daylight."

The boat drifted on, while Amos tried to straighten out his thoughts and grew more deeply tangled in a web of confusion. What could any man who worshipped God devoutly do if he found his God was opposed to all else he had ever believed to be good?

A version of Kant's categorical imperative crept into his mind; somebody had once quoted it to him—probably Doc. "So act as to treat humanity, whether in thine own person or in that of any other, in every case as an end withal, never as a means only." Was God now treating man as an end, or simply as a means to some purpose, in which man had failed? And had man ever seriously treated God as an end, rather than as a means to spiritual immortality and a quietus to the fear of death?

"We're being followed!" Doc whispered suddenly. He pointed back, and Amos could see a faint light shining around a curve in the stream. "Look—there's a building over there. When the boat touches shallow water, run for it!"

He bent to the oars, and a moment later they touched bottom and were over the side, sending the boat back into the current. The building was a hundred feet back from the bank, and they scrambled madly toward it. Even in the faint moonlight, they could see that the building was a wreck, long since abandoned. Doc went in through one of the broken windows, dragging Amos behind him.

Through a chink in a wall they could see another boat heading down the stream, lighted by a torch and carrying two Mikhtchah. One rowed, while the other sat in the prow with a gun, staring ahead. They rowed on past.

"We'll have to hole up here," Doc decided. "It'll be light in half an hour. Maybe they won't think of searching a ruin like this."

They found rickety steps, and stretched out on the bare floor of a huge upstairs closet. Amos groaned as he tried to find a position in which he could get some rest. Then, surprisingly, he was asleep.

He woke once with traces of daylight coming into the closet, to hear sounds of heavy gunfire not far away. He was just drifting back to sleep when hail began cracking furiously down on the roof. When it passed, the gunfire was stilled.

Doc woke him when it was turning dark. There was nothing to eat, and Amos' stomach was sick with hunger. His body ached in every joint, and walking was pure torture. Doc glanced up at the stars, seemed to decide on a course, and struck out. He was wheezing and groaning in a way that indicated he shared Amos' feelings.

But he found enough energy to begin the discussion again. "I keep wondering what Smithton saw, Amos? It wasn't what we saw. And what about the legends of war in heaven? Wasn't there a big battle there once, in which Lucifer almost won? Maybe Lucifer simply stands for some other race God cast off?"

"Lucifer was Satan, the spirit of evil. He tried to take over God's domain."

"Mmm. I've read somewhere that we have only the account of the victor, which is apt to be pretty biased history. How do we know the real issues? Or the true outcome? At least he thought he had a chance, and he apparently knew what he was fighting."

The effort of walking made speech difficult. Amos shrugged, and let the conversation die. But his own mind ground on.

If God was all-powerful and all-knowing, why had He let them spy upon Him? Or was He still all-powerful over a race He had dismissed? Could it make any difference to God what man might try to do, now that He had condemned him? Was the Presence they had seen the whole of God—or only one manifestation of Him?

His legs moved on woodenly, numbed to fatigue and slow from hunger, while his head churned with his basic problem. Where was his duty now? With God or against Him?

They found food in a deserted house, and began preparing it by the hooded light of a lantern while they listened to the news from a small battery radio that had been left behind. It was a hopeless account of alien land-

179

ings and human retreats, yet given without the tone of despair they should have expected. They were half-way through the meal before they discovered the reason.

"Flash!" the radio announced. "Word has just come through from the Denver area. Our second atomic missile has exploded successfully! The alien base has been wiped out, and every alien ship is ruined. It is now clear that the trouble with the earlier bombs we assembled lay in the detonating mechanism. This is being investigated, while more volunteers are being trained to replace this undependable part of the bomb. Both missiles carrying suicide bombers have succeeded. Captive aliens of both races are being questioned in Denver now, but the same religious fanaticism found in Portland seems to make communication difficult."

It went back to reporting alien landings, while Doc and Amos stared at each other. It was too much to absorb at once—the official admission of two races, the fact that bombs had been assembled and tried, and the casual acceptance of suicide missions. It was as if God could control weather and machines, but not the will of determined men. Free will or . . .

Amos groped in his mind, trying to dig out something that might tie in the success of human suicide bombers, where automatic machinery was miraculously stalled, together with the reaction of God to his own thoughts of the glow he had felt in his early days. Something about men . . .

"They can be beaten!" Doc said in a harsh whisper.

Amos sighed as they began to get up to continue the impossible trek. "Maybe. We know God was at Clyde. Can we be sure He was at the other places to stop the bombs by His miracles?"

They slogged on through the night, cutting across country in the dim moonlight, where every footstep was twice as hard. Amos turned it over, trying to use the new information for whatever decision he must reach. If men

180

could overcome those opposed to them, even for a time . . .

It brought him no closer to an answer.

The beginnings of dawn found them in a woods. Doc managed to heave Amos up a tree, where he could survey the surrounding terrain. There was a house beyond the edge of the woods, but it would take dangerous minutes to reach it. They debated, and then headed on.

They were just emerging from the woods when the sound of an alien plane began its stuttering shriek. Doc turned and headed back to where Amos was, behind him. Then he stopped. "Too late! He's seen something. Gotta have a target!"

His arms swept out, shoving Amos violently back under the nearest tree. He swung and began racing across the clearing, his fat legs pumping furiously as he covered the ground in straining leaps. Amos tried to lift himself from where he had fallen, but it was too late.

There was the drumming of gunfire and the earth erupted around Doc. He lurched and dropped, to twitch and lie still.

The plane swept over, while Amos disentangled himself from a root. It was gone as he broke free. Doc had given it a target, and the pilot was satisfied, apparently.

He was still alive as Amos dropped beside him. Two of the shots had hit, but he managed to grin as he lifted himself on one elbow. It was only a matter of minutes, however, and there was no help possible. Amos found one of Doc's cigarettes and lighted it with fumbling hands.

"Thanks," Doc wheezed after taking a heavy drag on it. He started to cough, but suppressed it, his face twisting in agony. His words came in an irregular rhythm, but he held his voice level. "I guess I'm going to hell, Amos, since I never did repent—if there is a hell! And I hope there is! I hope it's filled with the soul of every poor damned human being who died in less than perfect grace. Because I'm going to find some way——"

He straightened suddenly, coughing and fighting for breath. Then he found one final source of strength and met Amos' eyes, a trace of his old cynical smile on his face.

"——some way to urge Lucifer to join us!" he finished. He dropped back, letting all the fight go out of his body. A few seconds later, he was dead.

6

. . . Thou shalt have no other peoples before me . . . Thou shalt make unto them no covenant against me . . . Thou shalt not foreswear thyself to them, nor serve them . . . for I am a jealous people . . .

Exultations, XII, 2-4.
THE BOOK OF MAN

Amos lay through the day in the house to which he had dragged Doc's body. He did not even look for food. For the first time in his life since his mother had died when he was five, he had no shield against his grief. There was no hard core of acceptance that it was God's will to hide his loss at Doc's death. And with the realization of that, all the other losses hit at him as if they had been no older than the death of Doc.

He sat with his grief and his newly-sharpened hatred, staring toward Clyde. Once, during the day, he slept. He awakened to a sense of a tremendous sound and shaking of the earth, but all was quiet when he finally became conscious. It was nearly night, and time to leave.

For a moment, he hesitated. It would be easier to huddle here, beside his dead, and let whatever would happen come to him. But within him was a sense of duty that drove him on. In the back of his mind something stirred, telling him he still had work to do.

He found part of a stale loaf of bread and some hard cheese and started out, munching on them. It was still too light to move safely, but he was going through woods again, and he heard no alien planes. When it grew darker, he turned to the side roads that led in the direction of Wesley.

In his mind was the knowledge that he had to return there. His church lay there; if the human fighters had pushed the aliens back, his people might be there. If not, it was from there that he would have to follow them.

His thoughts were too deep for conscious expression, and too numbed with exhaustion. His legs moved on steadily. One of his shoes had begun to wear through, and his feet were covered with blisters, but he went grimly on. It was his duty to lead his people, now that the aliens were here, as he had led them in easier times. His thinking had progressed no further.

He holed up in a barn that morning, avoiding the house because of the mutilated things that lay ón the doorstep where the aliens had apparently left them. And this time he slept with the soundness of complete fatigue, but he awoke to find one fist clenched and extended toward Clyde. He had been dreaming that he was Job, and that God had left him sitting unanswered on his boils until he died, while mutilated corpses moaned around him, asking for leadership he would not give.

It was nearly dawn before he realized that he should have found himself some kind of a car. He had seen none, but there might have been one abandoned somewhere. Doc could probably have found one. But it was too late to bother, now. He had come to the outskirts of a tiny town, and started to head beyond it, before realizing that all the towns must have been well searched by now. He turned down the small street, looking for a store where he could find food.

There was a small grocery with a door partly ajar. Amos pushed it open, to the clanging of a bell. Almost immediately a dog began barking, and a human voice came sharply from the back.

"Down, Shep! Just a minute, I'm a-coming." A door

to the rear opened, and a bent old man emerged, carrying a kerosene lamp. "Darned electric's off again! Good thing I stayed. Told them I had to mind my store, but they wanted me to get with them. Had to hide out in the old well. Darned nonsense about . . ."

He stopped, his eyes blinking behind thick lenses, and his mouth dropped open. He swallowed, and his voice was startled and shrill. *"Mister, who are you?"*

"A man who just escaped from the aliens," Amos told him. He hadn't realized the shocking appearance he must present by now. "One in need of food and a chance to rest until night. But I'm afraid I have no money on me."

The old man tore his eyes away slowly, seeming to shiver. Then he nodded, and pointed to the back. "Never turned nobody away hungry yet," he said, but the words seemed automatic.

An old dog backed slowly under a couch as Amos entered. The man put the lamp down and headed into a tiny kitchen to begin preparing food. Amos reached for the lamp and blew it out. "There really are aliens—worse than you heard," he said.

The old man bristled, met his eyes, and then nodded slowly. "If you say so. Only it don't seem logical God would let things like that run around in a decent state like Kansas."

He shoved a plate of eggs onto the table, and Amos pulled it to him, swallowing a mouthful eagerly. He reached for a second, and stopped. Something was violently wrong, suddenly. His stomach heaved, the room began to spin, and his forehead was cold and wet with sweat. He gripped the edge of the table, trying to keep from falling. Then he felt himself being dragged to a cot. He tried to protest, but his body was shaking with ague, and the words that spilled out were senseless. He felt the cot under him, and waves of sick blackness spilled over him.

It was the smell of cooking food that awakened him finally, and he sat up with a feeling that too much time had passed. The old man came from the kitchen, studying him. "You sure were sick, Mister. Guess you ain't used to going without decent food and rest. Feeling okay?"

Amos nodded. He felt a little unsteady, but it was passing. He pulled on the clothes that had been somewhat cleaned for him, and found his way to the table. "What day is it?"

"Saturday, evening," the other answered. "At least the way I figure. Here, eat that and get some coffee in you." He watched until Amos began on the food, and then dropped to a stool to begin cleaning an old rifle and loading it. "You said a lot of things. They true?"

For a second, Amos hesitated. Then he nodded, unable to lie to his benefactor. "I'm afraid so."

"Yeah, I figured so, somehow, looking at you." The old man sighed. "Well, I hope you make wherever you're going."

"What about you?" Amos asked.

The old man sighed, running his hands along the rifle. "I ain't leaving my store for any bunch of aliens. And if the Lord I been doing my duty by all my life decides to put Himself on the wrong side, well, maybe He'll win. But it'll be over my dead body!"

Nothing Amos could say would change his mind. The old man sat on the front step of the store, the rifle on his lap and the dog at his side, as Amos headed down the street in the starlight.

Amos felt surprisingly better after the first half mile. Rest and food, combined with some treatment of his sores and blisters, had helped. But the voice inside him was driving him harder now, and the picture of the old man seemed to lend it added strength. He struck out at the fastest pace he could hope to maintain, leaving the town behind and heading down the road that the old man had said led to Wesley.

It was just after midnight when he saw the lights of a group of cars or trucks moving along another road. He

185

had no idea whether they were driven by men or aliens, but he kept steadily on. There were sounds of traffic another time, on a road that crossed the small one he followed. But he knew now that he was approaching Wesley, and he speeded up his pace.

When the first dawn light came, he made no effort to seek shelter. He stared at the land around him, stripped by grasshoppers that could have been killed off if men had worked as hard at ending the insects as they had at their bickerings and wars. He saw the dry, arid land, drifting into dust and turning a fertile country into a nightmare. Men could put a stop to that.

It had been no act of God that had caused this ruin, but man's own follies. And without help from God, man might set it right in time.

God had deserted men. But mankind hadn't halted. On his own, he'd made a path to the moon and had unlocked the atom. He'd found a means, out of his raw courage, to use hydrogen bombs against the aliens when miracles were used against him. He had done everything but conquer himself—and he could do that, if he were given time.

Amos saw a truck stop at the crossroads ahead and halted, but the driver was human. He saw the open door and quickened his step toward it. "I'm bound for Wesley!"

"Sure." The driver helped him into the seat. "I'm going back for more supplies myself. You sure look as if you need treatment at the aid station there. I thought we'd rounded up all you strays. Most of them came in right after we sent out the word on Clyde."

"You've taken it?" Amos asked.

The other nodded wearily. "We took it. Got 'em with a bomb, like sitting ducks; we've been mopping up since. Not many aliens left."

They were nearing the outskirts of Wesley, and Amos pointed to his own house. "If you'll let me off there . . ."

"Look, I got orders to bring all strays to the aid station," the driver began firmly. Then he swung and faced Amos. For a second, he hesitated. Finally he nodded quietly. "Sure. Glad to help you."

Amos found the water still running. He bathed slowly. Somewhere, he felt his decision had been made, though he was still unsure of what it was. He climbed from the tub at last and began dressing. There was no suit that was proper, but he found clean clothes. His face in the mirror looked back at him, haggard and bearded as he reached for the razor.

Then he stopped as he encountered the reflection of his eyes. A shock ran over him, and he backed away a step. They were eyes foreign to everything in him. He had seen a shadow of what lay in them only once before, in the eyes of a great evangelist; and this was a hundred times stronger. He tore his glance away to find himself shivering, and he avoided them all through the shaving. Oddly, though, there was a strange satisfaction in what he had seen. He was beginning to understand why the old man had believed him, and why the truck driver had obeyed.

Most of Wesley had returned, and there were soldiers on the streets. As he approached the church, he saw the first aid station, hectic with business. And a camera crew was near it, taking shots for television of those who had managed to escape from alien territory after the bombing.

A few people called to him, but he went on until he reached the church steps. The door was still in ruins and the bell was gone. Amos stood quietly waiting, his mind focussing slowly as he stared at the people, who were just beginning to recognize him and to spread hasty words from mouth to mouth. Then he saw little Angela Anduccini, and motioned for her to come to him. She hesitated briefly, before following him inside and to the organ.

The little Hammond still functioned. Amos climbed to the pulpit, hearing the old familiar creak of the boards. He put his hands on the lectern, seeing the heavy knuckles and blue veins of age as he opened the Bible and made ready for his Sunday morning congregation. He straightened his shoulders and turned to face the pews, waiting as they came in.

There were only a few at first. Then more and more came, some from old habit, some from curiosity, and many only because they had heard that he had been captured in person, probably. The camera crew came to the back and set up their machines, flooding him with bright lights and adjusting their telelens. He smiled on them, nodding.

He knew his decision now. It had been made in pieces and tatters. It had come from Kant, who had spent his life looking for a basic ethical principle, and had boiled it down in his statement that men must be treated as ends, not as means. It had come from Rover's passive acceptance of the decision of a god who could do nothing for him, and from the one rebellious act that had won Anne his respect. It had been distilled from Doc's final challenge, and from the old man sitting in his doorway, ready to face any challenger.

There could be no words with which to give his message to those who waited. No orator had ever possessed such a command of language. But men with rude speech, and limited use of what they had, had fired the world before. Moses had come down from a mountain with a face that shone, and had overcome the objections of a stiff-necked people. Peter the Hermit had preached a thankless crusade to all of Europe, without radio or television. It was more than words or voice.

He looked down at them when the church was filled and the organ hushed.

"My text for today," he announced, and the murmurs below him hushed as his voice reached out to the pews. "Ye shall know the truth and the truth shall make men free!"

He stopped for a moment, studying them, feeling the decision in his mind, and knowing he could make no other. The need of him lay here, among those he had always tried to serve while believing he was serving God through them. He was facing them as an end, not as a means, and he found it good.

Nor could he lie to them now, or deceive them with false hopes. They would need all the facts if they were to make an end to their bickerings and to unite themselves in the final struggle for the fullness of their potential glory.

"I have come back from captivity among the aliens," he began. "I have seen the hordes who have no desire but to erase the memory of man from the dust of the earth that bore him. I have stood at the altar of their God. I have heard the voice of God proclaim that He is also our God, and that He has cast us out. I have believed Him, as I believe Him now."

He felt the strange, intangible something that was greater than words or oratory flow out of him as it had never flowed in his envied younger days. He watched the shock and the doubt arise and disappear slowly as he went on, giving them the story and the honest doubts he still had. He could never know many things, or even whether the God worshipped on the alien altar was wholly the same God who had been in the hearts of men for a hundred generations. No man could understand enough. They were entitled to all his doubts, as well as to all of which he knew.

He paused at last, in the utter stillness of the chapel. He straightened and smiled down at them, drawing the smile out of some reserve that had lain dormant since he had first tasted inspiration as a boy. He saw a few smiles answer him, and then more—uncertain, doubtful smiles that grew more sure as they spread.

He could feel himself reach them, while the television camera went on recording it all. He could feel his regained strength welding them together. He could feel them suddenly one and indivisible as he went on.

But there was something else. Over the chapel there was a glow, a feeling of deepening communion. It lifted and enshrouded him with those below him. He opened

189

himself up to it without reserve. Once he had thought it came only from God. Now he knew it came from the men and women in front of him. Like a physical force, he could sense it emanating from them and from himself, uniting them and dedicating them.

He accepted it, as he had once accepted God. The name no longer mattered, when the thing was the same.

"God has ended the ancient covenants and declared Himself an enemy of all mankind," Amos said, and the chapel seemed to roll with his voice. "I say to you: He has found a worthy opponent."

PURSUIT

1

Fear cut through the unconscious mind of Wilbur Hawkes. With almost physical violence, it tightened his throat and knifed at his heart. It darted into his numbed brain, screaming at him.

He was a soft egg in a vast globe of elastic gelatine. Two creatures swam menacingly through the resisting globe toward him. The gelatine fought against them, but they came on. One was near, and made a mystic pass. He screamed at it, and the gelatine grew stronger, throwing them aside and away. Suddenly, the creatures drew back. A door opened, and they were gone. But he couldn't let them go. If they escaped . . .

Hawkes jerked upright in his bed, gasping out a hoarse cry, and the sound of his own voice completed the awakening. He opened his eyes to a murky darkness that was barely relieved by the little night-light. For a second, the nightmare was so strong on his mind that he seemed to see two shadows beyond the door, rushing down the steps. He fought off the illusion, and with straining senses jerked his head around the room. There was nothing there.

Sweat was beading his forehead, and he could feel his pulse racing. He had to get out—had to leave—at once!

He forced the idea aside. There was something cloudy in his mind, but he made reason take over and shove away some of the heavy fear. His fingers found a cigarette and

191

lighted it automatically. The first familiar breath of smoke in his lungs helped. He drew in deeply again, while the tiny sounds in the room became meaningful. There was the insistent ticking of a clock and the soft shushing sound of a tape recorder. He stared at the machine, running on fast rewind, and reversed it to play. But the tape seemed to be blank, or erased. '

He crushed the cigarette out on a table-top where other butts lay in disorder. It looked wrong, and his mind leaped up in sudden frantic fear, before he could calm it again. This time, reason echoed his emotional unease.

Hawkes had never smoked before!

But his fingers were already lighting another by old habit. His thoughts lurched, seeking for an answer. There was only a vague sense of something missing—a period of time seemed to have passed. It felt like a long period, but he had no memory of it. There had been the final fight with Irma, when he'd gone stalking out of the house, telling her to get a divorce any way she wanted. He'd opened the mail-box and taken out a letter—a letter from a Professor . . .

His mind refused to go further. There was only a complete blank after that. But it had been in midwinter, and now he could make out the faint outlines of full-leafed trees against the sky through the window! Months had gone by—and there was no faintest trace of them in his mind.

They'll get you! You can't escape! Hurry, go, GO! . . .

The cigarette fell from his shaking hands, and he was half out of the bed before the rational part of his mind could cut off the fear thoughts. He flipped on the lights, afraid of the dimness. It didn't help. The room was dusty, as if unused for months, and there was a cobweb in one corner by the mirror.

His own face shocked him. It was the same lean, sharp-featured face as ever, under the shock of nondescript, sandy hair. His ears still stuck out too much, and his lips were a trifle too thin. It looked no more than his thirty years. But it was a strained face now—painted with weeks of fatigue, and greyish with fear—sweat-streaked and with nervous tension in every corded tendon of his throat. His somewhat boney, average-height figure shook visibly as he climbed from the bed.

Hawkes stood fighting himself, trying to get a grip on himself, but it was a losing battle. Something seemed to swing up in the corner of the room, as if a shadow moved. He jerked his head toward it, but there was nothing there.

He heard his breath gasping harshly, and his knuckles whitened. There was the taste of blood in the corner of his mouth where he was biting his lips.

Get out! They'll be here at once! Leave—GO!

His hands were already fumbling with his underclothing. He drew on briefs jerkily, and grabbed for the shirt and suit he had never seen before. He was no longer thinking now. Blind panic was winning. He thrust his feet into shoes, not bothering with socks.

A slip of paper fell from his coat, covered with big sprawled Greek letters. He saw only the last line as it fell to the floor—some equation that ended with an infinity sign. Then psi and alpha, connected by a dash. The alpha sign had been scratched out, and something written over it. He tried to reach it, and more papers spilled from his coat pocket. The fear washed up more strongly. He forgot the papers. His wallet lay on the chair, and he barely grabbed it before the urge overpowered him completely.

The doorknob slipped in his sweating hands, but he managed to turn it. The elevator wasn't at his floor, and he couldn't stop for it. His feet pounded on the stairs, taking him down the three floors to the street at a breakneck pace. The walls of the stairway seemed to be rushing together, as if trying to close the way. He screamed at them, until they were behind and he was charging out of the front door.

A half-drunken couple was coming in—a heavy, older man and a slim girl he barely saw. He hit them, throwing them aside. He jerked from the entrance. Cars were streaming down West End Avenue. He dashed across, paying no attention to them. His rush carried him onto the opposite sidewalk. Then, finally, the blind panic left him, and he was leaning against a building, gasping for breath, and wondering whether his heart could endure the next beat.

Across the street, the fat man he had hit was coming after him. Hawkes gathered himself together to apologize, but the words never came. A second blinding horror hit at him, and his eyes darted up toward the windows of his apartment.

It was only a tiny glow, at first, like a drop from the heart of a sun. Then, before he could more than blink, it spread, until the whole apartment seemed to blaze. A gout of smoke poured from the shattered window, and a dull concussion struck his ears.

The infernally bright flame flickered, leaped outward from the window, and died down almost as quickly as it had come, leaving twisted, half-molten metal where the window frames had been.

They'd almost gotten him! Hawkes felt his legs weaken and quiver, while his eyes remained glued to the spot that had lighted the whole street a second before. They'd tried —but he'd escaped in time.

It must have been a thermite bomb—nothing but thermite could be that hot. He had never imagined that even such a bomb could give so much heat so quickly. Where? In the tape-recorder?

He waited numbly, expecting more fire, but the brief flame seemed to have died out completely. He shook his head, unbelieving, and started to cross the street, to survey the damage or to join the crowd that was beginning to collect.

The fear surged up in him again, halting his step as if he'd struck a physical barrier. With it came the sound of an auto-horn, the button held down permanently. His eyes darted down the street, to see a long, grey sedan with old-fashioned running-boards come around the corner on two wheels. Its brakes screeched, and it skidded to a halt beside Hawkes' apartment building.

A slim young man in grey tweeds leaped out of it and came to a stop. He threw back heavy black hair with a toss of his head and ran into the crowd that parted to let him through. Someone began pointing towards Hawkes.

Hawkes tried to slide around the corner without being seen, but a flashlight in the young man's hands pin-pointed him. A yell went up.

"There he goes!"

His feet sounded hopelessly on the sidewalk as he dashed up toward Broadway, but behind came the sound of others in pursuit, and the shouting was becoming a meaningless babble as others took it up. There was no longer any doubt. Someone was certainly after him— there'd been no time to turn in an alarm over the fire in his apartment. They'd been coming for him before that started.

What hideous crime could he have committed during the period he couldn't remember? Or what spy-ring had encircled him?

He had no time to think of the questions, even. He ducked into the thin swarm of a few people leaving a theater just as the pursuing group rounded the corner, with the slim young man in the lead.

Their cries were enough. Hands reached for him from the theater crowd, and a foot reached out to trip him up. Terror lent speed to his legs, but he could never out-distance them as long as others picked up the chase.

A sudden blast of heat struck down, and the air was golden and hazy above him. He staggered sideways, blinded by the glare. The crowd was screaming in fear now, no longer holding him back. He felt the edge of a subway entrance. There was no other choice. He ducked down the steps. His vision slowly returned, and he risked a glance back at the street—just as the whole entrance came down in a wreck of broken wood and metal.

A clap of thundering noise sounded above him, drowning the hoarse screams of the people. The few persons in the station rushed for the fallen entrance, to mill about it crazily, as a train pulled in. Hawkes started toward it, and then realized his pursuers would suspect that. Whatever frightful weapon had been used against him had back-fired on them—but they'd catch him at the next stop.

He found space at the end of the platform and dropped off, skirting behind the train, avoiding the high-voltage rails.

The uptown platform held only three people, and they seemed to be too busy at the other end, trying to see the wreckage, to notice him. He vaulted onto it, and dashed into the men's room. The few contents of his coat pocket came out quickly, and he began to stuff them into his trousers. He shoved the coat into a garbage can, wet his hair and slicked it back, and opened his coat collar. The change didn't make much of a disguise, but they wouldn't be expecting him to come out so near where he entered.

His skin prickled as he came out, but he fought down the sickness in his stomach. A few drops of rain were beginning to fall, and the crowd around the accident was thinning out. That might help him—or it might prove more dangerous. He had to chance it.

He stopped to buy a paper, maintaining an air of casual interest in the crowd.

"What happened?" he asked.

The newsstand attendant jerked his eyes back from the excitement reluctantly. "Damned if I know. Someone says a ball lightning came down and broke over there. Caved in the entrance. Nobody's hurt seriously, they say. I was just stacking up to go home when I heard it go off. Didn't see it. Just saw the entrance falling in."

Hawkes picked up his change and turned back across Broadway, pretending he was studying the paper. The dateline showed that it was July 10, just seven months from the beginning of his memory lapse. He couldn't be-lieve that there had been time enough for any group to invent a heat-ray, if such a thing could exist. Yet nothing else would explain the two sudden bursts of flame he had seen. Even if it could be invented, it would hardly be used in public for anything less than a National Emergency.

What had happened in the seven blanked-out months?

2

The room was smelly and cheap, with dirty walls and no carpet on the floor, but it was a relief after the hours of tramping and riding about the city. Hawkes sat on the rickety chair, letting the wetness dry out of his clothes. He looked at the bed, trying to convince himself that he could strip and warm up there while his clothes dried. But something in his head warned him that he couldn't— he'd have to be ready to run again. The same urge had made him demand a room on the ground floor, where he could escape through the window if they found him. They could never find him here—but they would! Sooner or later, whatever was after him would come!

It had seemed simple enough, before. There had been three friends he could trust. Seven months couldn't have killed their faith in him, no matter what he'd done. And perhaps he'd been right, though there'd been no chance to test it.

He'd almost been caught at the first place. The two men outside had seemed to be no more than a couple of people waiting for a bus. Only the approach of another man who resembled Hawkes had tipped him off, by the quick interest they had shown.

The other places had also been posted—and beyond the third he'd seen the grey sedan with the running boards, waiting.

There had been less than twenty dollars in his wallet, and most of that had gone for cab fares. He'd barely had enough left for this dingy room, the later edition of the newspaper, and the coffee and donuts that lay beside him, half-consumed.

He glanced toward the door, listening with quick fear as steps sounded on the stairs. Then he drew his breath in again and reached for the newspaper. But it told him as little as the first one had.

This one mentioned the two mysterious explosions of "ball lightning" in a feature on the first page, but only as curiosities. They even gave his address and listed the apartment as being in his name, though apparently not currently occupied. But no other reference was made to him, or to the chase.

He shook his head at that. He couldn't see a news-paperman refusing to make a story of it, if there were any other news about him to which they could tie the burning of his apartment. Apparently it wasn't the police who were after him, and he hadn't been guilty of anything so ordinary as murder.

Outside the window a sudden scream sounded, and he jerked from the chair, reaching the door before he realized it was only a cat on the prowl. He shuddered, his old hatred of cats coming to the surface. For a minute, he thought of shutting the window. But he couldn't cut off his chance to retreat through the garbage-littered backyard.

He returned to his search, beginning an inventory of the few belongings that had been in his pocket. There was a notebook, and he scanned it rapidly. A few pages were missing, and most were blank. There was only a shopping list. That puzzled him for a minute—he couldn't believe he'd taken to using lipstick as well as cigarettes, though both were listed in his handwriting. The notebook contained nothing else.

He stuffed it back into his pockets, along with his key-ring. There were more keys than he'd expected, some of which were strange to him, but none held any mark that would identify them. He put a few pennies into another

198

pocket—his entire wealth now, in a world where no more money would be available to him. He grimaced, dropping a comb into the same pocket.

Then there was only his wallet left. His identification card was there, unchanged. Behind it, where his wife's picture had always been, there was only a folded clipping. He drew it out, hoping for a clue. It was only an announcement of those killed in an airplane crash—and among those found dead was Mrs. Wilbur Hawkes, of New York. It seemed that Irma had never reached Reno for the divorce.

He tried to feel some sorrow at that, but time must have healed whatever hurt there had been, even though he couldn't remember. She had hated him ever since she'd found that he really wasn't willing to please his father by becoming another of the vice-presidents in the old man's bank, with an unearned but fancy salary. He'd preferred teaching mathematics and dabbling with a bit of research into the probable value of the ESP work being done at Duke University. He'd explained why he hated banking; Irma had made it clear that she really needed the mink coat no assistant professor could afford. It had been stalemate—a bitter, seven-year stalemate, until she finally gave up hope and demanded a divorce.

He threw the clipping away, and pulled out the final bit of paper. It was a rent receipt for a cold-water apartment in what had once been called Hell's Kitchen—from the price of forty dollars a month, it had to be a cold-water place. He frowned, considering it. Apartment 12. That might explain why his own apartment had been unused, though it made little sense to him. It would probably be watched by now, anyway.

He jerked to his feet at a sound on the window-sill, but it was only a cat, eyeing the unfinished donut. He threw the food out, and the cat dived after it. Hawkes waited for the touch of ice along his backbone to go away. It didn't.

This time he tried to ignore it. He picked up the paper and began going through it, looking for something that might give him some slight clue. But there was nothing there. Only a heading on an inside page that stirred his curiosity.

Scientist Seeks Confinement

He glanced at it, noting that a Professor Meinzer, formerly of City College, had appeared at Bellevue, asking to be put away in a padded cell, preferably with a strait-jacket. The Professor had only explained that he considered himself dangerous to society. No other reason was found. Professor Meinzer had been doing private work, believed to relate to his theory that . . .

The panic was back, thick in Hawkes' throat. He shoved himself against the wall, his heart racing, while he tried to fight it down. There was no sound from the hall or outside. He forced his eyes back to the paper.

And the paper was surrounded by a golden haze. It burst into a momentary flame as the haze flickered out. Hawkes dropped the ashes from his clammy hands. He hadn't been burned!

You can't escape. Run. They'll get you!

He heard the outside door open, as it had opened a hundred times. But now it could only mean that more were coming. He jerked for the open window.

Something came sailing through the air to hit the sill. Hawkes screamed weakly, far down in his throat, before his eyes could register the fact that it was only the cat again.

Then the cat let out a horrible beginning of a sound, and its poor, half-starved body seemed to turn inside out, with a churning motion that Hawkes could barely see. Blood and gore spattered from it, striking his face and clothes.

He froze, unable to move. Either they were outside in the yard, or whatever frightful weapon they used could work through a closed door. He tried to move, first one way, then the other. His feet remained frozen.

Then steps sounded in the hallway, and he waited no longer. His legs came to sudden life, hurling him over the carcass of the cat and outside. He went charging through the refuse, and then leaped and clawed his way over the fence. The alley was deserted, and he shot down it, to swing right and into another alley.

It wasn't until his muscles began to fail that he could control himself enough to stop and stumble into a darkened spot among the garbage cans, spent and gasping for breath.

There was no sign of anyone following. Hawkes had no idea of how they could trace him—but he was beginning to suspect that nothing was impossible, judging by the results of their weapons. For the moment, though, he seemed to have shaken off pursuit. And the physical fatigue had apparently eased some of his terror.

What had shocked him into losing seven months out of his memory—and still could drive him into absolute terror at the first sign of them?

He couldn't go back to the room, and his own apartment was out of the question. The rain had stopped, mercifully, but he couldn't walk the streets indefinitely, dirty and bedraggled as he was. He tried to think of something to do, but all of his schemes took money, which he no longer had.

Finally, he arose wearily. Maybe the apartment for which he had the rent receipt was watched—but he'd have to chance it.

He'd been accidentally heading toward it, and he continued now, turning right and up the Avenue that would take him to the apartment. He tried to hurry, but the best his tired muscles could do was a slow shuffle.

Light was beginning to show faintly in the sky, but it was still too early for more than a few cars and a chance pedestrian. At this hour the Avenue was used by only a few cruising cabs. He shuffled along, trying to look like a man on his way home after too much night out. The cat-blood on his clothes bothered him, until he tried weaving a little as he walked, imitating the drunks he had seen often enough.

He passed an all-night diner, and fished for his pennies. But there were several men inside. He went on, past Fifty-Ninth Street, and up West End Avenue, heading for the apartment, which should be near.

He was just reaching the right block when a grey sedan sped past, heading downtown. There were running boards on it, and behind the wheel sat the slim young man who'd given chase to Hawkes before.

Hawkes tried to duck, but the sedan braked to a stop and began backing toward him. It was beside him before he could realize more than the old clamor of his brain telling him to run, that he couldn't escape.

A window of the car slid open, and the driver leaned far to the right. "Will Hawkes," the young man called. "How about a lift?"

The smile was pleasant and the voice was casual, as if they were old friends. There was no gun in the man's hands. It might have been any honest offer of a ride.

Hawkes braced himself, just as a patrol car started to turn onto the Avenue. He opened his mouth to scream for help, but his vocal cords were frozen. The young man followed his eyes to the patrol car, and frowned.

Then the grey sedan lifted smoothly upwards to a height of twenty feet, turned sharply in mid-air, lifted again, and apparently made a smooth landing on top of a parking garage!

There had been no roar of jets and no evidence of any means of propulsion.

The patrol car went on along the Avenue, heading for a diner. The officers inside apparently had missed the whole affair.

Hawkes' cowardly legs suddenly came unfrozen. He was conscious of them churning madly. With an effort, he got partial control of himself, managing to focus on the house numbers.

There were no watchers outside the number he wanted,

though they could have been in rooms across the street. He had no choice now. He leaped up the steps and into the hallway. His eyes darted around, spotting a door that led out to the side, probably into an alley. He drew himself together, hiding behind the stairs.

But there was no further pursuit for the moment. The fear that seemed to come before each attack was missing. Maybe it meant he was safe for the moment—though it hadn't warned him of the car the young man was driving.

Heat rays! Levitation! Hawkes dropped to his knees as fatigue and reaction caught up with him again, but his mind churned over the new evidence. As a mathematician, he was sure such things could not exist. If they did, there would have been an extension of math well in advance of the perfection of the machines, and he'd have known of it as speculative theory, at least. Yet, without such evidence, the devices apparently existed.

The police weren't in on it, that much was certain. It was more than a hunt for a criminal. What had been going on during the months he had missed?

His mind shuttled over the spy-thrillers he had seen. If some nation had the secrets, and he had discovered them . . . But the heat ray would never have been used openly, then; they wouldn't tip their hand. No nation would let such a weapon get into another nation where its secrets might be discovered.

And if the weapon belonged to the United States, the young man would never have levitated to avoid police at the greater risk of tipping off anyone who saw that such things could be done.

Nothing made sense—not even the crazy feeling of fear that had warned him on some occasions and failed him this last time. The only explanation that was credible was the totally incredible idea that some life, alien to earth and with strange unearthly powers, was after him—or that he was insane.

He fumbled through a pack of cigarettes until he located the last one, streaked with sweat that was still pouring down from his armpit, and lighted it. It was all answerless—just as his sudden need for smoking was.

3

Hawkes crushed out the cigarette and began climbing the wide stairs slowly. It was probably an ambush into which he was heading—but without this place, he had no chance of resting. He stared at the numbers painted on the dirty red doors, and went on up a second flight of stairs. The number he wanted was at the end of the hall, dimly lighted. He dropped to the keyhole but found it had been filled long ago, probably when the Yale lock was installed.

He put his ear against the door and listened. There was no sound from inside except a monotonous noise that must be water dripping from a leaky faucet. Finally he climbed to his feet and reached for his keys. The third one he tried fitted, and the door swung open.

He fumbled about, looking for a light switch, and finally struck a match. The switch was a string hanging down from a bare bulb. He pulled it, to find he stood inside one of the old monstrosities with which New York was filled—a combination kitchen and bathroom, with a tiny closet for the toilet in one corner. There was an icebox, a dirty stove, a Franklin heater connected to the chimney, a small sink, and a rickety table with four folding chairs. In a closet, cheap china showed.

He went through, into the seven-by-twelve living room. There was a small radio, a worn sofa, two more folding chairs and a big typing table. The rug on the floor had been patched together. Then he breathed more easily. Over the back of one of the chairs was a sports jacket which he recognized as his own. He jerked it up suddenly and began going through the pockets, but it had already been emptied.

It didn't matter—he no longer cared why he should be

in a place so totally unlike any his usually neat habits would have led him to. It was his.

Then, as he came into the bedroom, he hesitated. It was smaller than the living room, with a bed that took up half of one wall, and two dressers jammed into the remaining space. One corner held a rickety closet—and hanging on a hook on one side was a man's raincoat and hat, both at least five sizes too big for him. His eyes darted about, to find a strange mixture of things he remembered as his and possessions which he would never have owned. On one of the dressers was a small traveling case, filled with the cosmetics and appliances which only a woman would use.

He jerked open the closet, and his nose told him before his eyes that it held only female clothing! Yet on the shelf his old hat rested happily.

He could make no sense of it—the place looked as if several people lived in it, and yet it wasn't really fitted for anyone to spend his whole time there. It had none of the accumulation of property that should be found in any permanent residence. He went out of the bedroom, passing the typewriter desk. The typewriter was an old, standard Olympia—a German machine he'd refitted with the Dvorak keyboard which he had learned for greater efficiency. He was sure nobody else would want it.

The dishes were dusty, and there was no food in the ice-box; from the smell, there had been no ice in it for weeks.

Now, though, it began to fit—a place where it was convenient to stop in, but not a place in which to live. And perhaps he had been in the habit of lending it to others. Though why he shouldn't have used his own apartment was something he couldn't understand.

But it was possible there was no record of this place.

He began shucking off his shirt as he went back through the living room—until the marks on the rug caught his eyes. Something heavy had rested there recently—there had been other desks about, or heavily laden tables. And a bit of paper under the sofa could only have come from one of the complicated computing machines used in high-power mathematics. He scanned the fragment, making no sense of it, except to observe that it was esoteric enough to belong to any new branch of theory. For a second, the heat-rays and levitations entered his head—but none of the symbols fitted such a branch of physical development.

What had been going on here—and why had the machines been removed so recently that their traces still looked fresh?

He shook his head—and froze, as a key turned in the lock.

There was no time for flight. She stood in the doorway, blinking at the light before he could turn. She, of course, was the girl whom he'd barely noticed when he knocked the couple down as he charged out of his apartment.

Of course? He puzzled over that. He'd almost expected it—and yet, now that he looked more closely, he couldn't even be sure that she was the same. She wore an identical green jacket, but nothing else fit, because he had no other memory of that girl. This one was two inches shorter than he was, with dark red hair and the deepest blue eyes he had seen. She looked like an artist's conception of an Irish colleen, except that her mouth was open half an inch, and she was studying him with a look of being about ready to scream.

"Who are you?" He forced the words out at her.

She shook her head, and then smiled doubtfully. "Ellen Ibañez, naturally. You startled me! But you must be Wilbur Hawkes, of course. Didn't you get my wire?"

He watched her, but there had been no stumbling over his name, and no effort to make it sound too casual. Apparently, the name meant nothing to her. He shook his head. "What wire?" Then he plunged ahead, quickly. "You've heard of amnesia? Good. Well, I've got it—partially. If you can tell me anything about myself before yesterday, Miss, I'll . . ."

He choked on that, unable to finish. And behind the surface emotions, his mind was poised, sniffing for danger. There was no feeling of it, though he kept telling himself alternately that she had been the girl at the door and that she obviously had not been.

He'd seen her before. The tilt of her head, that unmatchable hair . . .

"You poor man!" Her voice was all sympathy, and the bag she was carrying dropped to the floor as she came over. "You mean you *really* can't remember—at all?"

"Not for the last seven months!"

She seemed surprised. "But that was when you answered my advertisement. I never saw you—though you did call me, and your voice sounds familiar. You sent me the check, and I mailed you the key. That was all."

"But I must have given you references—told you something—"

Again, she shook her head. "Nothing. You said you were a teacher at CCNY, but that you were quitting, and wanted a place to use as an office. You didn't care what it was like. That's all."

Hawkes felt she was lying—but it could have been true. And in his present state he probably believed everyone was other than they seemed. He remembered the grey sedan rising to the roof—and the cat turning inside out—

Sickness hit at him. He groped back towards a chair, sinking into it. He'd almost found a refuge, and even hoped that he could find some of the missing past. Now . . .

He must have partially swooned. He heard vague sounds, and then she was putting something against his lips. It was bitter and hot, though it only remotely resembled coffee. He gulped it gratefully, not caring that it was sweet and black. He saw the bottle of old coffee powder, caked with age, and heard the water boiling on the stove. Idly, he wondered whether he'd bought the jar originally or she had. Then his senses snapped back.

207

"Thanks," he muttered thickly. He groped his way to his feet, his head slowly clearing. "I guess I'd better go now."

She forced him back into the chair. "You're in no condition to leave here, Will Hawkes. Ugh! Your shoes are filthy. Let me help you . . . there, isn't that better? Whatever you've been doing to yourself, you should be ashamed. You're going straight to bed while I clean some of this up!"

His head had sunk back on the table, and everything reached him through a thick fog. It wasn't right—girls didn't act that way to strange men who looked as if they'd come from a Bowery fight. Girls didn't take a man's clothes off. Girls didn't . . .

He let her half carry him into the bedroom, and tried to protest as she put him between clean sheets. He stared at the view of his lavender shorts against the fresh whiteness, while things seemed far away. He'd played with a girl named Ellen once, when he was eleven and she was nine. She'd had bright copper hair, and her name had been—what had it been? Not Ibañez. Bennett, that was it. Ellen Bennett.

He must have said it aloud. She chuckled. "Of course, Will. Though I never thought you'd be the same Will Hawkes. I knew it when I saw that scar on your shoulder, where you cut yourself sliding down our cellar door. Go to sleep."

Sliding down—sliding down into clouds of sleep. Sleep! She'd drugged him! Something in the coffee!

He jerked up, reaching for her, but she ducked aside, drawing on the tops to a pair of frilly pajamas. "Ellen, you—"

"Shh!" She pulled a robe over the pajamas and lay down, outside the blankets. "Shh, Will. You have to sleep. You're *so* tired, *so* sleepy . . ."

Her voice was soothing, and the fingers along the base of his neck were relaxing. He reached out a last inquiring finger of doubt for the feeling of danger, and couldn't

208

find it. This was as wrong as the other things had been wrong—but his mind let go, and he was suddenly asleep.

He awoke slowly, with a thick feeling in his mouth. Drugged! And the sense of danger had failed him again! He swung over sharply, reaching for her, but she was gone.

His clothes lay beside him, neatly pressed, and he grabbed for them. There was a pair of socks, too large, but better than none. His muscles felt wrong as he began dressing, but the feeling wore away. The clock said that less than two hours had passed. If she'd put a drug in the coffee, it must have been one to which he was less sensitive than the average. She'd probably never suspected that he would waken.

A trace of fear struck through him, but it was weaker than before, and it seemed normal enough under the circumstances. He fumbled over the shoelaces, and then grabbed up his coat.

She'd bring *them* back. Maybe they'd used her as a spy!

But he couldn't understand why she'd bothered to press his clothes. And the apartment still puzzled him. Even if her story was true, it simply wasn't the sort of place where a girl like her would live. Nor was it fixed as she might have arranged a place, even allowing for what he might have done to it in seven months.

He reached automatically for the lock in the dim hall, and realized his hands knew the door, whatever else was true. Then he went out and down the stairs. He heard a babble of kids' voices, part in English and part in a sort of Spanish. That meant that things were normal, to the casual observer along the street. But he knew it was poor evidence that things really were as they should be. He stood in the comparative darkness of the hall, staring out. Nothing was wrong, so far as he could see.

Hawkes shoved past the women on the steps and headed toward the subway, trying not to seem in a hurry. His eyes turned up to the roof of the parking garage, but he could see nothing there; he'd half-expected that the slim young man would be parked up on the roof, waiting.

Then the fear began, mounting slowly. He jerked around quickly, scanning the street. For a second, he thought he saw the slim figure, but it was only a back turned to him, and it disappeared into a barber shop. Probably someone else.

The fear mounted a little, and he found his steps quickening. He cut around the corner, where men were crowded into a little restaurant. He was heading into a dead-end street, but there was an alley leading from it. He had to keep off the main streets.

Footsteps sounded behind him.

He moved faster, and the footsteps also speeded up. He slowed, and they kept on. Then they were nearly behind him, just as he reached the alley and jerked back into it, grabbing for a broken bottle he had spotted.

"Will!" It was a gasping wheeze. "Will! For God's sake, it's only me. I know everything—your amnesia. But let me explain!"

It stopped him. He held the bottle carefully, as the fat figure of an old man stepped softly around the corner, fear written on every aged wrinkle. It was the man he'd stumbled into when he dashed out of his apartment.

But the fear there matched his own so completely that he dropped the bottle. The other man stood, trembling, gasping for breath. Then he gathered himself together, though his pudgy hands still clenched tightly, showing white knuckles.

"Will," he repeated. "You've got to believe me. I know about you. I want to help you—if there's any help for you, God forgive us both. And God have mercy on Earth. It's worse than you can believe—and different. It's ..."

Horror washed over the old man's face. He stood, fighting within himself. Hawkes felt his own neck hairs lift, and he drew back. For a second, the fat man seemed to

210

waver before him, as if his body were only a projection. Then it quieted.

"It—it almost had me . . ."

He turned back to Hawkes, trying to control the quivering muscles in his face. But his victory was still incomplete when he suddenly leaped up.

"Get back, Will. Oh, God oh, God!"

He leaped outwards, his fat old legs pumping savagely. Then the air seemed to quiver.

Where he had been, there was only a dark cloud of smoke, spreading outwards in a rough equivalent of his shape. A spurt of steam leaped upwards savagely, and the smoke seemed darker. It began to drift on the air, touched a building, and left a spot of smudginess before it drifted on, getting thinner with each gust of wind. It was as if every atom of his body had suddenly disassociated itself from every other atom.

Disintegration!

Hawkes found his fingernails cutting his palms, and there was blood flowing from his bitten tongue. He heard a hacking moan in his throat. He struggled against something that seemed to be holding him down, then leaped at least ten feet, to land running.

The alley was twisted and narrow. He shot down it and around a corner. A warehouse stood there, and he barely avoided the loading trucks. He was back near the apartment building where he'd found the girl, and he leaped to a door that showed. It seemed to be locked, but somehow he got through it. He seemed to melt through the door, though he wasn't sure whether his lunge had smashed it or whether his fingers had found the latch in time.

He ducked around loose-hanging electric wires, under twisted pipes, and across a pile of junk around a hot-water heater. He twisted and turned, to come into complete darkness, and halt short, listening.

The fear was going—and there was again no sound of

pursuit. But he couldn't be sure. He'd heard no sounds before the fat man had leaped away, but *they* had been there.

Silently and thickly, he cursed. To find a man who seemed to be his friend, and who knew about him—and then to have them kill that man with such horrible efficiency before he could learn what it was all about!

He gagged in the darkness, almost fainting again.

Then, slowly, it was too much. For the moment, he could run no more, and nothing seemed to matter. He understood his sudden bravado no better than the unnatural cowardice that had been riding his shoulders, but he shrugged and moved forward.

The dark passage led out to steps, that carried him up to the sidewalk, in front of the building. Ellen Ibañez— or Bennett—was less than five feet from him, and her eyes were fixed firmly on his face.

4

She seemed surprised, but tried to smile. "I thought I left you asleep, Will," she said, in a tone that was meant to be bantering. " 'Smatter, the fuse blow?"

He accepted the excuse for his presence in the basement. "Yeah, it did. You left the iron on. I wondered what happened to you?"

"Nothing. Just shopping. There wasn't a bit of food in the place—and I must say, Will, you aren't much of a housekeeper. I bought pounds of soap!"

He followed her up the stairs, and his key opened the door for them. He was still operating on the general belief that they'd be least likely to spot him where they had already found him once. If the girl had tipped them off, then they had it figured out that he had run off, and probably wouldn't be back.

He hoped so, at any rate.

She was talking too briskly, and she was too careful not to mention that the iron was cool, with its cord wrapped neatly around the handle. He offered no explanation, but let her babble on about the strange coincidence of his being *the* Will Hawkes, and how she'd almost forgotten the childhood days.

"How come the Ibañez?" he asked finally.

"Stage name! I tried to make a go of the musicals, but it wasn't my line, I found. But the name stuck."

"And where'd you learn how to drug coffee that way?"

She didn't change expression. There was even a touch of a twinkle in her eye. "Waitress in a combination bar and restaurant. You needed the sleep, Will. And I guess I still feel as much of a mother to you as I did when you used to get hurt, so long ago."

She had things out of the bags now, and he saw that she had been doing a lot of shopping. There had still been time enough to call the slim young man, though—or, he suddenly realized, the fat man. He had no more reason to believe her an enemy than a friend. Then he corrected that. If she'd known enough to call the fat man, and had been his friend, she could have told him things. She'd denied knowing anything, though.

He couldn't understand why he trusted her—and yet, somehow, he did. Even if he knew she'd called them, he would still have to trust her. He was sure now that she was lying, and that she had been the girl he'd first noticed —but that meant she'd been with the fat man. And the fat man had seemed to be his friend. Or had the man been set to lure him out, but miscalculated and gotten only what had been meant for Hawkes?

His head was spinning, and he gave it up. He was a fool to trust her simply because the fear feeling subsided around her—but he had nothing better to do than to follow his hunches, and then try to play the odds as best he could.

"Cigarettes," she said, handing him a pack of his brand. "And some for me. Shoe dye—your shoes need it, and I couldn't find a shoe store. I did get a shirt though, and a tie. You'll find a hat in that bag. Size seven and a quarter?"

He nodded gratefully, and went in to change. The old shirt had caught most of the cat's blood, and he needed a fresh one. There were a couple of spots on his trousers, but they'd do. And the sports jacket matched well enough. He daubed the dye onto his shoes—one of the combined polish and dye things.

"Cold cuts all right?" she asked, and he called back a vague answer that seemed to satisfy her. He was staring at the shoe dye.

It worked fairly well, when he experimented. He daubed it onto his hair with a wisp of cotton. His hair began to mat down, but he found that combing it out as he went along removed the worst of the wax and still left some of the color. It worked better than he had expected.

He found a bottle of something that smelled of alcohol and belonged in her cosmetics, and began removing most of the mess. By being careful, he got the wax and most of the dye smell off, while leaving his hair darker.

"Better wash up," she called.

There was a razor among the things she had bought. He daubed some of the dye on his upper lip, where the stubble of a mustache was showing. It was easier there, if it didn't wash off in soap and water.

Some of it did, but when he finished shaving he felt better. It wouldn't pass close inspection, but he now seemed to have darker hair, and it had exaggerated the little beginning of a mustache enough to make some change in his appearance.

He waited for her to comment, but she said nothing. He waited for her questions about what he was going to do, and her explanations that of course he couldn't stay there. She said none of those things. She went on talking idly while they ate. It didn't fit.

Finally he stood up and began taking down the rope

that was strung up over one end of the room—to use as a clothes line, he supposed. She looked up at that. "What—"

"You can fight, if you want to," he told her. "Or you can save yourself the headache of being knocked out. Take your choice. People don't pay much attention to screams in a place like this. And I'm not going to harm you, if you'll take it easy."

"You mean it!" Her eyes were huge in her face, and there was a touch of fright then. She gulped visibly, and then seemed to go limp. "All right, Will. In the bed-room?"

He nodded, and she went ahead of him. She didn't struggle, until he was about to gag her. Then she drew her head aside. "There's money in my bag, if you're going out."

He swore, hotly and sickly. If she'd only act just once as a normal female should! Maybe Irma had been a hysterical, cold-blooded bitch, but she couldn't have been that much different from other women—even the fiction he'd read indicated that Ellen should be anything but so damned coöperative!

"If you'll tell me what's going on, I'll still let you go," he suggested, drawing her hands tighter together.

"I can't, Will. I don't know."

He had to believe her—he knew she was telling the truth, at least to a major extent. And that made it just that much worse. He bound the gag over her mouth as gently as he could, and closed the door behind him. Her big eyes haunted him as he turned to the telephone.

The information girl at CCNY could only tell him that Wilbur Hawkes had resigned abruptly seven months before, and no one knew where he was—they had heard he was doing government research. He snorted at that—it was always the excuse when nobody knew anything.

He tried a few other numbers, and gave up. Nobody knew—and nobody seemed to react to his name any differently from what they would have done had he remained a quiet, professorish man minding his own business, instead of being chased by . . .

He couldn't complete that. The idea was still too fantastic. Even if there were alien life-forms that were subtly invading Earth, why should they pick on him? What good could a little, unimportant mathematician do them—particularly if they had the powers he already knew they possessed? It was a poor answer, though no harder to believe than that any group on Earth could so suddenly come up with miracles.

Anyhow, men knew enough already to be pretty sure that Mars and Venus wouldn't have creatures that could invade Earth—and the other planets were hopeless. Perhaps from another star—but that would mean violating the theories of mass-increase when approaching the speed of light, and he wasn't ready to accept that yet.

This time, he went out of the building without looking first. It could do no good—they could hide from him, he knew, and he would only call attention to himself by looking around. With the change in appearance, he might get by, particularly with Ellen's money. He moved rapidly toward Broadway, where he found a little clothing store and a ready-made suit that nearly fit him. The salesman there seemed unconcerned when he insisted the cuffs be turned up at once, and that he wanted to wear it immediately. It took nearly an hour, but he felt safe, for a change. A five-and-ten furnished a pair of heavy-rimmed glasses that seemed to have blanks in them, and he decided he might get by.

There was no evidence of pursuit. He caught a cab, and headed for the library. Ellen had been well-heeled—suspiciously so for a girl who lived in a cold-water flat like that; he'd peeled fifteen tens from her wallet, and there'd been more, not to mention the twenties. His conscience bothered him a bit, but he was in no position to worry too much.

The library was still the puzzle of the ages to him—

he'd used it half his life, and still found it impossible to guess why such a building had been chosen. But eventually he found the periodical room, and managed to be given a small table with a stack of newspapers and magazines.

The mathematics magazines interested him most. He pored through them, looking for a single hint of the things he had seen. Einstein's work on a unified field stood out, but no real advances had come from it. It was still a philosophical rather than an actual attack on physics—as beautiful as a new theology, and about as hard to utilize. He skimmed through the pages, but nothing showed. No real advance had been made since his memory had blanked out, except for one paper on variable stars, which was interesting but unhelpful.

He threw them aside in disgust. He knew that it was useless to look in other languages. Work couldn't be done without some first stages that would be reported, and any significant new theory would be picked up and spread. Science wasn't yet that completely under political wraps.

For a second, he stopped as he came to a paper bearing his by-line. Then he grimaced—it was an old one, just published—his attempt to find how the phenomena of poltergeists could be fitted into the theory of the conservation of energy, and his final proof that the whole business was sheer rubbish. It would be nice to be able to get back to a life where he could fool around with such learned jokes.

The newspapers, beginning with the last day he could remember, were almost as barren of results. There was a story of some new political tension, but without the strange overtones that should be there if any of the major powers—where all the major scientists would tend to be —had found something new. He'd studied the statistical analysis of mob psychology at times, and felt sure he could spot the signs.

He skimmed on, without results, until he finally came to the current newspaper. This he read more carefully.

There was no mention of him. But he found something on the fat man. It was a simple follow-up to the story about the scientist who'd turned himself in at Bellevue— the man had mysteriously disappeared, three hours later. And there was a picture—the face of the fat man, with "Professor Arthur Meinzer" under it.

Hawkes shoved the magazines and papers back, then went through the series of halls and stairs that led him to the main reference room, inconveniently located on the top floor. He found the book he wanted, and thumbed rapidly through it. Meinzer was listed on the bottom of page 972—but as he looked for the important details on 973, a pile of ashes dribbled onto the floor.

It was no use. They'd gotten there ahead of him.

He made one final attempt. He called the College, asking for Meinzer, to find that nobody even knew the name! He was sure they were lying—but he could do nothing about that. Maybe it was only because of the publicity— or maybe because someone or something had gotten to them first!

Fear was growing in him as he came out on the street. He ducked into a crowd and headed slowly into a corner drug store, trying to seem inconspicuous, but it mounted. They were near—they would get him! Run, GO!

He fought it down, and found that it was weakened, either by his becoming used to it, or because the urgency was less than it had been.

He ducked into a phone-booth and called the newspaper, keeping his eyes on both entrances to the store. It seemed to take forever to locate the proper man there, but finally he had his connection.

"Meinzer," the voice said, with a curious doubtfulness. "Oh, yeah. Mister, that story's dead! Call up . . ."

The telephone melted slowly, dropping into a little cold puddle on the floor!

Hawkes had felt the tension mounting, and he was prepared for anything. Now he found himself on the outside, darting across 42nd Street against the light, without even remembering leaving the booth. He stole a quick glance back, to see people staring at him with open mouths. He thought he saw a slim figure in grey tweeds, but he couldn't be sure—and there were probably thousands of such men in New York.

He darted into a bank, wormed his way around the various aisles, and out the back entrance. A cab was waiting there, and he held out a bill.

"I'm late, buddy. Penn Station!"

The cab-driver took the bill and the hint, and accelerated forward, just as the light was changing.

Penn Station was as good a place to try to get lost from pursuit as any. Hawkes examined his wallet, considering trying to get a train out—but he'd used up nearly all he had taken from Ellen.

And all his careful disguise had proved useless. They weren't fooled—and this business of dodging was wearing thin. By now, they'd know his habits!

He drew out a coin, and flipped it. It came up heads. He frowned, but there was nothing else to do. He moved down the ramp toward the subway that would carry him back toward Ellen's apartment. He was probably walking into their trap by now, but the coin was right. He had to free Ellen. If they got him, it couldn't be much worse for him.

Then he shuddered. He couldn't know whether it would be worse for his country, or even his world. He couldn't really know anything.

5

It was growing dark as he walked down Sixty-Sixth, eying every man suspiciously, and knowing his suspicion would do no good. He was still trying to think, though he knew his thoughts were as useless as his suspicions.

If he could remember! His mind came up sharply

against leaving Irma and taking out the mail; then it went abruptly blank. What had been in the letter? It had been from a professor—it might have been from Professor Meinzer. That would tie in neatly. But Meinzer was dead, and he couldn't remember. They'd stripped him of his memory. How? Why? Were they trying to prevent his giving information to others—or were they trying to get something from him? And what could he know?

He'd dabbled with ESP mathematically enough to disbelieve in it, but now he found himself wondering if it could exist. Could they be tracking him by some natural or mechanical ability to read his mind? He strained his own mind to find a whisper of foreign thought, outside his own brain. He drew a blank, of course, as he'd expected.

There were no answers. They could play with him, like a cat juggling a mouse, letting him almost learn something —and then, always, they arrived just in time to prevent his success!

Put a rat in a maze where it can't learn the path, and it goes insane. But what good would he be to anyone if they drove him insane? And why bother with all that when they could silence him as well by killing him?

He'd forgotten to watch, and was surprised to find his feet on the steps of the apartment building. He glanced back, and bumped into someone.

"Sorry." The words came from beside him, automatically, and he turned to see the slim young man stepping aside. For a second, their eyes met squarely. A row of teeth flashed in a brief smile as the man started around him. "Guess I was thinking. Should have watched where I was going."

The man went on down the street, and turned in at the restaurant entrance.

Hawkes lifted a foot that weighed a ton and slowly closed his mouth. He'd been facing away from the street light—and his face might have been hard to see. Yet . . .

It didn't fit. The young man must have known him!

He blanked it from his mind. He couldn't believe that it was anything but lack of recognition. It was hard to see here, where the other was facing the light and he was in the shadow.

But it still meant that they were waiting, nearby.

He dashed up the stairs, expecting an ambush at both landings. The normal sounds of the apartment house went on. He listened at his door, but he could hear nothing but the same drip he had heard before. Slowly, he inserted the key and went in. The same small bulb was on. He crept along, trying to move silently on floors that insisted on creaking. The living room was as he had left it, and he caught sight of Ellen on the bed.

He found a mirror over one of the dressers, and used that to study more of the bedroom. It seemed as empty as before.

Finally, he stepped inside. There was no one there but Ellen, and she seemed to be asleep, doubled up in a position that might have made the unkind cords easier to stand. She moaned slightly as he untied her gently, but she didn't awaken. Her breathing was regular, and her breath had the odd muskiness of someone who has slept.

He found a bottle of liquor on the shelf where she had put it, and rinsed out a couple of glasses. It was good liquor—good enough to take without mixers, as they'd have to do.

She came awake when he called her, rubbing her eyes and then her wrists, where the cords had left a mark. But she was smiling. "Hi, Will. I knew you'd come back. Hey, not on an empty stomach."

"You need it—and so do I," he told her. "Bottoms up!"

They were big glasses. She gasped over it, but she downed it, then reached for the water he had brought as a chaser. She swallowed, and blinked tears out of her eyes. "I don't usually drink."

He made no comment, but refilled the glass. The liquor had less effect on him than he'd expected, though he'd

221

always had a good head for it. It took some of the edge off his worrying, though.

She giggled suddenly, and he frowned. She really couldn't take much on an empty stomach, it seemed. Then he shrugged. Let her drink—maybe if he could get her drunk he could find something out; at least, he might learn whether the slim young man had been there during the day.

"Like when you found your dad's cider," she said, and giggled again. "You got awful—hp!—awful drunk, Willy, didn't you? You were—so—funny!"

She was trying to be careful with her words already. She slid around, doing things that brought more honestly beautiful thigh into the light than Will had seen in ten years. He reached to adjust her dress, and she giggled again, sliding against him.

"'You kissed me then, Willy. Remember? Bet you don' remember!"

He began it coldly, deliberately. If he could work on her emotions enough, he'd crack the wall of evasion and lies, somehow. He reached for her, calculating what would arouse her without causing any shock to bring her back to her senses.

He hadn't counted on the quickness of her response, nor the complete acceptance of his right with which she took his advances. The liquor had reduced her to the stage of a little girl who completely trusted her companion. She seemed as unconscious of her body as a child might be.

Instead of protesting, she reached down and began unfastening the buttons on her dress. " 'Syour turn now, Willy. Put you to bed last night, you put me to bed t'night. Then you gotta kiss me good night. Nighty-night, nighty-night."

He felt like a heel at first. And then he began to feel like a man—any man around a beautiful girl half-undressed, and getting more so.

She slipped under the sheets, tossing out the last of her

clothing, and crooning happily. "Gotta kiss me good-night, Willy. Nighty-night!"

He yanked the pull-cord savagely, cutting off the light, then fumbling in the darkness. After what seemed hours of awkwardness, he slid in beside her, feeling her arms go around him in complete acceptance. To hell with them! They could chase him some other time!

He pulled her to him, while his blood beat in his neck, and he began to lose any conscious volition in what he was doing. He drew her tighter, while a great clot of emotion set fire to his brain. He—

Cold beyond anything he had known bit at him. A tremendous pressure within him seemed about to force him to explode outwards, and the shock jerked him into full awareness.

In a split second, he swung his eyes from the great, jagged landscape on which he stood, up an impossible range of mountains that were all harsh blacks and cold whites, to a cold black sky in which the stars were blazing specks without a flicker. He saw the Earth above him, bigger than the moon had ever been, and with the dim outlines of continents showing through the soft stuff that must be clouds.

He was on the moon! And naked, without air!

Almost at once, something clapped down around him, and the pressure let up, while heat seemed to leap into the rocks under his feet and make them comfortable. He gulped down the air that somehow seemed to stay close to him, instead of evaporating into the vacuum.

The moon! Now they had him!

Fear blazed in him—a stark, unreasoning terror that was like a physical thing. *Run—but you can't run! They've got you! You can't escape!*

The light blotted out, and then snapped on, more strongly. He stood in the kitchen of the cold-water apartment, still naked, with bits of chalky-dust between his toes.

He had no time for reason. His brain seemed to have jumped over a hurdle and come down in a puddle beyond, foul with the stuff it had found there. He heard Ellen shriek, and then cry out again.

He lurched into the bedroom, while she let out another gurgling cry as the light showed him in the doorway. She came out of the bed, leaping for him, crying his name. But he wanted none of her act. He shook her off.

"You damned alien! You filthy monster, disguised as a girl! When you get in a spot where I'm sure to find you out, you have a cute trick up your sleeve, but it won't work. You cān send me back there—back to the rest of your kind, from wherever they came. But you won't fool me into thinking you're human again. You can't pass one test!"

He wouldn't be fooled into thinking it was a dream, either. He'd been physically on the moon—the very dust on his feet proved that. They might drive him insane, but they wouldn't do it that way.

She was crying now, gasping out words that he only half heard. "I'm human, Will. Oh, I'm human!"

"Then prove it! Come here and prove it!"

She cried again at that, as he pulled her down with him. But slowly her crying quieted.

He awoke slowly, with sunlight streaming in the windows, and reached for her. He owed her more apologies than one, though he wasn't too sorry about most of it. She had proven herself human. And virginally so. Her complete surrender still left something warm inside him, where only the madness and the fear had been before.

Then he jerked upright, as he found her gone. He cursed himself for a fool, and listened for a stir and bustle from the kitchen, but there was none.

He was getting used to dressing with a feeling of dire pressure driving him on. He finished rapidly, and yanked the bedroom door open just as he heard the outer lock

224

click. She was coming in with a bottle of cream and a package of sausage as he reached the kitchen, and there was a smile tucked into the corner of her mouth.

And this time, he knew she wouldn't have betrayed him. Yet the fear lifted in him. He darted past her as she leaned to kiss him, heading for the door. The room seemed to quiver. The hall was filled with a faint golden haze!

He had to escape! He jerked backwards, caught her hand, and pulled her. "Ellen! We've got to get out!"

It was a half-articulate shout, and she resisted, but he began dragging her after him. Something fumbled at the lock, and a key slipped into it. The door opened.

Hawkes didn't know what kind of an alien he expected. He knew that men could never have thrown him instantly to the moon and back, not in another thousand years. It had to be a monster.

But he should have known that monsters here came in human form—they'd have to.

The fear rose to a shriek in his brain, and then died down as the human form entered. It was too normal— too familiar. A medium-sized man, dressed in a suit as inconspicuous as his own, wearing a silly little mustache that no outland monster should ever wear.

The creature jumped in, slamming the door behind it. "Stay there! You can't risk it outside now! We've got to—"

Hawkes hit the figure with his shoulder, in the best football fashion he could muster. It could try—but it couldn't keep him and Ellen here to be burned in their heat-ray bath, or treated to whatever alien torture they had in mind. He felt his shoulder hit. And he knew he'd missed. It was an arm that he struck against, and the arm brought him upright, while a second arm drew back and came forward with a savage right to his jaw.

He went out with a dull plopping sound in his brain. Then, slowly, an ache came out of the blackness, and the beginning of sound. He was fighting out of the unconsciousness, fighting against time and the monster who'd try to steal Ellen.

But Ellen's hands were on his head, and an ice-cold towel was wet against his forehead. "Will! Will!"

He groaned and sat up. The other—alien or human—was gone.

"Where—?" he began.

She was trying to help him to his feet, and he got up groggily, with his head beginning to clear.

"He just ran out Will." Ellen was crying, this time almost silently, with the words coming out between shakes of her shoulders. "Will, we've got to get out. We've got to. There are men coming for you. They'll be here any minute. And it's wrong—it won't work! Oh, Will, hurry!"

"Men? Men are coming?" He'd almost forgotten that it could be men who were after him.

"I called them, Will. I thought I had to. But it won't work. Will, do anything you like, but *get out!* They're fools. They . . ."

He opened the door and peered out into the hall, which seemed quiet. He'd been a fool again. He'd trusted her for some reason, as if a body and loyalty had to go together. They'd been smart, picking a virgin for the job. It must have cost them plenty, unless they'd twisted her mind somehow. Maybe they could do it.

But he knew that whatever they looked like, it couldn't be men who'd meet him out there.

"Why?" he asked, and was surprised at the flatness of his voice.

She shook her head. "Because I'm a fool, Will. Because I thought they could help you—until *he* came! And because I was still in love with you, even if you'd forgotten me."

But the fear inside him was drowning out her words, and the golden haze was faint in the air again.

"Okay," he said finally. "Okay, don't burn her too, now that she's done your dirty work. I'm coming."

The haze disappeared slowly, and he started down the stairs, still holding her hand.

6

There were uniformed men with guns in the street. He'd heard shooting as he came down the stairs, and had shoved Ellen behind him. But it was silent now. People with dazed, frightened faces were still darting into the houses, leaving the street to the men with the guns.

Hawkes marched forward grimly, perversely stripped of fear, even though he was sure some of the men out there were monsters and others were their dupes. He tapped one of the men on the shoulder.

"Okay, here I am. The girl goes free!"

The man spun around as if mounted on a ball bearing and pulled by strings. The gun fell from his hands. His emotion-taut face loosened suddenly, seemed to run like melted wax, and congealed again in an expression of utter idiocy. He gargled frothily, and then screamed—high and shrill, like a tortured woman.

Suddenly he was a lunging maniac, racing up the street.

Now the others were running—some toward cars and some toward the corners, running desperately on the flat of their feet, without any spring to their motions.

Hawkes jerked his eyes down toward the big parking garage near which most of them had been posted, and the glow that had been in the corner of his vision was gone. The men seemed to be coming out of a trance. They were breaking away, some in uniform and some in plain clothes, dropping their guns and fleeing.

Three men alone were left.

Hawkes ducked back into the hall of the apartment, dragging Ellen with him. The glass of the door was somewhat dirty, but it made a dim mirror in front of him. He could see the slim young man and two others frantically gathering up the dropped guns and piling them into a car. Two of the men took off, but the leader turned up the street, moving deliberately and heading for the apartment house.

Hawkes could make no sense of it—unless it was another of the seeming tricks designed to drive him out of his mind. He had decided he was one of the rats in the maze that didn't go crazy—the pressure could drive him out of his mind temporarily, but it couldn't keep him insane.

He didn't wait to see what had happened, or whether the sirens that were sounding now were reinforcements for the men with guns, or the real police. He didn't bother with the slim young man anymore. They'd apparently used their dupes to frighten out the people, and then had scared off the dupes—the poor humans who didn't know what it was all about. Now two of the three were gone with the evidence, and the third monster was coming.

But Hawkes had escaped before. Sooner or later, they'd catch him—once they were sure he wouldn't be driven insane.

Or was this the beginning of insanity—a delusion of power, a feeling that he could escape? He could never know, if it were. He had to assume that he was sane.

He lurched inside and back behind the stairs, while the young man in the grey tweeds went up them. Then he headed out into the street. The siren was near now—and tardily, he realized that the siren might herald the coming of the real monsters. It was as easy for them to be a cop as any other human!

He jerked open the door of the nearest car, pulled Ellen in, and kicked the motor to life. He gunned away from the curb, tossed it into second, and twisted around the corner, straight toward the siren that was nearest. At the last minute he jerked to the side of the street, to let the police car shoot by. "Never run from a tiger—run toward it. It sometimes works, and it's no worse."

The car was a big one, and the motor purred smoothly. He glanced down at the dash, and frowned. There was no key in the switch. For a second he stared at it, and then grinned. He'd picked a monster's car, apparently— they'd done a neat job of duplicating, but they didn't need all the safeguards that humans used, and the switch had obviously been a dummy.

He looked at the buttons on the dash, wondering which would make it levitate. But he had no desire to test it, nor to stay in an auto which could probably be traced very easily.

He braked to a halt outside the subway and led Ellen down.

"We're down to the last hole," he told her as the train pulled out of the station. "How much money do you have?"

She shook her head, and held up her arm. "I left it, Will."

They were beyond the last hole, then. He realized now that as long as they'd been in a crowded apartment house, filled with other humans, it had proved a tough nut to crack for the aliens. But on the move . . .

"Maybe we have a chance," he told her. "If humans were after me, it'd be tough—but these things have to avoid the police."

She looked at him, misery on her face. "There are no aliens, Will. Those men you saw were police—and F.B.I. men. That's where I reported you."

He stared at her, but she was serious.

"But there was nothing about me in the papers, Ellen."

She pointed across the aisle. Spread over two columns on a front page, an older picture of him showed plainly. And even at the distance, the heading was boldly legible.

$100,000 REWARD FOR THIS MAN!

He stared at the figure twice, unbelieving. He was no longer alone against a small group of humans or aliens. Now every living human on the face of the planet would be looking for him!

He could feel their hot breath on his neck, feel eyes staring at him through the papers. Fear began to rise in him, to be halted as the train ground to a new station. Ellen jerked him out, and he moved with her. It wasn't safe to stay too long with one group, until they began to wonder and compare faces!

"But what—"

She shook her head. "Nothing, Will. I don't know. What can we do?"

He'd been wondering, while they moved quietly through the people and up the stairs. There was no place left. He had only a few dollars and some change, and that would be of no use. They'd have to dig a hole in the ground and pull it over them . . .

It joggled his memory, and he grabbed her hand and jerked open the door of a cab that was waiting for the light. He barked out an address at the corner of Tenth Avenue and one of the streets below Twentieth. The driver got into motion, not bothering to look back. It was near enough to where Hawkes wanted to be—an old warehouse, with a loading platform. He'd played there as a kid, climbing back under it and digging holes down into the damp, soft earth, as kids have always done. He'd been by there since, and it had remained unchanged.

Sooner or later, the aliens would locate them. But it would give them a chance to rest—perhaps long enough for him to waylay someone at night and steal enough for them to leave town. That wouldn't be much help—but it was all he had left to count on.

He saw trucks loading there as he paid the cab-driver. His heart sank abruptly, until he studied the way the big trailer was parked. If he watched carefully, he could slip under it from the side, and there was a chance he wouldn't be seen.

Luck, for once, was with him as he drew Ellen under the trailer and the platform. The old holes were covered with rubble, but he scraped it aside and found an entrance barely big enough for them to wiggle through. Then

230

they were in a dark pocket under the back of the platform, barely big enough for them to sit upright. The hole had seemed bigger when he was a kid.

Outside, he heard a boy's voice yelling. "Monster attacks cops! Monster kills five cops! Extra Paper!"

Now he was a monster—to be shot on sight, probably.

"I shouldn't have brought you into this, Ellen," he said bitterly. "I should have left you. You don't even know what's going on—you haven't the faintest idea. If it were just humans, as you think . . ."

She snuggled against him in the coldness of the little cave. "Shh. I got you into it. I—I ratted on you, Scarface!"

But he couldn't reply to her attempt at humor. There was no fear now—not even the relief of fear. He'd felt brave for a few minutes, back in the hallway of the apartment. Now the chips were down, and sunk. They were here, in a dank hole, without food, and without a chance, while all the world above searched for him to kill him—and while still-unknown aliens with unknown reasons played out their little game with consummate skill that would inevitably locate him.

It might take them a day—they probably would do nothing to him until night came, and the warehouse street was deserted! Ten more hours!

If he only knew what they wanted of him, or why? If he could remember!

He sat there, numbed within himself. Ellen leaned her head forward onto his lap, and he began stroking her hair softly. He'd have liked to have had a chance with her. One night wasn't enough for a whole life. He reached down to draw her face to his . . .

Fear hit him, as something rustled behind him. He tried to turn and look, but his neck refused. The fear grew to panic, and swelled higher as the golden haze began to spread around the little cave. Then his muscles snapped his head around sharply. The slim young man was crawling toward them, holding something that looked like a

231

flashlight. Behind it, he could see the tense lips drawn back over clenched teeth. The man wasn't smiling now. He opened his mouth, just as the thing like a flashlight sprang into light.

No time seemed to elapse, but suddenly Ellen and the young man were both gone, and he sat in the dark hole alone. He let out an animal cry and dashed out, crawling through the opening, and kicking the rubble back as he went. He slipped out, and under the trailer. But there was no sign. They'd taken her, and left him unconscious!

He groaned, trying to figure. He'd always gone back to the same place to hide, since he'd found it. They must expect him back there. They'd take Ellen there and wait for him, drugging her, changing her mind, setting her up to use against him. The first time hadn't worked, but they'd try it again. It had to be that. If they hadn't taken her there, he had no way of finding her, and he had to find her.

He began running down the street, forcing himself to believe she was there. Then he slowed. It would do no good to have them all notice him, here on the street. Someone might recognize him then. He turned around, walking back to the bus stop.

He hunched down on the seat of the bus, which seemed to crawl up Tenth Avenue. But no one noticed him in the almost empty vehicle. There was nobody at his bus stop and the street seemed deserted until he turned the corner to the apartment-house.

There men were drawing up in cars—men with guns in their hands. He made a final dash for the apartment entrance. This must be the real show—for which the other had been only a dress rehearsal to throw him off balance. Well, they could wait.

He fumbled with the lock, until he finally got it open. Then he jumped in, slamming the door shut behind him. Ellen stood there, and the creature that had assaulted him before was pawing at her. But he had no time for the monster.

"Stay there!" he shouted at her. "You can't risk it outside now! We've got to—"

He saw she wasn't listening to him. He had to get rid of the creature somehow, if he could get it far enough away from her. Then they'd find some way to get outside without going out through the entrance.

The creature sprang at him awkwardly. His left arm darted down to catch one shoulder, and his right hand swung back and up. There was a savage satisfaction in seeing the creature crumple.

Ellen's voice reached him. "Will! Will, before I go crazy . . ."

"You're free," he told her. "Go down the fire escape and leave that thing here. I'll get rid of them out front somehow."

He shut the door again, and went down. The words had sounded brave enough, but there had been no courage behind them. Fear still rode him, like the little golden haze that again hovered over him, showing they had spotted him.

He walked out with it thick around him, rising slowly in temperature. They had him—but Ellen might get away. He walked down the steps, his hands up. They drew back, surprise and something else on their features, their eyes on the haze that surrounded him. They were shouting, but he couldn't hear the words over the shrieks of the people along the street, rushing inside or trying to drag their kids to safety.

Hawkes doubled his legs under him and leaped. He was still attacking the tiger—the slim young man, down by the parking garage, directing the new crop of dupes.

His charge carried him there, while the young man slipped aside. Then someone fired a gun.

He heard the young man yell hoarsely. "No shooting! Stop it! Damn it, NO SHOOTING!"

They weren't paying any attention to the shouts. Bullets ticked against the building. Hawkes ducked frantically, physical fear knotting his stomach.

Suddenly he seemed to jerk upwards, to find himself suspended in mid-air, fifty feet off the ground, just beyond the edge of the roof. He stared down at the men, dizzy with the height, but no longer surprised by anything. The men were pointing their guns upwards, while the young man leaped about among them. Bullets were splatting out, though none came near Hawkes. They seemed to ricochet off the air a few feet in front of him.

The slim young man drew back. And now the rubble and stones along the street began to lift, and to drive savagely at the attackers. A gale swept along the street, though Hawkes could feel no breath of air, and the force of it was enough to knock most of them down.

They got up and began running, dashing away from the super-science that the young man seemed bent on turning against his own troop of dupes, now that they were out of control.

Hawkes came drifting downward. He started to cry out in fear, until he noticed that the ground was coming up at him slowly, and that he was slipping sideways. He landed around the corner, as gently as a feather.

Surprisingly, everyone was gone when he risked a glance at the scene of the fight, except for the young man, who was darting into the apartment house. Then Hawkes cursed, as the creature with whom he had fought came running out, with Ellen behind, to leap into a car and drive off. The sound of sirens grew louder, and a police car swung onto the Avenue.

Hawkes straightened up slowly as it hit him. It had been the same scene he'd gone through before, this very morning—but with himself in the middle! He shot a glance at the sun; it was still to the east, though his memory of the day indicated that it should have been after noon.

Time! They'd twisted him back through time—the weapon that had looked like a flashlight must have tossed him hours backwards, instead of knocking him out. He'd been attacking himself there in the hallway of his apartment! He'd knocked himself out. And the fight he had just been through was the same fight that he had seen come to its end before!

Now, his younger self and Ellen must be just fleeing toward the hideout under the loading platform, with the slim man still following. If he could get there in time, before the man could run off with Ellen. . . .

7

The paper he'd found kept the other passengers on the bus from seeing him, but he was too deep in his own thoughts to read it. His eyes roamed back to the story of the cop-killing monster—not about him, but about a seemingly harmless florist in Brooklyn who'd suddenly gone berserk and rushed down the streets with a knife. He'd been wrong about the headline.

And he'd been wrong in thinking anyone would try to kill him on sight. The reward notice and picture of himself were in front of his eyes—but it was a reward for information, and there was a huge box that proclaimed he was *not* a criminal and must not be harmed, or even allowed to know he was recognized.

The new facts only confused the issue. He twisted about in his mind, trying to explain why the young man had left him to drift down, and had gone rushing into the apartment. He had been ready to be collected—and he'd been left uncollected!

The girl had said there were no aliens. Now he wondered. She had known more than he'd found out from her—she'd known his brand of cigarettes, even. And there had been that shopping list, with the lipstick on it—the same type he now remembered her using. He'd known her before—and not just as a little girl. That tied him in with Meinzer, who was a mystery in himself.

He puzzled over it. The things that had happened to him had always been preceded by violent emotion, instead of followed by it. Usually, it had been fear—but sometimes some other emotion, as had been the case just before he was suddenly shifted to the Moon. Whenever he seemed on the verge of discovering something or emotionally upset, it hit at him. Did that mean he was only susceptible to the phenomena when off balance? It still didn't account for the fact that some of the things hadn't directly affected him at all.

The more he knew, the less he knew.

He got off the bus and headed for the warehouse. This time he had to wait before he could see a chance to dart under the trailer and into the entrance. He noticed that the grey sedan was parked nearby.

They were still there! He heard Ellen's voice, sounding as if she had been crying, and then an answer from the other. He felt his way carefully over the rubble, working as close as he could. Now, if he sprang the few feet . . .

". . . must be a time-jump," the man's voice said, doubtfully. "I tell you, Ellen, those damned fools were firing at him, up there in the air, while you were still with him in the apartment. That time shift is an angle on this psi factor stuff we hadn't expected."

The voice stopped for a moment. Then it picked up again. "Drat it! I wish you hadn't called the F.B.I. on him—they got rattled when he came out looking like a saint in a halo and jumped fifty feet up to float around. Some fool started shooting, and the rest joined in."

"I had to—he was talking about alien monsters. I thought he was going crazy, Dan. I couldn't tell him anything—I promised him I wouldn't, and I kept my promise. But I thought enough of them might catch him, somehow . . . Dan, can't we find him now? He needs us!"

Hawkes lay frozen. He tried to move forward, but his body was tensed, waiting for more. If something happened now . . .

"Alien monsters?" Dan's voice grew bitter. "It is alien —and a monster. This psi factor . . ."

The words blurred, and seemed to echo and re-echo

236

inside Hawkes' head. That made twice he'd heard them mention the psi factor—the strange ability a few people claimed they had to perform seeming miracles. Men who had it could make dice roll the way they wanted. Young girls sometimes had it before puberty, and could throw heavy objects around a room without touching them; they didn't even know they were the cause of the motion, but blamed it on poltergeists. Other men caused strange accidents—fires, for instance—the old salamander legend!

There'd been a piece of paper—psi equals alpha; the psi factor was the beginning for mankind. But it had been wrong. He'd changed that, on the other side. It should have read psi equals omega, the absolute end.

He gasped hoarsely, and heard their startled voices stop, while the flashlight beam swung around, picking him out in the darkness. He felt Ellen and her younger brother, Dan, pulling him forward into the little cave with them, and he heard their voices questioning him. But his head was spinning madly under the sudden flood of memories that the missing key word had suddenly brought back.

The letter from Professor Meinzer had been about his paper on poltergeists, which the old man had seen before publication. Meinzer had been doing research on the psi factor for the government, and he needed a mathematician —even one who proved something that he knew wasn't true, provided the mathematics could handle his theories.

Hawkes' head was suddenly brimming with mental images of the seven months, during which he had worked on the mathematics to tie down the strange pattern of brain waves the old professor had found in the minds of those who had the mysterious psi factor. Dan had worked with them, in the little cluttered apartment, building the apparatus they needed. It was through Dan that Ellen had been hired, as a general assistant and secretary.

There had been only the four of them, working in deepest secrecy in a dingy three-room apartment which the government had felt was more suitable to maintain complete security than any deeply buried laboratory could have been. Ellen made a pretense of living there, and it was a neighborhood where no landlady worried about the men who went to a girl's place, provided everything was quiet.

They'd succeeded, too—they'd found the tiny bundle of cells that controlled the psi factor, and learned to stimulate them by artificial wave trains and hypnosis. But the small group in the top division of the government to whom they were responsible had demanded more proof.

Hawkes had treated himself secretly, not knowing that Meinzer had done the same two days before. And both had learned the same thing. The wild talents appeared, but they couldn't be controlled. Meinzer hadn't found security in the hospital, hard as he'd tried to find it. He'd gotten up in the middle of the night and walked through the solid wall, unable to stop until he was back with the group.

Hawkes had tried another way to stop the wild abilities that operated without his conscious control. He'd prepared a new hypnotic tape, worded to make him forget everything he knew, or even the fact that he had worked on the psi factor. He'd put in commands that would make him avoid any reference to it, so that he couldn't learn accidentally. He'd ordered his brain to have nothing to do with it. He'd drugged himself with a combination of opiates and hypnotics that should have knocked out a horse. Then he'd telephoned Dan to have men pick him up in an hour and keep him drugged. He'd turned on the tape recorder and stumbled back to the bed.

He groaned as he remembered his failure. "It's the ultimate, absolute alien, all right—the back of a man's own mind," he said. "It's Freud's unconscious, with no censor. The psi factor is controlled by that, and not by the conscious mind. And the id is a primitive beast—it operates on raw impulse, without reason or social consciousness. Every man's unconscious is back in the jungle, before civilization—and we've given that alien thing the

238

greatest power that could exist when we wake up the psi power."

"Meinzer thought it was controlled, for a while," Ellen said. "He came when Dan and I called him. I went with him up to your apartment, while Dan called the men to carry you away. But we couldn't reach you—Meinzer barely touched the tape-recorder when something seemed to pick us up and drive us out of the room and down the stairs. We were just going back when you came out."

She shuddered, and Hawkes nodded. He'd obviously used that psi factor to throw off the drugs at the first sign of anyone near him. He told them sickly what had happened to the old man.

"So I killed him," he finished bitterly.

Dan shook his head. "No. Your psi factor works differently. You control heat and radiation, you can move yourself or any object in space for almost any distance, instantly if you want, and it seems you can do the same through time. But you can't disintegrate things, as Meinzer could. He had a suicide urge—we knew that before. When it got out of control again, he blew himself up— just as your dominant urge to protect yourself did all those things around you."

Hawkes grimaced. It wasn't pleasant to know that he'd been doing all the things he'd blamed on monsters. He'd somehow remembered that someone was supposed to come to get him, and he'd run out in wild fear, while his unconscious mind blasted the apartment with heat to destroy all traces. He'd blasted down the subway entrance with another bolt of energy to make his getaway. The poor cat had surprised him, and been killed—the only really evil thing he had done. His unconscious gone wild had tossed Dan's car two hundred feet to the roof of the garage. When it had found him losing control emotionally with Ellen, it hadn't let his conscious brain give it the information it needed—it had simply thrown him completely off Earth, pulled air to him, and warmed the rocks. Then, when it found the Moon unfit for life, it had thrown him back to his own world. It had tossed him hours back in time this morning, lifted him into the air while it pelted his "enemies" with rocks, and built a wall around him by throwing the bullets back instantly.

And it had somehow clung to the implanted idea that he must not find out about himself. It had destroyed anything where the written word might give him a hint, and it had even melted the telephone so that he couldn't continue listening to other evidence.

It had probably done a thousand other things that he couldn't even remember, whenever its wild, reasonless fears were aroused and it decided that he had to be protected!

"You should have killed me," he told them. But he knew that they couldn't have done it.

"We had to let you sweat it out. You made us promise not to tell you anything, and we thought you might be right," Ellen told him. "We thought that it might adjust after while. All we did was to try to pick you up, until we knew it was impossible."

"Until Ellen tipped off the Government men," Dan added. Hawkes could imagine what their reaction had been to a man with his power running wild. He was surprised that they had even bothered to make an attempt to see that he wasn't harmed.

He shrugged helplessly. "And where does it leave us now—beyond this hole in the ground?"

"The Government's put about fifty specialists on the notes you and Meinzer left," Dan answered, but there was no assurance in his voice. "They're trying to find some way to bring the psi factor under the control of your logical rational mind."

He got to his knees and began crawling out of the little cave, while Hawkes tried to help Ellen follow him. Outside, Dan knocked off the dirt from his clothes and headed for his sedan.

Hawkes followed, for want of anything better to do.

He knew the answers now—and he was worse off than

ever. Instead of a horde of outside aliens, he had one single monster in his own skull, where he could never fight it, or even hope to escape it. He was the ancient Golem, the horror created by arcane knowledge to destroy all before it.

The power had been meant as a hope for the world. A man who could work such seeming miracles might have ended the threat of war; he'd have been the perfect spy, or better at attack than a hundred hydrogen bombs that had to smash whole cities to remove a few men and weapons. But now the world was better off without him. So long as he still lived, there would be nothing but danger from the alien monster in his head. He had no idea of his limits—but he was sure that it could trigger the energies of the universe to move the whole world out of its orbit, if that seemed necessary for his personal survival!

8

Hawkes leaned forward cautiously as the grey sedan moved up Tenth Avenue. His finger found the gun in Dan's coat pocket, and he pulled it out stealthily.

He knew that the only answer for him was suicide. He had to destroy himself, since no one else could!

He propped it up, pointing at his head, and his thumb pressed back on the trigger, further and further, until he felt sure the smallest change would set it off. Then he waited for the rough spot in the street or the sudden stop at a light that would do the trick before he could stop it.

The car lurched—and the gun suddenly vanished, leaving his hand empty.

His responses were too quick—and his mind wasn't waiting, once it knew there was danger. He slumped back on the rear seat, trying to think. Drugs were out—he knew his system could throw them off.

But he couldn't remove himself!

He lifted his wrist to his teeth, and bit down savagely. If he could sever an artery . . . Pain shot through him, and he stared down at the blood.

Then the blood was gone, and the wound was closing before his eyes, until only smooth flesh remained. His mind could juggle the cells back into their original form.

It would have to be sudden, complete death.

And no death was that sudden! For a fraction of a second, there'd be life left—and during that split second the damage would be repaired, or he would be shifted from danger.

There was no way out—unless he could pull himself to another planet, or throw himself back into the dim past. But that would take voluntary control, and he knew now that was hopeless; hours of effort had shown him how impossible that was. He hadn't been able to lift a crumb of bread from the table deliberately, in his original tests after he had treated himself.

He was faced with a problem that had to be solved—and there was no possible solution that he could find.

No man could face that dilemma forever without going insane. Hawkes shuddered, trying to picture what might happen if he went mad and the wild talents began operating at every whim of his crazed mind!

Ellen shouted suddenly, grabbing for the wheel. Hawkes felt himself tense and begin lifting from the seat of the car. But there was no visible danger, and Dan was slowing to a halt at the curb. Hawkes' body dropped back slowly.

"Dan," Ellen was whispering hoarsely. "Dan, we can't. If we take him back, they'll find him, and they'll know what he can do. They'll kill him. Eventually, they'll kill Will!"

Hawkes started to protest, but Dan's words cut him short.

"You're right, sis. They'll wait their time, until he won't know when to expect it—and then they'll drop an H-bomb on him, if they have to. That's faster than any nerve impulse!"

He swung back to face Hawkes, reaching for the door of the car. "Get out, Will—and get as far away as you can. I'm not going to drive you to your death. They'll get you eventually, but I won't be the one to make it easier for them!"

Hawkes jerked. The old fear came back suddenly.

You can't escape! They'll get you. Run! GO!

He screamed, as the golden haze flickered again. He could wipe out the Earth, but he couldn't survive then. He could move back in time, but it would only mean other dangers—no man could stay awake forever, and he was used to civilized living.

The haze hesitated, while the sense of danger mounted. Then it was gone, as if the beast in his head had found no answer.

Suddenly the grey sedan lifted again, to a height of fifty feet above the tallest building. It shot forward, hesitated, and came down softly on a deserted side-road in Central Park.

His mind felt as if it were going to split. Dan and Ellen stared at him speechlessly.

You can't survive alone! No power is enough by itself! They'll get you! You are your own death-sentence! RUN! DON'T RUN!

Hawkes put his hand to his splitting skull, trying to force words through the agonies of pain, while slow understanding began to reach him.

"Dan! The scientists . . . get me there!"

Then his mind seemed to clamp down on itself, and he was unconscious. He could protect himself from almost anything—except his own brain!

He was conscious of no pain, but only of irritation. There was a needle touching his arm; his mind got rid of it!

He opened his eyes slowly, to find himself the center

of a group of men, while a white-clothed doctor stood staring at an empty hand that must have held a hypodermic.

Ellen cried out suddenly and ran to him, cradling his head in her hands. He found her arm with his own hand, and stroked it slowly.

"You've found the answer?" he asked. Then he nodded, while the weight that had lain on him so long began to lift. His voice was suddenly positive. "You found it!"

One of the men pushed forward, but Dan shook his head, and came over to stand beside the cot where Hawkes lay. "No, Will. They didn't find it—you did! You found what we should have known—your unconscious mind may be a wild beast, but it isn't insane. When it was shocked into realizing that it couldn't save you by itself, it finally looked for help from your conscious mind. Then it knocked you out—knocked itself out, too—until we could work on you."

"I realized I needed outside help," Hawkes said slowly. "But how? Convince a girl troubled by poltergeists that she is the cause of them, and they'd go away. But nobody knows how to talk to the unconscious, so she has to outgrow her trouble. All you psychiatrists have been driving yourselves crazy for years, trying to find a way to reach the unconscious directly."

"Touché," an older man said, and there was a faint sound of amusement from some of the others. "Communication is the problem, of course. But this psi factor *is* the means of communication! You told us that yourself while unconscious and undergoing our hastily improvised hypnotic education of your brain. Apparently, the psi ability was developed gradually by the unconscious as a way to reach the conscious mind; it didn't work too well up to now, but it was meant as a channel of communication. Your trouble was that the link hadn't been fully developed by your treatment. We simply used your own technique to improve the relationship between conscious and unconscious. The only fault with the treatment you and Meinzer gave yourselves was that you stopped too soon. Now you should have full conscious control of all your abilities."

Hawkes dropped back comfortably onto the cot. He reached out for a glass of water, lifted it to his lips, and then put it back—without using his hands. He thought of his clothes, and they were suddenly on him, over the single white garment he had been wearing. Another thought took that away, to leave him normally dressed.

Whether they were entirely correct or not in their theories, the psi factor was no longer wild. He had it under full control!

He sat up, just as three men entered the crowded room. One wore the uniform of a four-star general, but the familiar faces of the two civilians told Hawkes at once that they were more important than any general could be.

He was about to become officially the National Arsenal and replacement for all the armies, navies, and air-corps they had ever dreamed of having. He'd also become their bridge into space, their means of solving the secrets of the planets, and probably their chief historical tool, since nothing could ever be secret from him.

It was going to be a busy life for him, and for the others like him who would now be carefully selected and treated!

He grinned faintly as he realized that they didn't know yet just how important he was. He wasn't going to be a National Resource—he'd be a World Resource. This power was too great for any local political use, and no man who had it along with the full correlation of his conscious and unconscious mind could ever see it any other way.

But right now, he had other pressing business. He grinned at Ellen. "You don't mind a small wedding, do you?" he asked.

She shook her head, beginning to smile. He reached for her hand. This psi factor was going to be a handy thing

to have around, with its complete control of space and
time.

"I'm taking a two-week honeymoon before we talk
go away. We'll be back in ten minutes!"

Honolulu looked lovely in the moonlight, and June
business," he told the approaching three men. "But don't
was the perfect month for a wedding.

www.ingramcontent.com/pod-product-compliance
Lightning Source LLC
Chambersburg PA
CBHW051311250626
47155CB00014B/1033